The Half-Forgotten Stone

REVISED EDITION

The Half-Forgotten Stone

REVISED EDITION

Q E DANIELS
ZACK DANIELS

ISBN: 978-1-7331252-3-9

Other versions:

eBook, revised version ISBN: 978-7331252-2-2

eBook, original version ISBN: 978-1-7331252-0-8

paperback, original version ISBN: 978-1-7331252-1-5

Cover art: Q. E. Daniels

This book is a work of fiction. All of the characters, names, places, and incidents are products of the authors' imaginations. Any resemblance to actual events, organizations, or persons, living or dead, is entirely coincidental.

❀ Created with Vellum

To the irrepressible optimism
of a special aunt,
who won several bouts with cancer during her life,
but lost to the last in a close decision.
When Death finally came to visit,
she was surprised.

Chapter One

BLURRED VISION

IF THUNDERSQUAT HAD ANY DOUBTS about whether to intrude, the glares from the circle of old barbarians made it clear.

Nobody got hurt this time. Pretty sure.

Not like they're gonna do anything about it. Grandfather hadn't even said a word yet.

The elders had raged deep into the moonlit night. Pauses grew longer and the comments shorter, brief jabs into the crawling night with words that burned. They argued from a deep-seated conviction about the way things ought to be. And what ought to be was not the way things were.

"As I was saying," UncleCousin Sumac began, returning to their previous point in the stalemate after a suitable exchange of glances and head shakes.

It was obvious to everyone what they needed to do. Yet what was clear to one was foggy to the rest, and none could grasp how the others failed to see it. Despite their splintered views, they could agree on a single point. The problem was a certain young barbarian, the grandson of the old chief.

Thundersquat couldn't listen to another round of the same complaints. Not that he'd call himself impatient. When he was hunting, he could wait all day for the right game to come along. That was just natural. He liked to eat more than he hated to wait. But don't ask him to sit around and listen to a bunch of old barbarians flap their jaws without saying anything worth hearing.

He spotted the bearskin in the center of the circle. "See you got my gift."

UncleCousin Sumac whipped his head around, fresh claw marks visible across his face. "It was the middle of the night, you dung beetle."

"Meat was fresh."

"It was still alive!" Sumac's face roiled through three shades of purple. He fixed Grandfather with a satisfied sneer. "Tell that empty-headed fool what the Council decided."

Grandfather stood. In the starlight his face looked like the wall of a weathered canyon. His eyes were set far back in the shadows, beneath a rocky overhang.

The bear thing might've played out better in my head.

"Council hasn't decided anything yet," Grandfather growled. "But we've met too many times about you. Things you've done."

"Brought people together. Gave them something to talk about."

Some of the others discovered a sudden interest in the bearskin. A few looked off into the distance.

Grandfather's mouth was fixed in a thin line. "Some of us were known to talk before you came along."

Thundersquat had seen rival chieftains crumple under that glare. They didn't know him like he did.

"Council wants to know what you're still doing here. Why haven't you gone on a quest, like everybody else?"

"Hadn't got around to it."

"Time you did," Grandfather said.

"Got my reasons."

"You'd just botch it up anyway," said UncleCousin Sumac.

Grandfather threw a hard stare in Sumac's direction.

Thundersquat smirked.

The chief fixed his piercing eyes on the young barbarian. "What I believe—what any of us believes—means nothing. Up to you now. Take on the challenges you were meant to face. Find out what you're made of."

"Maybe he doesn't want to know," Sumac said. "Might be too much for him."

That set off nods and murmurs across the Council.

"Never gonna get rid of him."

"Pushed us too far."

"He's a menace."

"He's young. Might just need a little more—"

"Can't coddle him forever, just because of his father!"

"Enough!" Grandfather snapped. The Council became still. The bugs stopped chirping. Grandfather took a long, deep breath.

"Because you're my grandson...because of your father..." His voice wavered. "One last chance."

"Or what?"

"You heard them. Banishment. Or skin you alive."

The young barbarian glanced at the bearskin rug. In his imagination, though, he saw the rest of the bear. "Want my vote?"

"Go. Come back a new man. Or not at all."

Clearly, Grandfather's having a bad day. The young barbarian stalked off, headed north in the windswept wasteland.

A behemoth of a stallion trotted up alongside him, his

coat flashing silver in the moonlight. Despite his size and maturity, Bolstrus moved with the restless energy of a young colt. The steed also answered to Not-gonna-tell-you-again and Trampling-on-my-last-nerve.

They paused at the top of the ridge. If you went far enough, it blocked your view of the village. Home. A hodge-podge of makeshift shelters thrown together from animal skins, grass, rocks, and dirt. A tornado would've laid them out better. The people could pick up and leave on a moment's notice and not worry about anything left behind. And they often did. In fact, when he was younger, he was one of the things they left behind. Regularly. He didn't blame them. Most of the time when they got the notion to go, he hadn't been around. He used to sneak away. From the time he could walk, he couldn't wait to see what else was out there.

Until that day. He shook off the memory and eased into a steady jog over the craggy ground. His heart still skipped when he fixed an eager eye on the horizon. But an invisible tether to the village stretched like it might snap and always pulled him back.

The barbarian made a beeline north—assuming the bee in question had an inner ear infection. Bolstrus galloped ahead, circling back now and then to adjust course.

A few weeks later, the barbarian plunged into the clouds that blanketed the mountains. Somewhere in all the mess was a cave and the strange woman who lived there. Fenestral Smogen. People wouldn't say much about her. But they'd break into a sweat when they heard her name, and some of them would shake.

The path snaked up and around. He could scarcely see far

enough to warn him of the next curve. He stopped often to feel his way around. As the wind whipped around, his hair lashed at his face from every direction. He couldn't see; couldn't hear. Neither could anything else out there, he hoped.

In the gray before dawn, a voice scraped through the mist, deep and gravelly, like a donkey braying through a sore throat. "Visions. Show me who's coming. Never say when. Brilliant."

A voice like that could start a rockslide. The sound bounced around; it was hard to pinpoint. He crouched sideways and slid his front foot forward. The silver stallion pawed at the ground. He reached back and placed a hand on the stallion's forehead. They waited.

A squat figure hobbled into view. She leaned hard on her cane and stretched. Bones crackled like dried twigs underfoot. "Sleep is overrated, but I like it once in a while. Not that I'd ever complain."

"Took a shortcut."

"They always do. Let's get this over with." The hooded cloak shielded Fenestral Smogen's face in shadows. She moved closer.

Hands clasped behind his back, his fingers drummed a silent beat in the swirling wind. "How long does this take?"

"Can't receive your quest until I read your soul." Her top lip curled up on one side. "That won't take long. First, I have to give you a name. Used to be more ceremonial, but...it is what it is."

She gazed upward and sniffed. Her eyes narrowed. One eye closed while the other scanned him from top to bottom. "They call you Thundersquat."

"Well, yeah, but that's just something UncleCousin Sumac came up with. Rest of them figured it was good enough till I came to you and got a real name. Main reason to come here."

"Fits you. Keep the name."

"But—"

"Now, let's get on with it." She clamped down on his forearm with her free hand. "Steady. You won't be standing when this is done."

The seer took a quick breath. Her tiny chin shot out from among folds of flesh. A whorl of red, like hot ashes, zipped around the rim of her eye sockets. A purple beam of light fired from her eyes and locked onto his. "Hold still. This won't take ver—"

The light flickered out, and she staggered back, wheezing, her eyes unfocused. She pressed her hand over her collarbone.

From what they told him, he was ready to feel something scary, disturbing to think about, maybe even painful. But he didn't feel a thing. Her—maybe not so lucky. "We done?"

"Oh yeah." Fenestral Smogen huddled over the cane and rocked in time to her wheezing until it fizzled out. "We're done."

"What happens now?"

"We die."

"What do you mean, we die?"

"I mean, it's all up to you. Same thing."

"What's all up to me?"

She stared at the ground. "Just wanted to pass my remaining days in peace. Hand out quests, conjure up names. Maybe sell hats."

The barbarian shifted from one foot to the other. "Aren't you supposed to tell me something?"

"High point of my life. Come and gone, like a restless butterfly."

"What do I have to do?"

The seer snapped upright and jammed her cane into the ground. "I'll tell you when I think you're good and ready. Exactly as written."

"Ready as I'll ever be."

Fenestral Smogen looked off to the side and blew out a ragged breath. "Patience is a dog-blasted virtue."

She raised a hand to eye level and rotated it slowly. It quivered. She wrapped it around the hand leaning on the cane. "The prophecy. Whispered, sage to sage, across ten generations. Had to fall out on my watch."

Her gaze snapped back to the present. She flashed a look that he'd seen more than a few times—the kind that came with a punch. "Okay, barbarian, listen close, ready or not.

"When stars are misaligned,
Let tangled fate unwind,
Unless you find the Half-Forgotten Stone.
When held, it can reveal
Endeavors to conceal,
Releasing secrets better left unknown.
Hidden, undetected,
No longer recollected
By the last to wield the power of the Stone:
A failure to recall
Ignited destiny's fall.
See cherished rules of order overthrown.
But let the Stone be found
And placed in hallowed ground,
Enshrouded somewhere known to one alone.
Or by divine decree:
The world will cease to be."

She poked him in the chest with her cane. "Well? Told you. What do you have to say about it?"

Thundersquat shrugged. He turned his back, arms folded. "Not my idea to come here."

"The gods must be out of their ferzuken minds. Do you understand what it means, 'cease to be'? All of us, gone. The people. The others. Gone. Animals. Plants. Gone."

"Doesn't sound good."

"Do you have even a smidgen of curiosity about the Stone? Because—I don't know—none of us will be here if you don't find it?"

Thundersquat cocked an ear in her direction. He could smell a lecture coming. He didn't have time for this.

"Generations pass without word of the Half-Forgotten Stone. Sought by those who hunger for power, who scour the far corners of the earth for the slightest edge over others." She leaned an elbow on the cane and held her hand in front of her like she was holding something heavy. She waved the other hand in circles above it. "Whoever holds the Stone can discover things that are hidden."

"Even from long ago?"

"If that's where you're fool enough to look. But the secrets unleashed by that Stone can tear people apart. Sooner or later, for better or worse, somebody always loses it."

"Sounds like we need the Stone to find it."

"Well, we don't have it," she said. "And if you think it's dangerous when it's found, the Stone's even worse when it's lost. If we don't find it, the world as we know it will end."

"One little rock?"

"It's complicated," she said. "Gets its power from Meandyra, the Braider of Time."

"Never heard of her."

"Well, she's heard of you. Thinks you're the answer."

"Gonna take her word for it?"

"Not my call. Just find the Stone."

"Got something else to do," he said.

"What you have to do doesn't matter. The Stone locks the Braid of Time in place. Lose the Stone, time starts to unravel."

"What if it did?"

"Chaos. Complete chaos." She hooked her cane on his arm and pulled him partway around. "The Braid of Time records everything. All our hopes, fears, and regrets; where we've been, where we choose to go next. A loose thread for the odd and unexpected. If it unraveled, it might brush up against a braid from another time and place."

"Another braid?"

She glanced both ways, grabbed a handful of buckskin, and yanked him close. "It's not the only braid she's working on. Imagine other worlds, more than you can count. Each with its own story, its own braid. Each braid with a sacred Stone to hold it in place."

"Other worlds...?"

"Gets worse. Those other worlds are the same as this one: the same people, making different choices. Creating their own history. To us, it's what could've been, what almost was. Somebody else's reality—nearly us but not us. Not exactly here, not quite now. So close you can feel it, but you can't touch it, unless—"

"The Braids of Time brush up against each other."

The seer released him. "You get this, don't you, barbarian?"

"Not sure that's a good thing."

"It's not. Unless you're the one who can do something about it."

"What if I don't?"

Her knuckles whitened around the cane. She spoke loud and fast. "Our time will get mixed up with fate and chance from other worlds. Anything could happen, and we'd never see it coming." She blew out a long breath. "Bottom line, you have to find that Stone."

"Where was the Stone last?"

"Blisteria, east of the Badlands. Futhark the Meddler forgot where he hid it."

"Why did he hide it in the first place?" Thundersquat asked.

"Couldn't sleep, for one. Always on guard—too many others wanted it." She searched the sky. "Could've been afraid of it. The Stone does something to you."

"Like what?"

She belched. "It grabs you. Won't let go. Like it's alive."

"Where was this Meddler when he lost it?"

"Do I really have to answer that?"

"Well, where would you start, if it was you?" he asked.

Her gaze rambled over the ground. "You might try the sorcerer king. Futhark the Meddler trained him."

"Where do I find this sorcerer king?"

Fenestral Smogen squinted to the left. "A shiny black palace."

One of her eyebrows took a deep dive. "Or swimming in a pond somewhere."

"Narrows it down."

"Don't be sarcastic. I see images. Might be exactly what they seem. Could mean something else—something deeper. Symbolic. You people have no idea what it's like to be a seer. We can see, but we don't really know." She cast her eyes to the side and slowly exhaled. "Not that it's any of your business, but it's not what I thought it would be when I went into it."

"Just find it? Nobody has to know what to do with it?"

"Hide it somewhere safe. Find a caretaker—someone not under its power. Just don't touch it. You'll find out things you never wanted to know."

"Don't need a Stone for that to happen."

"You're not taking this seriously. The gods have chosen you. Everything depends on it."

"How long is this supposed to take?"

"Until you find it. Why?"

He hesitated. "No reason."

"Twelve moons, maybe less." Fenestral Smogen jabbed a bony finger into his forehead. "Whatever's in that hard head of yours, set it aside."

"Don't want to leave the Badlands."

"Suit yourself. Take one last look."

Thundersquat jerked free. He leaped upon the stallion. "Better not take that long. If I decide to do it."

"Dramblunkit, is it not sinking in what's at stake here?"

Thundersquat wheeled around and galloped away into the mist. The stallion hurtled the two of them into the blind curves with reckless abandon. The barbarian's adrenaline surged. *Not my fault if the Braider of Time can't keep track of things.*

Chapter Two

LEAP FROG

THE SORCERER KING surfaced in the cover of the reeds. Before him, the long-legged bird posed like a statue, skewered into the mirrored shallows of the pond. Sunlight glinted off the saber-like beak. He used to think it was beautiful, until he found himself on the menu.

If fast enough, someone could survive out here for five years, maybe ten at the outside. He never thought it would get to twelve, thirteen, whatever it was. Looking back, it all ran together. As Wolfmini floated, he could almost fool himself. In the old days, he could snag a dragonfly in mid pirouette and reenter the water with hardly a ripple. Not so now. He'd belly flop. And probably miss the dragonfly. The mere thought of moving made him mindful of the stubborn sluggishness in his back and limbs. It was his cue to rejuvenate. He began the painstaking process of transforming his amphibian body into a younger version of himself. The sorcerer king had undergone the procedure enough times that his thoughts were free to wander. He rattled off the chant mindlessly to himself, keeping one eye on the bird.

This wasn't his life. The few moments he could steal into his human body, that's what's real. He didn't think he could've pushed through without those leaps, all too brief and not without cost. That pressing fatigue that comes with distant magic... Vulnerability to predators while he was in leap phase...

His human body had gone through changes as well, perhaps more evident because he only visited it once in a while. The last time he'd popped in, his joints had been stiffer, the range of motion less. He wouldn't dream of tampering with the aging process in his real body. It wouldn't matter. He can't turn back time for everyone else. For his daughter. Lost time. A punctuated life. You could give up in a hurry if you dwelt on all that you missed. He stopped going down that road a long—

The bird lifted a leg and slid a webbed talon forward. It unfolded its wings, flapped hard a few times, and sailed to the other side of the pond. Wolfmini completed the chant and lay back in the shadows to allow the transformation to unfold. His eyes and nostrils pierced the surface while his body floated just below. The more warmth he could absorb now, the easier it would be to get through the cold night. The bird waded off to the left and disappeared around the bend.

What haven't I tried? Years of ideas, none that worked. If he tried to tell somebody where to find him, the words jammed, and the spell jerked him back into the frog. Can't leave a note—same thing. Wolfmini sank below the surface and glided to one of his safe places, careful not to disturb the reeds. He could keep his body still, but the restless crashing in his mind was something else entirely. But he wasn't getting anywhere. He could think of another plan tomorrow, hit it fresh. For now, he had to see his daughter once more.

Wolfmini awoke squatting in his study, immersed in

documents. He stood and stretched. Pain shot up his lower back and slowly dissipated. The sorcerer king combed his fingers through his neatly trimmed beard. *So good to be back.*

He scanned the scrolls for something familiar—anything that would give him a hint as to what he was doing when his last visit came to an abrupt stop. It clicked right away: signs in the night sky, patterns he'd picked up from the pond that he needed to check out. He traced the paths of the five stars through the heavens. The two slowest were almost upon each other. All five crossed at a point just beyond. They'll meet within the year.

Wolfmini spread his hands flat on the scroll and leaned forward. Old teachings slogged through the sludge in his brain. *What was it what's-his-name said to watch for...? Futhark the Meddler, that's it, there was something...*

He flipped through the parchments scattered across his desk. *Before this. There. All five stars coming together. Past the gobbledegook.*

The croaking was already a constant hum in the background. The sorcerer king clasped his hands behind his neck and squeezed his head between his forearms. *Confounded croaking. Can't slip away yet.* He read, "A time of shifting power; freedom ripped away; traditions overturned; conflict tearing friends and families apart; cataclysmic disaster."

Wolfmini drew a long, slow breath and allowed his mind to clear. He pushed away from his desk and dragged himself into the hallway. His dignity held him upright. It was not lost time that nagged at him now. There was none of it left to lose.

The sorcerer king spotted Blundren in the courtyard. Streaks of gold vanished from her auburn hair as she entered the palace shadows. Another brushing wouldn't be too much to ask. His daughter's dress was simple, like always, a dull blue with a grayish tinge. The bottom hem of her dress was tattered and spattered with mud. For some reason she always wanted to go off into the woods. He'd never go back there, if he could help it.

The maiden next to her was new to him, as far as he knew. Her full dark hair captured him with a slow dance, falling in loose curls to a point halfway down her back. With each step, fine fabric clung to her ever so briefly, setting off a cascade of sparkles that hinted of the curves underneath. A subtlety in the way she moved gently latched onto his attention and drew him in, as if a spell were being cast. The sorcerer king shook his head and focused on the surroundings until they drew close. "Greetings, ladies."

"Your Eminence." The maiden bowed her head slightly.

"Father." Blundren offered just enough of a nod to be polite. "This is my friend, Dekatria, the one I was telling you about."

"Ah, yes." He scanned the splotchy archives of his mind, hoping to settle on something familiar. "From the market."

"Yes," Dekatria said. "That's where we met."

"You're a priestess?"

"In training. I hope to be some day."

Wolfmini stooped over and plucked a leaf from the hem of Blundren's dress. "It's good to see that some of the young still value the old ways."

"How can we not?" Dekatria asked.

"My room is this way." Blundren pushed past her father.

The smell of the pond. "Wait."

The young ladies turned.

"No time. End of the—" His mouth kept moving, but the words dried up. "...F-f-fi..."

They glanced at each other and back at him. Blundren's

eyes widened, and her face flushed. She turned and hurried up the stairs.

Blasted croaking. Losing her. His spirit imploded; the familiar suction ripped him away from her. With webbed fingers, he parted the reeds. The dim outline of the two young ladies faded. Heart pounding, the sorcerer king screamed a warning before the connection vanished. "Croak!"

His last image until he could link up again: her cold eyes stabbing at him. A look that said, "You didn't just do that in front of my friend." *Still worth it.*

A flurry in the water slapped him into high alert. He ducked and dove left. He felt the splash behind him. The sorcerer king zigzagged through the reeds with powerful kicks. A long beak grazed his thigh. He veered right and down. After a quick bounce off the bottom, he dipped under a log. Wolfmini pressed a hand over his injured thigh and stilled the palpitations in his heart. He was in for a long wait. That bird could watch fruit ripen.

The highly charged energy spent itself out, and the sorcerer king sagged against the log. One eye closed; the other drifted to half-mast. *Can't get that careless again. Too much at stake. For now, just a brief glimpse. All I ask. Once in a while. And not to wake up as an hors d'oeuvre.*

"So that was the sorcerer king?" Dekatria asked.

"Yes, that was my father." Blundren felt heat rise to her face.

"How long is he going to squat like that?"

"Hours. Maybe days. He won't talk when he does that. Just sits there." *No wonder I never brought anybody home.*

"You mean he's done it before? Why does he do it?"

"Who knows?" *Ceased to be funny a long time ago.* "Eventually he'll stand up and talk to me, but he'll act like it never happened."

"Maybe he's under some kind of spell. I can ask the high priest. If he'll talk to me." Dekatria's eyes sparkled as she leaned in. "He caught us. We carved icons out of stone and tried to connect them to each other's souls."

"Some people believe things like that."

Dekatria drew her head back. "I believe things like that."

"I'm sorry. I don't mean to suggest…" *Well, yes, I did.*

Her friend scaled back the enthusiasm in her voice. "The high priest lost control. He threw one of the girls against the wall. Her hair turned green, fell out, and sprouted out of her knees."

"Did you actually see it? Or did he just tell you about it?"

"I know what I saw."

Careful. Not many chances to make friends around here. "They had to be working together."

"How can you say that? You weren't even there." Dekatria's smile was gone.

Too far. But the truth is what it is. "There has to be some other explanation."

"Explain this. I scratched an icon and made my lab partner itch all over. She couldn't stand it and dove into the purification pool. She lost her mind and spun her icon around four or five times in the palm of her hand. I got so dizzy I threw up in the pool."

"Power of suggestion. It'd be hard to prove it was anything more."

"The priest tried to kick me. He tripped and fell into the pool. He sat up, wiped his eyes, and caught a full load of projectile vomiting from three directions."

"That would've been worth seeing." *Better. Find something positive to say.*

"He cancelled class."

Blundren laughed. "Maybe the old ways do have some value."

The princess knelt down and pulled a sheet of parchment from under her bed. "Sorry if I made you uncomfortable. But my father used to show me how he did what he did. Sorcery is just a bunch of tricks, nothing more."

"You shouldn't say things like that," Dekatria said. "Something might happen."

"Like what?"

"I don't know."

"Exactly." Blundren spread the old manuscript on the bed. "Here. You might want to see this. I borrowed it from my father's study."

"Is that a magic spell?" Dekatria caressed the air above the sacred script. "The old language. Don't you feel it?"

"I never have. I'll never understand how people let themselves get caught up in it."

"You're the one who's missing something." Dekatria folded her arms. "Do you even care how you come across?"

"People have a hard time with my questions. But things always make sense, if you know where to look." *Truth or friendship—is that what it always boils down to?*

"If you're so sure there's nothing to it, then why don't you try it?"

"Yeah, why not? The evidence will speak for itself." Blundren rolled up the manuscript. "Let's take this out into the woods, where no one's watching. See what it doesn't do."

"Do you know what you're getting into?"

"I promise you we have nothing to worry about."

"But what if something bad happens?"

"Just as likely that something good will happen. Most likely, nothing will happen at all."

"The old ways are nothing to trifle with."

"On that point we can agree," Blundren said. "Now, how to get past an overprotective father…" *An absent one, to be more accurate. With strict rules. Please, this one time, let him be gone.*

No such luck. They found the sorcerer king, still squatting, leaning against the wall in the great hallway. The crevices beneath his eyes were deep. One eye was open but not focused.

"Father, we're thinking about going to the market next week."

His eye blinked.

"I'll speak to you later about it," Blundren said.

"Can I help you, Highness?"

Just when I thought it couldn't get any worse. She conceded half a smile to the cherubic figure who had slinked up behind them. Jermbog had all the appeal of rotting celery. Globules of oil leached through his bloated pink cheeks. The grimace that was his best approximation of a smile offered more gums than teeth. Jermbog had taken it upon himself to make sure her father's rules were followed, to the letter. "Dekatria, let me introduce you to my father's chief administrator, Jermbog."

"Chief Magistrate of All Things Pertaining and Otherwise." Jermbog bowed and hijacked Dekatria's hand. He held her gaze as he drew her fingers to his lips. She freed her hand and stowed it behind her back, wiping her fingers on her dress.

Blundren shot her an apologetic glance. Bad enough that she let her own big mouth get in the way, but then there was this greasy administrator and her loony father. If Deketria could overlook all that, she'd be a friend she didn't deserve.

Jermbog presented his gums again and ushered them away. "His Eminence has asked not to be disturbed."

"Too late."

"Highness, I heard you mention Market Day. Are you sure you want—"

"Nothing's going to happen. But we'll take guards with us." *Typical.*

Chapter Three

KEEPING WATCH

ON THE RIDGE overlooking the village, Thundersquat leaned back against a gnarled, misshapen tree. Without turning his head, he waited for his grandfather to sidle up next to him. Thundersquat knew he was there for the last hour. Still, he never saw him sneak out of the village. He could envision the old chief's face lighting up. "Almost had me, Grandfather."

"Used to get you all the time."

"Taught me well."

"Received your quest?" Grandfather asked.

"More or less."

"Usually, a man's gone for a while after that."

"Haven't gone," Thundersquat said.

The old chief nodded. "Still remember what the Council told you?"

"Not going into the village."

"Good. Some think you look better with skin," the old man said.

"Not gonna test that theory."

Grandfather pointed to a horned toad that baked in the sun on a nearby rock. "No bigger than half my thumb when I first saw him. Every day of his life you can find him. Even when we pick up the village and move, you'll find him there. Asked my good friend Horned Toad, 'Why have you given up everything in a horned toad's life to watch over us?'"

"What did he say?"

"Nothing. He's a horned toad."

Thundersquat picked up a pebble and flipped it back and forth. *Grandfather thinks I should go, or he wouldn't have brought it up.* "Whoever decided that a man had to have a quest?"

"Always been that way."

Thundersquat's face grew warm. "Plenty of challenges out there. Crazy woman in a cave can't tell me which one to take on."

"Unless that's your challenge. And she's only crazy if she's wrong."

"Well, she ain't right," Thundersquat said. "Think I oughta go?"

"Only you can decide that."

Thundersquat tossed the pebble. "Anybody ever *not* do what the quest told them to do?"

"Some tried. But they say your challenge will find you, come at you another way, until you have no choice."

"Maybe this time it'll be different."

"Maybe so," Grandfather said. "Somebody has to be the first. What did she tell you to do?"

"Find some stone. Half-Forgotten Stone. Sorcerer king might know where it is, wherever he might be."

"What would happen if you didn't find it?" the chieftain asked.

"Wouldn't be good."

The old man's knees popped when he climbed to his feet.

He patted Thundersquat on the shoulder. He glanced at the horned toad. "It's a great comfort to know that someone's always watching over us."

The chief lowered his voice. "Watch him. Never really trusted Horned Toad."

Grandfather leaped like a young goat down the ridge, from one foothold to another. A couple farts escaped in sync with his landings. He flashed a grin at Thundersquat as if to say, "Still got it."

Thundersquat placed his hands behind his head and leaned back against the tree. *Grandfather didn't exactly tell me to leave.*

No one stirred in the village below. From the shallow ridge, Thundersquat could see well past next week. Things looked safe enough to slip away for a while, if he wanted to. But there was no way he could take off long enough to hunt for the Stone.

A blast of high-pitched chirps, like a thousand cicadas, exploded on his left. He spun into a fighting stance. Energy coursed through his veins, and his head was on fire.

A whirlwind, no higher than his shoulder, churned the dust into a choking fog. In its center a dark form took shape, giving off a low moan that swelled into a grating caterwaul. The dust settled, and the chirping wound down. Fenestral Smogen shivered, eyes bugged out. She sputtered, "Whoa! She didn't do that. She didn't just do that."

Thundersquat reeled in his impulse to crush and otherwise dismember her. *Things don't sneak up on you out here. It's just wrong.* "Who? Did what?"

"Braider of Time. Sent me here. Didn't ask. Just did it.

Whoa! It was like chomping on an icicle, only you're the icicle." The seer stomped and huffed like she wanted to put someone out of her misery. She scanned the horizon. Her body went slack, and her jaw dropped. She raised an eyebrow at the barbarian and viewed the panorama again. "Never saw so much of nothing. What were the gods thinking when they slapped this place together?"

Her tone caught him by surprise. Thundersquat took another gander at the rolling wasteland, dotted with lonesome sprigs of grass and scrubby trees. Granite towers blinked through the haze on the horizon under a cloudless sky. A person could catch a glimpse of eternity out here.

She shoved her face in close to his. "Why are you still here?"

Thundersquat gestured toward the ramshackle huts and shelters scattered below. The people stood outside, staring at the ridge. "If I left, what would happen to them?"

"What would anybody in their right mind worry about out here—besides starving to death?"

"Be surprised."

"What's gonna be left of that village when the whole world is demolished?"

"Just an old legend," he said. "People down there are real."

"Look, the Braider of Time pops in on me several times a day. Middle of the night even. Has to check on every ferzuken detail. If you don't go, she'll keep hounding me. I won't have any peace."

His eyes darted around. *Lived in that cave by herself too long. Still, something sent her here. Out of nowhere.* He swallowed. "Take my chances right here."

"When was the last time anything bad came this way?"

"That's the point," he said. "Overdue."

"That's not how it works."

"No way I'm gonna find that Stone," he said.

"Not sitting here, you're not."

"Not a lot to go on," Thundersquat said.

"It's a quest, dramblunkit. It doesn't come with a chart."

"Can't be sure that sorcerer king knows anything."

"That's the only clue we've got. Find him." Dust started to swirl around her. "No. Oh, no. Go! Now! Nonono—"

The chirping whirlwind swallowed her up.

The walls of Thundersquat's chest squeezed in. *People popping in and out. Don't need it.*

Then again, maybe something like that happened to Father. Warriors scoured the ground for weeks. Grandfather could track a grasshopper in a sandstorm. No trace. Maybe the Stone could tell what happened back then. But they're asking him to go off to who knows where, looking for something no one can remember. *Not likely.*

He folded his arms and leaned against the tree. *Nothing's gonna happen to my village. Not as long as I drew breath.*

The afternoon heat bore down, and the shade provided scant relief. He could usually count on a breeze, if not a stiff wind. But not today. The barbarian drifted off to sleep.

Thundersquat pressed against the wall in a darkened hallway. He slid his toe across the floor, smooth as ice or polished bone. He wasn't supposed to be here, wherever here was.

Torchlight flickered around a figure seated behind a white slab on the far side of the cavernous room. "If it please thee, barbarian, approach."

Thundersquat peered around the entry. They were alone. His eyes reverted to the seated figure. His heart skipped. He hadn't moved, but there he was, across the room, the white slab no more than an arm's length away. The seated figure leaned forward on his elbows.

The man's hairline receded to the midline of his skull, his thinning hair combed over the top into a ponytail that hung down to the right, resting on his shoulder. His vest, several sizes too small, hung open. A gold earring looped through the lobe of his left ear. "Thou hast the honor and privilege of addressing the god of Stipulations and Particulars, Axiom Punctilio."

Thundersquat nodded. A dream. Only way a god would ever venture into the Badlands. *Could be a good time to wake up. Wouldn't hurt to see what he has to say first.*

"One would not reasonably expect a barbarian to be versed in the proper protocol." Axiom Punctilio twirled a pointer and read from the parchment laid out on the slab. "Thou wilt note the fine print under heading 3(b), line ii, pursuant to the Standard Operating Procedure in the Event of Undue Delay in Seeking One's Quest: Whereas, as it may apply to an otherwise inordinate delay in pursuit of a duly assigned quest, the individual determined through reasoned inquiry to be responsible for said delay will forfeit an item deemed precious or otherwise significant, at the discretion of the deified entity presiding. That would, of course, be me."

"That would, of course, mean what?"

"Thou hast taken far too long to initiate thy quest. Hence the imminent loss of something of value, which has been designated to be..." Axiom Punctilio skimmed the scroll with the pointer until he brought it to an abrupt stop. He raised his eyes level with those of the barbarian. "...yon stallion, of silver hue."

"Bolstrus? Not taking the horse."

The god shrugged. "One has minimal degrees of discretion in these matters."

"Doesn't belong to me. Just hangs out with me because he wants to."

"Irrelevant."

"What if we were about ready to leave?"

"Thou hast not heretofore shown a pattern of careful planning."

"Never too late to start something new."

Axiom Punctilio pursed his lips and nodded slowly. "Another day would not be considered unreasonable. Less paperwork. Thou hast until sundown tomorrow to commence thy undertaking."

Thundersquat brushed aside a drop of sweat that rolled down his forehead. "Why are you doing this?"

The god narrowed his eyes and rested his chin on his thumb. He tapped his forefinger against his cheek. "Thou didst not hear this from me. The hateful clause was invoked by the Braider of Time."

"Heard of her."

"She did nothing irregular, not at first. Simply pointed out rules and procedures which are already in effect. Duty demands that we implement them." He sighed. The god looked to the left and leaned in, lowering his voice. "But she didn't have to threaten my bonus."

"What bonus?"

"A shiny new temple. For umpteen gazillion eons of dedicated service." He smiled and gazed off into the distance. "Staffed by seventy-three nearsighted vestal virgins. Every last one of them allergic to gold and silver."

Heat rushed up the barbarian's neck. "So, you steal my horse or you don't get your bonus?"

"The seizure of property is mandated by law. And one's

bonus, once earned, will be rendered in full, regardless of the whims of a deity. But if thou dost not comply, the evil shrew threatened to give them 20/20 vision and to tell them about platinum." The god slouched over and traced idle circles on the marble slab.

Thundersquat, still fuming, gave a noncommittal stare, never having seen a temple or a vestal virgin and not sure what the fuss was all about. *Not my business what the gods want to do to each other.*

Axiom Punctilio locked eyes with the barbarian without lifting his head. He shrugged. "How many vestal virgins would stay, under those conditions? Worst of the bunch, perhaps; not enough to keep the eternal flame burning. Before long the temple would crumble. Ruins. Overgrown ivy. Mold." The god sighed. "We would lose our accreditation. The worst part? Pitying smiles from gods who used to grovel before me." He pushed up from the slab. "Thou art dismissed."

Thundersquat awoke, drenched in sweat. The sun was high overhead.

Bolstrus nudged his shoulder.

Ten years together. Circle of life might have to close a little early. He recalled the day he met the silver stallion.

Grandfather warned him. Told him never to come out here alone again. Father wouldn't like it either. Should be back any day. He couldn't exactly do what they said. He'd spotted the herd again. The boy slid a dry shrub in front of him and moved in close.

Two stallions were at a standoff. Their coats were splattered with froth and caked in dust. If either had any quit inside, they'd have to tear each other apart to find it. The old gray stallion reared. The brown bay feinted left and body-slammed him. The gray stallion struggled to regain his footing. The challenger rammed him again, and the gray toppled over. The brown bay rose high in the air and drove his hooves into the fallen champion, over and over. The old gray rolled into him as the bay backpedaled. The challenger lunged at him once more and pounded without mercy, until the old gray lay still. The new victor stood over the gray body, bellowing smoke in the frosty air.

A scream of outrage echoed across the wide expanse. A silver colt charged at the new champion, who waited, sides heaving. A powerful kick sent the colt tumbling. The stringy colt rolled to his feet and flung himself at the stallion. A second kick knocked him to the ground again. The brown bay trotted toward the colt, head high, ears forward. The colt flew into the stallion, who chopped him down once more. The bay surged at the colt.

Enough. The boy snatched up a rock. The brown bay reared. He let the rock fly. Got him, full in the cheek.

The boy froze as the stallion caught him in his sights. He wheeled and skedaddled, thundering hooves behind him. *What a sorehead.* At that point he realized that there was nowhere to run, no shelter in sight.

That's when the colt joined in. He grabbed a mouthful of the stallion's tail and jerked back. They harassed that brown bay for hours, he and that silver colt. *Best day of my life.*

Then Grandfather came. The herd sauntered off. The brown stallion was done anyway. The warriors stayed back. "Is Father back already? Don't tell him I was out here alone again. Can the colt come with me?"

He couldn't remember who else was there. Couldn't remember the exact words. Just that look. That look. That stone face: grim, tired, suddenly years older. The way the light glinted off tears deep in the shadows. "Where's Father?"

Worst day of my life.

Thundersquat swallowed. He'd learned several hard truths that day. Rules to live by. Never get close to anybody. Something bad is bound to happen. If you let anybody in, you have to protect them at all costs.

Bolstrus shoved him, snapping the barbarian back into the present. Thundersquat slapped the stallion on the rump and dashed off. The stallion chased him down, nipped him on the shoulder, and cantered away. They chased each other for the rest of the afternoon. At last, Thundersquat dropped into the dirt, drenched in sweat. He placed his hands behind his neck and studied the sky, while Bolstrus chewed on tufts of grass nearby. *No way the gods are taking that horse. Can't leave the village, either, not for long. One day to make up my mind.*

Chapter Four

THE LEAST HIGH DRUID

"SOMETHING'S CHANGED, spider. I feel it." The Least High Druid addressed his sole companion, a hairy spider that claimed the narrow patch of sunlight on the stone floor. The holy man squatted on a rectangular block in the sparsely furnished room. He balanced his elbows on his knees, his fingers interlaced. He stroked the underside of his beard with his thumb. The druid unfolded his spindly arms and legs and shuffled over to the window, a vertical slit the width of the hand that he rested on the stone sill.

The realization hit him like a slap of icy water. It was the middle of the day, but the colors blended and faded as if it were just before dusk. It was hardly enough for most people to notice, even if they did pay attention. *If it's what he thinks it is... But who would know what it's supposed to feel like? Nobody would be alive who went through it before. What else could it be? It's happening: the ancient prophecy—the Half-Forgotten Stone.* "Somebody grew careless. I have an idea who."

It was hard to tell if the spider was listening. Clueless, like all the rest.

"If I had it to do over again..." The Stone had been right there, within reach. He could've grabbed it, stashed it somewhere, and gone back for it later. His hand tightened on the windowsill. Futhark the Meddler made a mistake back then. Said it was meant for somebody else. Somebody more worthy, he implied.

Footsteps approached. The Least High Druid stretched his arms high. Eyes closed, he mumbled rhythmic nonsense, laden with mystic import. Someone smashed through the door. There was no mistaking the purposeful stride of Snartglobber, the head chieftain of the Qrudds. At least half a dozen others shuffled behind him and settled to the left. The druid felt the leader's hot breath on his cheek. A faint floral scent wafted from the blue paint that adorned the left half of the chieftain's face. The druid heard the necklace of five bear claws whip around and bounce on the chieftain's chest as he reversed course and strode away. The tiny herd of hangers-on scrambled for the exit. The door slammed.

The Least High Druid, still mumbling, opened his eyes enough to see the door. He lowered his arms and leaned against the window. Sorcery creeps the head chieftain out. Buys him time to think.

"You know, spider, when I first came to this land, it wasn't so bad. Told fortunes, healed the sick. Minor stuff. When the great one brought me into his castle, it was a heady thing. Didn't seem so cold, empty, or confining back then. But it's different now. Nowhere near what I expected. Then again, what is?"

Far away, a hawk floated motionlessly, going nowhere in a slow circle. "Now they need me more than ever. I may be the last hope for mankind."

The spider repositioned a couple of its legs.

"World's coming to an end, and here I am, trapped. Trained monkey for a blue-faced peacock." He shook his head and gritted his teeth. "Worst year of my life."

The hawk dipped and veered right, and a few powerful strokes soon carried him out of sight. "What am I going to do, spider? I have to be free!"

He snatched a sandal from his foot and slammed it hard. His chest heaved, and heat rushed to his skull. The druid slowed his breathing and restored his heartbeat to its former calm. His jaw was still clenched.

When he crushed the spider, he felt as if he'd bitten a tiny chunk out of the life force that writhed around and through him. But he didn't care. For now, he had to sulk. Nothing against spiders, but he was angry. It felt better if somebody paid. An impenetrable barrier erupted and filled his pores, cutting him off from the spiritual realm for now. He stilled his mind and felt connected once more. *Can't be like the rest of them. Higher standard and all that.*

The stone floor was cold as he limped over to the wall. A slab of rock lay slightly askew across two small boulders, covered with a jumble of gourds and small clay pots filled with various powders and concoctions. The druid retrieved an empty vial. He scraped the spider splatter from his sandal. He'd never come across a spell that actually used this goop. But the audience craved a dash of eerie repugnance, and he had to provide them that flavor. It was particularly true for a certain head chieftain of the Qrudds.

Despite years of study and commitment, it was still a struggle. The druid strove to be more in sync with the spirits of all that moved, as well as those of all that did not move. The more attuned he could be, the more he could influence the course of events. His chance of survival was better that way. The trick was to discover when to create, when to destroy, and when to toss out illusions or misdirection. Timing was everything. All the rest was show.

No matter how good he got, there always seemed to be something just out of reach. The druid never truly knew how the next moment would unfold, or how best to react to whatever came. He shrugged off a passing regret at the disturbance he'd caused when he flattened the spider. He was not above nature, nor apart from it—just one more fallible creature stumbling through life. *More gifted, perhaps. Without question.*

The druid strolled back over to the window slit. The sight of the blue vista of the hills to the west caused his forehead to knot up. *Maybe the second worst year of my life.*

Footsteps signaled another pending onslaught of Snartglobber and his entourage. The Least High Druid pinpointed where the head chieftain would likely stick after he swaggered into the room. From there he faced the wall, seemingly lost in thought. The Qrudd chieftain threw open the door and assumed the same commanding stance he had probably taken since he'd begun to walk. Half a dozen men and three dancing girls formed a semicircle around him. The druid turned his head, wearing the slightly disoriented look of someone who had just awakened. He added a touch of surprise, as if he'd just become aware of their presence. The hangers-on were new replacements—not a good sign, but not unexpected. The dancing girls may have been the same as the last time he'd seen them. "Greetings, great one. You've come to test me again, I see."

"Yes!" Snartglobber said. "What am I going to test you about today?"

"You're testing my ability to read your mind."

"Yes! You've passed the first question. If you fail the

remainder, what'll happen to this poor man here?" The chieftain shoved the tallest man forward. The tall man turned a shade paler.

The Least High Druid studied the head chieftain's face. *Should've thought this through. Hard to read a mind like that. No evidence of forethought. A few fleeting echoes of shallow reactions.* "I believe you want to tell me that."

"Yes again! We'll skin him alive!" Snartglobber reviewed his audience with a smile.

The tall man's eyes widened.

"Very well. I accept the challenge."

The unfortunate man stopped breathing.

"Don't keep me waiting, holy man."

"I suspect you have a plan. To inflict more misery on the kingdom of Blisteria."

"They have no respect for the Qrudd ways. They'd destroy us if they could." His eyes narrowed. "You're stalling. What are the details of my plan?"

"Details? Well...it's obvious. You were thinking about Blisteria... The villagers...they lack courage."

"Ah, but everyone knows that." Snartglobber reached for the hilt of his dagger.

Think. Stall. "More to the point, you were thinking that... the villagers in Blisteria...would...would crumple under the challenges that the Qrudds face each and every day."

"Rodents. The Qrudds are tigers next to them." He slid the dagger from its sheath.

Work the problem. "You want to send me to the sorcerer king. As an emissary."

The edges of Snartglobber's mouth turned up, but his eyes were still cold. He moved in closer. "Why would I want to do that?"

The splatter stain from the spider was still evident. *That'll be me, if I'm not careful.* "You want me to demand that he give you something. Something valuable. Land. Half of his land."

"And why would he ever do that?"

"Only one reason. I'm sure you're already thinking this." The druid squinted into the head chieftain's eyes. He broke eye contact and tilted his head. His face relaxed. "His daughter. You're right; his daughter. We kidnap her. He'd have no choice, but to give us whatever we asked, if he wants her back. Which I'm sure he would."

Snartglobber raised his eyebrows. The six men and three dancing girls raised theirs. "You're almost right."

The tall man wet himself.

"I want more than half his land. Arrange to have her kidnapped. But you stay here. I want you close."

"As you wish." *Meet them where they are and take them as far as you can.*

Snartglobber slammed the dagger home in its sheath. "I was right to bring you into my inner circle."

The tall man was the first out the door. The hangers-on scrambled to follow. The dancing girls lingered a bit, mesmerized by his powers. *One of the perks.*

The girls rushed out to catch up with the others. Snartglobber swung the door almost to a close. The cool eyes of the chieftain held his—the look of a cougar savoring its next meal. *Who does this prancing windbag think he's playing with? Serious matters are afoot, and he has no idea.*

The door shut, and the druid was alone once more. So, he was in the ever-shrinking inner circle now. It might just provide the opportunity he was looking for. *To be free again. To save the world. Show them all.*

Chapter Five

JUMP START

SCREAMS ECHOED ALL ABOUT, drowned out by howling wind; stinging rain battered him from the side. Grandfather stood alone with spear ready. A monster two or three times his size surged forward. Thundersquat's legs could not move. He could only watch in horror. Thundersquat jerked awake, heart racing, soaked in sweat. The image slowly faded.

The barbarian looked around in the silent dawn and took in the fact that nothing ever happened here. Not since, well... He was sure Grandfather was okay. Dreams don't mean anything. Still... *Wouldn't hurt to check.*

UncleCousin Sumac crawled out of his lean-to and stretched. Thundersquat tapped him on the shoulder. Sumac jumped like someone had dropped a handful of hailstones down his shirt.

"What are—you're not supposed—"

Thundersquat touched Sumac's lips. "Good to see you, too. Where's Grandfather?"

"How should I know? Like a ghost, that man."

"Haven't seen him in a couple of days."

"Me neither. That's what he does."

"Did he say anything?"

Sumac shook his head. "Last time we talked, it was about you. Probably your fault."

"What did he say?"

"Talked about you not going on your quest. Might have to go himself."

That sent the barbarian's heart racing. "Haven't seen him since?"

"Nope." Sumac's eyes darted around the village. "You're not supposed to be here."

"Leaving now. Just checking on Grandfather."

"I'm calling the rest of the Council."

"You do that." Thundersquat combed the ground around the village three times. Beyond the ridge, he searched in expanded semicircles. He discovered a partial footprint, maybe a day old. Grandfather's, no doubt. Probably just out hunting.

He took his bearings from the tree on the ridge and followed a direct line away from the village in a more or less eastward direction. The stallion fell in behind him. The barbarian turned up another sign, a thousand strides to the east. He encountered another partial footprint a couple thousand strides farther. He never knew Grandfather to leave such a clear trail. *Must be slipping. Unless he wants him to find him. What is he up to?*

He took a final look back at the ridge that now concealed the village. *Have to fend for themselves for a while. It'll be okay. Just a dream. Nothing's gonna happen.*

∾

At the eastern edge of the Badlands, a series of ridges lay in rumpled folds as far as he could see. In the distance a twisted mountain rose above the rest. Thundersquat caught a glimpse of it through the trees now and then. He used it to stay oriented. The forest thickened the farther he went in. It bombarded him with sounds and smells: rustling leaves, birds, bugs, things moving in the shadows. Bolstrus was as jumpy as a sand flea. Back in the Badlands, they could see forever. There was plenty of time to react if anything happened. Out here, if you blinked, you were some creature's lunch.

Never should've come. Only gonna get worse. But this is where the trail leads. If the old man needed him, he was gonna be there.

A strange aroma intruded and strengthened as they moved deeper into the woods. Thundersquat traced the smell to a clearing near a small pond. They stopped at the edge. The smell seemed to emanate from an old tree, very wide at the base of the trunk, across the clearing. Smoke escaped from a hole in the tree, about as high as he could reach.

Something wasn't right. The leaves and brush around the tree were missing. The area was spotless. This was completely backward. They wouldn't be able to hear anybody come up on them. Ripe for an ambush. Ever since he entered the woods, he couldn't take a step without making noise. Put predators and prey alike on alert. Who would be fool enough to clear that advantage away?

They watched. They listened. The stallion stayed among the trees, while the barbarian ventured out into the clearing. He split his attention between the surrounding trees and the ground. Scrape marks on the trees. Emerging from the pond, two sets of footprints—one of them Grandfather's. Off to the side, a worn patch revealing a large cat print and a few long strands of hair—a lion, maybe. He circled the old tree and inspected the cracks in the bark.

A chunk of earth and tree between the roots swung open. Thundersquat seized a creature by the throat and pinned it against the tree. Bolstrus charged out of the bushes and reared. A small troll, with receding red hair and skin slightly tinged with green, stared wide-eyed at the stallion.

Thundersquat allowed his racing heart to slow to a fast jog. "Don't sneak up on me like that."

"Sorry," the troll said in a hoarse whisper.

Thundersquat set him down and raised an eyebrow. He loosened his grip but kept his hand in place around the troll's throat. "Don't stink like other trolls."

"I can't help that. Will you please let me breathe?"

They stared at each other for a long moment. Bolstrus retreated into the woods.

Thundersquat released the troll.

The troll rubbed his neck. "You're a barbarian? From the Badlands?"

Thundersquat nodded.

"Are you going to kill me?"

"Not today."

"Are you going to tear the place up?"

"Too much to do. Anybody else come through here? An old man?"

"Inside. You must be the one he's waiting for."

Thundersquat breathed a sigh of relief. He hadn't noticed how worked up he'd been.

"Have you eaten?" the troll asked.

"Can always eat."

"I go by the name Smidgel."

The barbarian nodded.

"Do you have a name?" The troll gestured toward the doorway.

The barbarian hesitated. "Thundersquat."

"Seriously?"

"Call me what you want." The barbarian stepped past the troll and squeezed through the opening toward the beckoning aroma.

"Sorry. I didn't mean to imply anything. I'm sure it's a fine name."

Thundersquat attacked the spiral stairway four steps at a time. As he approached the bottom of the stairs, he could see a hearth that had been dug out of the wall to the right. It was still smoking. An oval room had been dug out of the earth below the tree. The floor was perfectly level, with a curved edge at the base of the walls. A column of earth mushroomed out from the middle of the room, such that it was much wider at the ceiling. Roots jutted out from the top of the column and draped across the ceiling to reenter the earth near the top of the walls.

Thundersquat ducked to keep his hair from getting entangled in the roots and peeked around the column. Grandfather sat against the back wall. Relief swept over the barbarian. Before the old man stretched a cross section of a tree, honed and smoothed. Several smaller sections of a tree trunk were distributed around it, about half as high. Thundersquat took a step toward his grandfather and froze.

Between the barbarian and his grandfather, a spotted lion with a scruffy black mane lay on his side. The animal looked gaunt, but the bulge in his stomach indicated that he'd eaten recently.

The lion raised his head and looked the barbarian over. He growled.

"He's our guest, Mudcat," the troll said from behind the barbarian.

The lion moved his head to where he could see the troll and looked sideways at the barbarian.

No one moved.

The lion sputtered.

"Manners," the troll said.

The lion pulled up, stretched, and dragged himself over to the wall on the left, where he plopped down and rolled over onto his side.

"Sorry," the troll said. "We don't get a lot of barbarians out this way. One maybe ten, twelve years ago. Now two in one week."

Thundersquat kept his eye on the lion. "Ten, fifteen years ago... My father?"

"Can't know for sure," Grandfather said. "Right time frame."

"He didn't stay long," Smidgel said. "He seemed lost."

"Sounds like him." Grandfather dug into a pile of food stacked in front of him on top of a flattened bowl. "Got to try some of these. Calls them pancakes."

The troll set a pile of pancakes in front of the barbarian. "Blueberry cinnamon."

Thundersquat tore an edge and set it on his tongue. Warm, light on the tongue, it almost melted in his mouth. He plopped down on one of the seats and stuffed a whole pancake into his cheek. "What are you up to, Grandfather?"

"Out for a walk. Stopped at the pond for a drink. Troll invited me in."

"Just out for a walk."

"Yep."

"Ever left the Badlands before?"

"Nope."

"Pretty far walk." Thundersquat swallowed. He closed his eyes and savored the taste. "Worth the trip. Didn't know trolls could cook."

"I had to learn, because of a condition I have."

"What condition?"

"I was born with it. The red hair's a tipoff. It's very rare. You know how trolls throw themselves onto a fresh kill, if they can get it?"

"Came across a troll once. Chewing on a rotten carcass. Kept batting the buzzards away."

"Exactly. That's what most trolls do. But I can't."

"Don't like it raw?" Grandfather asked.

"That's not it, exactly. I do miss the taste." Smidgel paused. "I wish I were like all the others. You see, when I first learned to talk, I found that I could understand animals."

"In their language?" Thundersquat asked. "Not just guessing from how they move?"

"Yes. I didn't know at first that the others couldn't do it." The red-haired troll's face tightened. "Most trolls have conversation over dinner while they wolf it down. I had conversations *with* dinner before it became dinner. It was unbearable. When I could no longer stand to eat meat, I started eating plants and vegetables."

"Not me," Thundersquat said. "Wouldn't miss a meal, no matter what it said."

"It was hard to get used to at first. Over the years, I taught myself to cook. The others wouldn't have anything to do with me."

"Found out where the sorcerer king lives," Grandfather said.

"What?" Thundersquat asked.

"Onyx Palace, on top of that twisted mountain. Troll here has heard of the Half-Forgotten Stone."

Smidgel wrinkled his forehead. "I can't say a lot about what I remember. But I'm pretty sure the sorcerer king knew something about it."

"Doesn't matter. Need to get back to the village."

"At least you know where to start looking, if you ever decide to try," Grandfather said.

"Might be a waste of time."

"Won't know until you do it."

"What's so important about a quest?" Thundersquat asked.

"Hard to say. Up to each of us to decide, after it's over."

"What about yours?"

"Still trying to figure it out," Grandfather said.

"Could've saved yourself all the trouble. Don't go in the first place."

"Then I'd be trying to figure out why not."

Thundersquat nodded slowly.

Grandfather tore off half a pancake. "The people don't have a lot of traditions. Can't seem to pay attention long enough to hand anything down. The quest is one tradition we managed to keep track of."

"Doesn't mean we have to keep doing it."

"What's keeping you?" Grandfather asked.

Thundersquat took in a deep breath. Grandfather wasn't letting this go. "Might be gone for a while."

"A lot of nothing can happen while you're gone."

"Maybe. What if something bad happened?"

"Nothing you can't handle," the old man said.

"I mean to the village. To you."

"Mm, hmm. Nothing you can't handle."

Thundersquat shook his head. "Had a dream. Monster."

"Might mean something. Might not."

"Didn't end well."

"Still just a dream. Probably nothing."

"What about my father?" Thundersquat asked. His face felt hot.

"That was real enough." Grandfather sniffed. "Can't put off living because you're afraid."

"Think I'm afraid?" That was one of the worst things his grandfather could have implied.

"Not of any challenge. But of what might happen to us if you're not around."

Thundersquat leaned back and slowly blew out to the side.

Grandfather said, "Remember what we say when we pack up and leave. 'Where we go, we don't know.'"

Thundersquat finished the statement, eyes cast downward. "Trouble can't find us."

Grandfather nodded.

"Want me to go?"

"Up to you. Nobody can decide that for you." Grandfather smiled. "Could start in the morning."

"Yeah. Back to the Badlands." Thundersquat glanced at the sleeping lion and addressed the troll. "How long have you lived with that animal?"

"A few years. He showed up one night in a terrible thunderstorm and never left."

"Safe to sleep around him?"

"So far."

The lion lifted his head and looked Thundersquat over.

"Sleeping outside tonight."

Thundersquat awoke early. He threw the door open and

scrambled down the stairs inside the old tree. Grandfather was gone.

"What's the matter?" the troll asked.

"Did you hear him leave?"

"No. I'm sorry."

"How did he get past me?" Thundersquat tried to conceal his concern. "Don't know if he went back to the Badlands or went the other way, toward that palace."

"Would you like Mudcat to try and locate his scent?"

The spotted lion grumbled and shifted his position, now facing away.

"Don't be so quick to judge. You don't know what he's capable of." Smidgel turned to the barbarian. "I might offer a word of advice."

Thundersquat nodded. "Can't hurt."

"Go to the sorcerer king. If you find him, you'll be closer to your goal and you'll be there if your grandfather needs you."

"What if he went back to the Badlands?"

"You can always go back there afterward. What can happen in that short a time?"

A lot, judging from the tightness in his chest. Still, Grandfather would be okay; he was sure of it. Almost. Thundersquat looked back and forth from the direction of the palace to the way home. His thoughts returned to what Grandfather said. No need to get bent out of shape over a dream. If he didn't go after the quest, he'd be thinking about it the rest of his life. Worse, Grandfather thought he was afraid. *That's it, then.*

He took a deep breath and began to stride toward the twisted mountain. "Can't be that far ahead of me."

"Wait! We'll come with you," the troll said.

"Only slow me down."

"Well, let us know how it turns out."

The barbarian tossed a backhanded wave without turning around. Something seemed off with all this. Usually, he was okay about not knowing things, but this wasn't one of those times.

Bolstrus fell in behind him.

Chapter Six

MARKET DAY

STEP ONE, LOSE the guards. Blundren led Dekatria to the chain of booths packed with people in the open square. One guard preceded them. Three others stayed in close proximity. It wasn't just the guards. Blundren could feel everyone's eyes on her, the daughter of the sorcerer king. And Dekatria's sensual beauty turned heads across the square. Melting into the background with the rest of the unnoticed could be quite a challenge. She pressed against a booth to allow a large peasant woman to squeeze by. A middle-aged man trudged behind, eyes glazed over. *The shopping dead.*

Blundren smiled. She leaned close to Dekatria. "Do what I do."

The young ladies examined every hand-woven basket, every collection of beads. They engaged every vendor in conversation. She used seventeen of the twenty-five levels of shopping she'd been trained in. The guards' eyes dimmed. One by one they checked out, retaining some ability to move but otherwise devoid of evidence of higher reasoning. Blundren approached the squad leader and pointed. "Is that shop safe? My father taught me to never place myself in danger."

The squad leader's eyes kept reverting to Dekatria. Her eyelids had a way of drifting down when she talked to the men. It didn't just draw them in; they leaped in.

If that's where their attention goes, then so be it. Use it. Keep the goal in mind.

The squad leader roused two of the guards and ordered them to check out the shop. When they returned, Blundren paused at the entrance. "You'll be here the whole time?"

"We'll be here until you come out." His eyes absorbed Dekatria.

Blundren gave him a mental thwack on the forehead. I'm over here, she almost said aloud.

Dekatria gifted him with a hint of a smile and a slight tilt of the head. Her eyelids closed to the sweet spot that ensnared his soul and wrapped him in a web of timeless intimacy. "It might be a while."

"Take as long as you want."

If she asked for a place to sit, he'd toss in the deed to his hovel.

The guards inspected each shop before they went in. Each time, Blundren took longer than before. Dekatria thanked the guards when they came out. The guards lit up like a bonfire, all four of them. As the morning wore on, the flames diminished. About midday, the squad leader nodded at her thanks with a reassuring smile that disappeared when he looked away.

Blundren caught Dekatria's eye. "Now."

The two young ladies hurried out the back into the alley. Trying to keep from laughing, they backtracked along the back edge of the village as casually as they could. At the edge of the woods, Blundren retrieved the manuscript that she'd hidden.

"You're quite the liar, Princess."

"Not so bad yourself. I wish I could see their faces when they figure it out."

They entered the woods. Blundren rolled out the parchment and studied it.

"Be careful," Dekatria said. "Words have power out here."

"It's okay. We won't disturb any angry spirits. This spell shows how to join the soul of a person with that of an animal. For the rest of your life, that animal will then be a special spirit guardian whenever there is any kind of trouble." Blundren glanced around the surrounding woods. "Maybe we should look for a rabbit or bird or something. It wouldn't be much of a guardian, but it may be enough to test the spell."

"Are you sure we should take chances with this? What if some bird that joins with your soul flies smack into a tree? Do you drop dead on the spot?"

"Nothing's going to happen."

Dekatria placed a hand on Blundren's forearm. "I'm serious. Suppose it backfires and something happens to me?"

Blundren gave her a sideways glance and rolled up the parchment. She searched the ground for signs of wildlife.

Dekatria held back. "Something's out here. I heard something."

"Don't let your fear run away with you." She spotted a rabbit, which promptly froze. "That's probably what you heard, over there."

"It sounded like it came from behind us."

"Sound bounces around out here. You never know where it comes from."

The rabbit scampered off as they drew closer. The rabbit dodged right and disappeared over a slight ridge. They spread out and poked among the bushes. The rabbit took off. Little by little, the pair made their way deep into the forest.

Dekatria pointed at the ground. "Is that from a wolf?"

Blundren examined the paw print. "I guess so. I don't know what else it could be..."

"Villagers speak of a white wolf who watches over the woods."

"I've been out here lots of times. I've never seen any signs of a wolf."

"Until now."

"I suppose."

"What if he's close?" Deketria asked. "Those tracks look fresh."

"Let's go a little farther. We'll be fine."

"We need to turn back."

The rabbit darted out from under a bush. Dekatria jumped. Blundren pounced on the rabbit and pinned it to the ground. She slid a palm under its chest and neck and clamped down on the loose skin over its shoulders. The rabbit squirmed and kicked as she handed it to Dekatria. The priestess held it close, and the rabbit settled down.

The princess unrolled the parchment and set rocks on the ends to hold it open. She raised her hands waist high, tilted her head, crossed her eyes, and wiggled her fingers. "*Amime mosdle sembel lumaled. Umo amimo, umo okulalum, ad edelmidadem.*"

"Did you feel anything?" Dekatria asked.

"No. As I expected."

"What do the words mean?"

"'Let our souls be forever joined, one mind, one set of eyes, for the rest of time.' It means we'd share the same distorted view of the universe for the rest of our lives."

An unseen force slammed into her. Something coiled

around her chest and squeezed. She felt like she was being pulled toward a nearby hedge, like she was falling sideways. She dug her feet in. The pressure dissipated and left her head swimming. Blundren sat down hard and stared at the ground. She gasped, "Let the rabbit go."

"You look pale," Dekatria said.

"Little lightheaded. Look at him run. My protector."

"So you're bonded with the rabbit now?"

"Hardly."

"Maybe we should catch it again to find out."

Blundren experienced the pleasant sensation of tearing into the rabbit's flesh, the warm blood trickling down her throat. She choked back the vomit that followed. She stalked off through the brush. She slapped branches out of the way. "Let's go home."

"Slow down—you'll get us lost."

"Keep up."

A bird sneezed. Blundren jerked to the side and dropped to a knee. A flock of birds took off.

"They sneeze when someone with great power comes near," Dekatria said.

"Folklore. It doesn't mean a thing." Blundren's sleeve snagged, and she ripped it free. She picked up the pace. Branches thrashed her about the head and shoulders. She didn't know what was worse, the urge to chow down on a live rabbit or the fact that she liked the sensation. Regardless, she needed to get away.

"There's a price to pay when you abuse the old ways," Dekatria called.

Blundren stopped. She allowed her heart to decelerate. She wouldn't ever abuse the old ways. She simply had a healthy disregard for anything patently ridiculous. She'd watched her father put on demonstrations over the years, when he wasn't lost to squatting oblivion. He'd explained to her how he did what he did. There was nothing to any of this. It was all show.

Dekatria caught up. "I'll have to go through a purification ritual to cleanse myself of what we've done."

"Save yourself the trouble. I'll just whip up a rainstorm." Blundren flicked her fingers at the sky. A vortex of black clouds charged across the sky and collided. The clouds exploded with pounding rain. In seconds, they were drenched. Blundren's head was spinning, like she'd stood up too fast.

"What did you do?"

"Nothing. It came out of nowhere."

"Let's get out of here before you do something else."

"Like what, stomp my foot and cause an earthquake?" Blundren slammed her foot into a puddle. "It's just not—"

A low rumble silenced her. The ground trembled. Blundren took a knee, trying not to pass out. A wavelike rocking as deep as her ankle went on for a count of thirty or more. Branches collided and debris rained down. Fighting the nausea, she met Dekatria's stare. "Come on! I didn't make that happen, any more than I can wave my arms and stop the rain."

She threw her arms up to illustrate. The downpour slowed to a trickle. Blundren dropped to all fours and steadied herself until the head spinning slowed down enough to regain her footing.

Dekatria stretched her hair and wrung it out. "I think I saw what I came to see."

"Don't get too excited," Blundren said. "The spell didn't work. I didn't join souls with the rabbit."

"What about the rainstorm? The earthquake?"

"Coincidence."

"Quite a few for one afternoon."

A cloud overhead turned the woods into layers of shadows. Blundren ducked her head, a reflex action, as if the skies were about to open up again. When nothing happened, she raised her head and smiled. "That time you know I didn't do anything."

A thunderous drone blared from above as hundreds of creatures dropped out of the sky and swarmed the princess, flinging her to the ground. Flapping, twittering animals clung to her. She twisted and flailed around. Tiny claws pinched her all over. She couldn't see. She couldn't breathe. "Dekatria!"

There was no answer. A group of bats lifted the princess off the ground and carried her away. She caught a glimpse of her friend watching from behind a tree at the edge of the clearing. *She's safe.*

A single beat of relief was swept aside by a crescendo of terror. The cloud of creatures whipped around and through trees. A branch broke against her shoulder and swatted several of the bats off. Blundren dropped. Others swooped in to grab hold. Several bats sneezed. Blundren slipped out of their grasp. Others took their place. She closed her eyes. More bats sneezed.

Blundren seesawed and rolled as the bats rotated in and out. She felt the urge to pray. The choppy snatch-and-glide flight carried her high above the trees toward the Onyx Palace. *Don't let go. Don't let go. Don't let go.*

Chapter Seven

SHAKEN UP

THE TINGLING ON THE SURFACE gave no hint of the ruptures that ripped through layers far below. Shaken and stirred, a deep stupor that stretched across centuries came to an abrupt end. A jolt of fear and outrage shocked a buried creature into a groggy state of awareness. *Move,* urged the whispers that stirred its soul. Bit by crumbling bit, the creature tore itself from the comfort of tightly pressed earth. The creature scraped and pulled itself forward through fractured rock. It consumed the freed particles and expelled the dirt behind. Each victory of claws over the earth's loosening grip drove the creature onward.

The creature poked a claw through to the surface and wriggled it at the nothingness beyond. It punched through. Its other fist followed shortly, then its face. A cool drape of muggy air and fresh smells assailed its nostrils, unlike those of the ancient bog it had once known. The creature rolled its head around, unsettled by the sudden lack of resistance. It let loose a wail from the depths of hell and recoiled from the unbuffered blast.

The creature stretched a limb, then another, and wriggled free. Everything was wrong. Unbalanced and stiff, the creature dragged itself forward in rigid jerks against unfamiliar gravity. A wisp of dark and light tumbled like a cloud inside its skull. Faded echoes of the past teased the edges of its mind. Others had passed this way before. *Surface ones...pain... surface ones. Find the One.*

Chapter Eight

INTO THE WOODS

SOMETHING YANKED WOLFMINI out of the pond. Hard slaps jarred the inside of his skull, as if someone had whipped him with a truncheon from within. The blurred silhouette in the bright light faded into Jermbog, doubled over in front of him, hands on his knees as he tried to catch his breath. The sounds of the words lingered until their meaning jolted the sorcerer king out of his clouded focus.

"Taken? What do you mean, taken? By whom?"

"Bats. A whole colony. Carried her over the palace."

The sorcerer king frowned. "Which direction?"

"East, Your Eminence."

"Summon the leader of the palace guards." Wolfmini had never seen Jermbog run before. The magistrate seemed to run a long time in the same place. Either that or his sense of time had been altered. The way his head pounded, that was a distinct possibility.

Regardless, his daughter was in grave danger, and otherworldly forces were clearly at play. He felt a sense of dread over what he was about to do. The sorcerer king's fingers trembled as he reached for two vials. He whispered a special incantation above the viewing pedestal. His hands rose with a flourish as he poured the liquids on opposite sides. They whirled around the stone bowl, met with a hiss, and released a yellow vapor. The solution settled and formed a clear, mirror-like surface. Wolfmini closed his eyes and emptied his mind of all thought. His eyelids floated halfway up. He peered into the solution, careful to keep his measured breath from rippling the surface.

An image came into focus. A wolf. His heart skipped. The liquid surface clouded over and became choppy. He let the liquid settle while he quieted the chemicals in his body. *There.* Flying creatures scrambled, loosely massed around a human form. The liquid surface jiggled. *Easy, don't lose the image.*

Bats darted away from Blundren; others zoomed in to take their places. The flock plummeted and dropped her on the ground in a gap in the woods before they scattered wildly. They gathered again in formation and resumed their flight eastward. His daughter sat in a tiny clearing, huddled over, her head down and her arms wrapped around herself.

Wolfmini slumped to the cold floor. Sleep clamored for his attention, demanding that he obey. The croaking grew louder. An image flashed of the wolf, but the flick of adrenaline it produced was not enough to offset the fatigue. He could barely make out the face of the guard. Words foundered, dodging his clumsy efforts to retrieve them. The guard faded.

Wolfmini awoke, stooped over in the amphibian squat that was far too comfortable. It felt as if a flock of woodpeckers were hammering against the inside walls of his skull. Jermbog and the chief of the guards hovered around him.

"My daughter?"

"No news yet, Your Eminence. We sent out several search parties."

"Let me know when you find her."

Once he was alone, fears for his daughter swarmed like angry bees. He paced while he weighed the options. He knew the odds of doing anything to help her out there were almost zero. He'd be at risk to predators every time he leaped back into the pond, and he couldn't always choose when the jump occurred. Worse, his daughter could walk right past him, and he wouldn't even see her. Wolfmini pressed both hands against the wall and searched the floor for a better answer. The safe move would be to sit and wait for information. Helpless. Worthless as a father. The prudent choice was not an option. *It must be now. I won't be in this body for long.*

The sorcerer king slipped out of the palace. As far as he knew, no one saw him hurry through the gardens and wind down the spiral path around the mountain into the woods. Beyond the minty fragrance of the deep forest, he detected the faint stench of rotting vegetation. Croaking followed, muffled by distance. He quickened his pace.

Blundren shivered in the tiny clearing, afraid to move but unable to sit still, either. The evening light would not last much longer. She paced in a circle, no longer sure which direction she'd come from. Scattershot flashes of trees looked the same on all sides. She pressed her fingers to her temples and sought to relax. She should have paused to get her bearings before she started running in circles. She knew it. But she couldn't stop herself. Just move, she screamed inside to herself. *Any direction. Get as far as I can.*

She threaded the trees and waded into knee-deep weeds

and vines. The heavy undergrowth tugged at her. The princess ripped out of the clutches of one vine only to be snared by another. She spun around. It felt just like the bats. She tried to quell her rising panic.

A tree beckoned. Blundren scrambled up the trunk in circular fashion, until the branches swayed under her weight. She settled into a crook of the tree and locked her legs and arms around the trunk as if to squeeze the life out of it. If something wants her for dinner tonight, they'll have to work for it.

She woke frequently throughout the night. Clouds blotted out the stars and buried the sliver of moon. In the overwhelming blackness, she wondered at times if she was moving. She was not entirely sure about up or down. She clung to the branches until her fingers cramped. Her first thought when she awakened fully was that she was still alive, even though she could not feel her arms or legs. After a few seconds, she dared to look. A quick check revealed no sign of having been devoured.

When the sun was well above the trees, she climbed down.

She never felt this alone, though she'd always been alone. This afraid—never. Judging from the rays that had penetrated the canopy earlier, she guessed where west was and plowed into the tangled vines again. She squeezed between two trees, ducked below a branch, and froze.

She stood face-to-face with a wolf, mostly white, at least a quarter larger than any wolf she'd ever seen. Granted, she'd never seen one this close. She couldn't outrun him, could never get up a tree in time. Yet she felt not one iota of fear. No, she felt intrigued.

The wolf's green eyes seemed to peruse her from the vantage of several lifetimes. After the sleepless terror of the night, she felt drained. It crossed her mind that waiting to become a meal should feel different than this. Not different. It should feel like something, not nothing, even if no more than a fraction of a preference not to be eaten. Blundren imagined his white fur splattered with her blood after he quite naturally tore into her flesh, but she only felt relief. And curiosity. *Is this what happens when you're about to die? You become objective about the whole thing?*

The wolf took half a step back and lowered his head. His ears folded against his skull, and he bared his teeth. Blundren crouched slightly and emitted a low growl. She showed her teeth to the wolf. She wondered if anything was stuck in them.

What am I doing? This is hardly a social event.

The wolf cocked his head. He ran his tongue across his teeth.

"What now, wolf?"

He faced away from her and glanced back in her direction.

"No way am I sniffing your butt." She was annoyed when the wolf rolled his eyes. *Since when do wild animals do that? Minor point, maybe. He might eat me, but don't judge me.*

The wolf held her gaze as he walked slowly into the forest.

Probably leading me to the pack—ravenous, half-crazed, ready to rip me to shreds. Outside chance he's taking me home to the palace. Sure.

Any sane person would avoid the greater risk. But her gut told her something different from the argument in her mind. And the wolf smelled okay. *Like that's a thing.* She followed him. "At least one of us knows where we're headed."

Late in the morning the wolf stalked a rabbit. The wolf crouched down, motionless for a minute, before he slowly moved forward. An image flashed in Blundren's mind of her teeth clamped on the rabbit's neck, shaking it vigorously back and forth. She cleared her head and glanced at the wolf. The wolf gazed intently at the rabbit. He slid another paw forward, but paused when the rabbit froze. Blundren couldn't contain her excitement any longer. Her whole body quivered. She charged. The rabbit spooked. The wolf flashed a canine at her.

"Sorry," Blundren said. "Don't make such a big deal out of it."

When the evening light dimmed, Blundren sat and leaned against a wide tree. Every inch of her legs screamed in pain. Her muscles tightened, and her calves trembled. She felt the wolf watching her. She spotted a tree a short dash away that she could probably climb. Another night in a tree, trying to hang on with these exhausted legs, was not likely feasible. The risk was not worth it. She kept her eyes open late into the night, shivering, but the cold helped her stay awake.

Hours later the wolf arose and took a step toward her. She lurched back against the tree. He shifted to the left, facing away from her. His forepaws slid forward, and he dropped his head. His breathing slowed as he drifted off to sleep. Blundren fought it but ultimately succumbed to the tyranny of micro-sleep.

The next day they found some berries. She stuffed her mouth full. Juice dribbled down her chin. They walked along a creek, and Blundren slipped. The wolf spun around and broke her fall. Both of them jumped back. She stepped past the wolf and knelt at the edge of the creek. The wolf eased alongside. Eyes on each other, they lowered their heads and lapped at the water. She splashed her face and combed her fingers through her straggly hair. They resumed their journey.

That night was just as cold as the one before. Again, the wolf waited for her to settle and took his position. When her eyes snapped open to check on the wolf, he blinked back at her, his eyes no wider than an unfocused slit.

On the third night, the wolf reclined next to her, parallel. A breeze stirred and rustled through the trees. She spread her numb fingers above his shoulder and let them drift down to the tip of his fur. He opened his eyes. She jerked her hand away. She touched him again and let her hand settle. He remained still. She felt his head and neck relax. After a while Blundren let herself lean against him. The warmth helped. She snuggled in and laid her head on his shoulder; sleep summoned them both.

Several days later, at the edge of the woods surrounding her village, the wolf halted. At the sight of the palace, a wave of emotion jammed up in her throat. Blundren placed a hand on either side of the wolf's face. She caressed the top of his head and scratched behind his ear. The wolf drew in and nuzzled her. They both sneezed.

Blundren pushed her legs up the spiral incline that encircled the twisted mountain. They were numb when she arrived at the courtyard, but nevertheless she quickened her pace and entered the Onyx Palace at a wobbly run. She fought back tears. "Father!"

Jermbog exited from the sorcerer king's study. He slammed the door behind him and leaned against it. His gaze flitted about. "His Eminence sends his apologies, Highness. He'll see you when he can. I can't interrupt him right now."

Her hands were blistered, and her lips were chapped. She hadn't bathed in a week; her hair hung in greasy strands along her face. She recalled the bats dropping her, then catching her, and her heart fluttered. Flashes of the dark night in the tree and her first face-to-face encounter with the wolf shot a chill through her body.

And her father couldn't be interrupted. She glared at the door behind Jermbog. "Tell him not to bother."

Alone and safe in her room, self-pity and fear fumed and fizzled in turn. She huddled on her bed, shaking. Her eyes filled with tears.

When she heard a noise behind her, she jerked upright and snapped her head to the right. Two feet above the floor, a tiny old man hovered in a wispy glow. *How wonderful. Now I'm seeing things that aren't there.*

"It's me, Herbert." He wore a big smile, like she was supposed to know who he was. Seeing and hearing things.

"Herbert." That was all she could think to say. She repeated herself. "Herbert."

"Herb."

"Herb." Her breathing was shallow.

"Sorry I'm running late. I'm the worst at making time conversions. What has it been, a week or more since your first act of magic?"

Sleep deprivation, most likely. Stress. A daydream gone wild? "I need to eat something."

"You question magic, do you? You remind me of your grandmother."

"My grandmother?" Talking to someone who didn't exist was surreal.

"Your father's mother. Are you a Querion, like her?"

"I never knew her. What's a Querion?"

"The Querions question everything. They believe in nothing. That is, nothing is all they believe in. They teach that you can't know for sure what something is, but you can be pretty sure that it's not nothing."

"I never heard it put like that, but it kind of makes sense." Intriguing idea, even if it came from a figment of her imagination. Blundren slowly repeated the phrase. "We can't know what something is, but there's one thing that it's not, and that's nothing."

"Yes! We like to say that they know nothing."

Right. "So, my grandmother was one of these Querions?"

"Did your father tell you anything at all about your family? She was almost impossible to train. And she had a very difficult time because both of her boys excelled in the old ways."

"Both of her boys... My father had a brother?"

"Has a brother."

"I have an uncle I've never heard about? Why not? Add that to a father who's never there for me—what's the difference? And now I'm talking to a little old man floating in the air." *Apparently, my hallucinations are supposed to stick to what's possible.*

"You don't believe that I exist? How did I train your family in the old ways for hundreds of years? Who do you think trained Futhark the Meddler?" He disappeared.

Blundren grabbed both sides of her head tightly and stared wildly around the empty room.

Chapter Nine

THE GREAT BEAR

THE BATS RETURNED without the sorcerer king's daughter. The Least High Druid looked straight ahead as they scattered, but his attention was on Snartglobber to his left. The Qrudd chieftain's eyes smoldered. He always glared at everybody like he knew they were going to screw up and he'd catch them when they did. Right now, he looked like he was ready to pounce. The sparkle in his eyes betrayed his eagerness.

The Least High Druid fought the impulse to flee. Fear was on the verge of catapulting his thoughts into images of future torture and pain, to the chieftain's inevitable delight. Instead, he steadied himself and concocted a story the chieftain would likely believe about what happened. He'd spin it from there. "Just as I thought. Princess Blundren is quite powerful."

Snartglobber's hand closed on the hilt of his dagger. His signature move had become old a long time ago, but the druid wasn't inclined to help the Qrudd make things more interesting. The chieftain was unpredictable enough.

Most people played it wrong. They wilted under the heat of that glare; they stumbled in to fill the silence. The druid waited a beat longer than expected and then made sure to maintain a casual tone. "Now that we've tested her, we have a better idea of what we're up against. The first thing we need to do is spread havoc through the Blisterian countryside. Create a diversion, while we move in and take her."

An edge of the head chieftain's mouth flicked upward, barely noticeable.

Got him.

The druid faced the floor and closed his eyes. He placed both index fingers against his temples. He raised his head, opened his eyes and let his face turn pale. The Least High Druid addressed the wall in a vacillating, conciliatory tone, as if he were searching for the right words. "Surely not... N-no question it would work. A bit extreme. But...to set the great bear loose on them..."

"Least High!" the chieftain whispered. "You'd disturb the great bear?"

The druid continued to address the wall. "That's pushing the boundaries of what we consider sacred."

Least High nodded slowly and turned toward the chieftain. He spoke in a low voice. "Long ago, in return for saving his life, the ancient spirit who dwells in the soul of the great bear made me a promise." He swallowed. "I can ask it one time, one time only, to do whatever I want. I've never asked." The druid squinted at the chieftain. "I've never told anybody. How did they know?"

"Who?"

"Them." The druid stared at the wall. He took a deep breath. "How important is this?"

Snartglobber relaxed his grip on the dagger. "Get it done." He headed toward the door.

The druid knew of no ancient spirit linked to the great bear. But it was a simple matter to slap together a mix that would block an animal's sense of smell for a while and confuse its sense of direction. It was an almost even chance that it would wander away from what used to be familiar. If the bear headed west, it should be enough to produce the desired effect. If any other direction, the druid would blame something he'd been concerned about all along and locate another bear. At least Snartglobber didn't ask about the main plan.

Snartglobber halted at the door and turned halfway. He narrowed his eyes. "What about the main plan?"

"We have people in place. Just need to create the opportunity." Too late, the druid realized he'd spoken too quickly.

"You don't have a clue, do you?" In one fluid motion, the chieftain flicked his dagger past the druid's ear. He smirked, apparently quite pleased with himself. "I like to keep my skills sharp."

Least High didn't flinch. The druid casually reached for the dagger embedded in the wall just behind him. With his thumb and forefinger, he rocked it loose and dangled it by the handle. The dagger transformed into a wriggling serpent. The druid gripped the snake by the tip of its tail and approached the Qrudd chieftain. "So do I."

The sneer vanished from Snartglobber's face. Least High couldn't help but feel satisfaction. He jiggled the serpent once and switched it back to a dagger. The druid flipped it and extended the handle toward Snartglobber. The chieftain snatched it out of his hand and strutted through the door a little too fast to be effective. The druid found it gratifying, but he set it aside. He had set a plan in motion and now he had to see it through. It may not work, but he'd be there every step of the way and wing it when necessary.

The holy man had never actually seen a great bear up close. At the workbench, surrounded by vials of flowers, roots, tree bark, and leaves, he calculated how much he'd need of each ingredient and doubled it. As he ground the necessary ingredients into powder, he envisioned the size of the great bear and doubled the amount again. His fingers trembled as he threaded them through the mix. The druid scraped the mix into a pouch and stashed it inside a leather satchel. He slung the satchel over his shoulder and headed out the door.

By midmorning the fetid signature of the village announced its presence long before the druid could see it. It was a sacred duty among all five clans of the Qrudds to spread their garbage around, evidence of their pride in marking their territory as their own. The stench was a blaring announcement, warning others to enter at their own risk. The Egg Stealers clan was particularly devout in this regard. A thousand strides away, the druid's eyes watered. It usually stopped after a day or two.

He headed for a grove of trees that jutted above the surrounding high grass. The village was just beyond the tree line. The children soon came running to crowd around him, jumping up and down.

"Least High! Least High!"

Several women hurried over as well.

"Please, Least High, my son is sick."

"My uncle can't get out of bed."

"Of course I'll look at them," the Least High Druid said.

Most of the remaining members of the clan arrived as one group. In the center was the chieftain, a necklace with a single claw from the great bear bouncing on his ample belly. "Least High! Stands in the shadows of the great one himself!"

"Thorn, my friend!"

They embraced. The druid draped his arm around the chieftain's shoulder, and they strolled toward the village. Thorn pointed. "A new long house since you saw us last."

Least High looked at the rectangular structure framed by animal skins sewn together and draped from poles along the exterior walls. A thatched roof sloped gently from front to back. The entry opened in the middle of the longer side. The druid smiled at his friend. "The whole village could gather in there."

"What's it like being so near to the great one?"

"Busy. His needs are many, and his demands never cease."

The leader of the Egg Stealers drew him close and lowered his voice. "I hear that the great one slew ten thousand trolls on a bridge. They say he was armed with a single claw from the great bear."

"Trolls do like their bridges. And as you know, the great one wears a necklace of five bear claws around his neck."

"Five, true. So he was better armed than they said."

"Had to be."

"Still—ten thousand."

"Staggers the imagination." They walked in silence. The druid placed a hand on the chieftain's shoulder. "My old friend, I seek your advice."

"Whatever you need, Least High."

"I travel with secret instructions from the great one himself. I must select a hunter from each of the five clans."

The chieftain's face darkened. He stifled a brief tremble. He swallowed. "Our best hunter was taken from us not long ago. You can have Rock Feet, whose skill is nearly as good. And I'll send out runners to the other clans that you may save time on your journey."

"You're most generous, as always. Now tell me of your loss."

Deeply saddened, the Least High Druid searched for the mother of the recently fallen. He forced a smile at the laughing children who encircled him like chicks crowding a mother hen. He tossed one of them high in the air, then looked away as if suddenly distracted. He caught the child with a sudden swoop. The children clamored for his attention even more. He couldn't help but wonder which of them might be the next to die.

They followed him into the long house. Heads turned. The woman he sought should've been here, barking orders, overseeing a large pot of stew. An older woman sliced meat off a bandicoot and tossed it in the pot. She inclined her head toward the back. Least High opened his eyes wide and pointed a finger at the children. They quieted down.

"If any of you move," he said, "I'll eat you."

The children collapsed, giggling.

"Wait here," the druid said. "I'll be right back."

Behind the long house, where the light was dim in the shadows of the trees, he found her sitting alone, head down. When he sat beside her, she took no notice. There was nothing he could do. Death was final and he couldn't change it. No trick of the mind would suffice. His helplessness at times like this was something he could never get used to. After a long while she moved her head slightly toward him. He placed his arm around her. "I'm so sorry, my old friend. Such an empty space he left behind."

A tear trickled down her cheek.

"He was one of my favorites," the druid said. "I expected him to be chieftain someday. Like his father."

～

The next morning, Least High Druid, Thorn, and Rock Feet headed back into the grassland toward the meeting place that had been arranged. They went slowly. Two dangers threatened any who ventured into the open, forcing them to scour the sky, while they stooped below the top of the grass. With the druid's height, such a maneuver took its toll on him. He rubbed his neck with both hands. He said nothing. It was not wise to admit to weakness among any of the five clans. When the others weren't watching, the druid popped up and stretched his lower back.

Halfway to their destination, they heard movement in the grass ahead. The men held very still. Three giant wingless birds with powerful legs and long necks walked with their heads above the top of the grass. Every now and then one of the twelve-foot-tall moas stood erect and looked around.

Suddenly, an object shot out of the sky. The men ducked. They heard a tiny explosion as the object struck one of the birds. The other two moas fled.

"Raptor," Rock Feet whispered.

The Least High Druid placed a hand on Thorn's shoulder. His heart was still racing from the unexpected attack. He could only imagine the scene being played out in the chieftain's head. His friend's son had fallen just like the moa, perhaps from the very same bird.

They waited for about an hour, giving the unseen raptor time to feast. At last, the bird rose into the air and flew lazily away. It was one-third the size of the giant moa it had slain, but its wingspan exceeded the length of two men laid end to end. They watched the raptor as it soared out of sight. No one said anything.

The Rock Slingers were already at Round Stones when the three arrived. Lumpface, chieftain of the Rock Slingers, approached Thorn and the Least High Druid. The two older chieftains grasped each other's forearms and looked at each other in silence. Lumpface then turned to the Least High Druid. "Old friend, it has been many months."

"Not by my choice, old friend. The great one keeps me very busy."

Lumpface had a deep, booming voice. Heads turned when he spoke. "I hear the great one can fly."

The druid paused, choosing his words carefully. When it came to the peoples' view of Snartglobber, a passion lurked beneath the surface. The Qrudds not only failed to see the flaws that were painfully obvious to him, but they were also willing to believe outlandish things. Still, there was no gain in challenging such beliefs. Blind spots had more than once proven to be useful. "I never saw anything like that."

"He's truly blessed by the gods," Lumpface said.

"No, I mean I never personally saw such a feat by anyone, anywhere. Excuse me."

The druid moved toward a young Rock Slingers' hunter. As he walked away, he could not help overhearing the chieftains' conversation.

"What did he say about the great one's feet?" Thorn asked.

"Unlike any he'd ever seen."

"I never knew."

"I guess that's why he had to learn to fly."

That afternoon the Raw Fish Eaters clan arrived from the river on the western edge of the Qruddlands, carrying spears. They were heavily tattooed and reeked from the fish oil they spread on their bodies to protect them from mosquitoes and gnats. The yellow-painted Jackal clan from the eastern forests followed, carrying their poisonous darts and blowguns. Toward evening the silent, cliff-dwelling Cloud Men with their blue-painted faces appeared from the highlands up north. The other clans had arrived with great fanfare. The three dozen Cloud Men, on the other hand, were simply there all at once, standing as a group grasping their longbows, one end resting on the ground. The Least High Druid gathered them all together and led them in a sacred feast to bless the mission.

At dawn the Least High Druid headed north, accompanied by a young hunter from each of the five clans. To pass the time, the young men exchanged weapons and taught each other how to use them. Midafternoon the following day, they spotted their target across the plains.

The great bear loped on a direct course toward two wolves. One wolf was sprawled across a carcass, sampling the feast, relaxed, as though he had nowhere else to go. The other napped alongside the carcass. The great bear surged forward at an astonishing speed, given his size. The sleeper awoke just in time to roll away. The pair of wolves scattered. The bear positioned himself above their carcass. For the next few hours, the wolves harassed him, taking turns. One wolf became sloppy and drew too close. The bear ended it with one swipe of a paw. The other wolf withdrew. The great bear settled down for a meal.

"He should be busy here for a while," the druid said. "Let's find a way to bring him to us."

The five young hunters and the Least High Druid continued toward higher ground. They came upon the trail of a mountain goat. Normally an Egg Stealer would have thrown a bola, which would wrap around its legs and trip it. The warrior could then run up and finish the prey off with a knife or spear. But instead, Rock Feet placed a smooth round stone in the hollowed end of the curved stick used by the

Rock Slingers. The trick was in knowing when to release. Before long they spotted the goat and worked their way in close. Rock Feet reached back and swung the stick in a long arc as he strode forward. The rock struck the ground. The goat took off.

Next up was the warrior from the Cloud Men. Rock Feet offered the curved throwing stick to the blue-faced warrior. The Cloud Man declined, offering the Egg Stealer another chance at the goat, now cropping a bush on a hillside. This time the angle was tougher, almost straight above. Only the goat's forequarters showed. Rock Feet took aim and let fly the stone. It caught the animal in the throat. The goat leaped back out of sight. They heard it collapse on the loose rock. The Rock Slinger slapped the Egg Stealer on the back. They clambered up the slope to finish off the goat. A quick slice and the deed was done.

Least High surveyed the surrounding area as he reached for his satchel. He hesitated. The smell of blood was sure to bring the bear, sooner or later. But this was a terrible position to lie in waiting. The bear would block any avenue of escape. The druid reached his hands out in front of him, palms down, fingers outstretched, and moved them in a slow circle as if he were trying to detect something. "This is unholy ground. We need to move out."

The Raw Fish Eater, largest of the five Qrudds, slung the goat over the back of his shoulders like it was nothing. The terrain sloped gently downward as they hurried around curves. To make matters worse, boulders were strewn about. The druid scanned the energy folding around each boulder, his attention bouncing from one to the next in random fashion as they rushed forward. Periodically they slowed briefly to listen. The five warriors, though young, were seasoned hunters. Two of them were familiar with terrain like this. The druid could rely on them to give ample warning of anything amiss.

The great bear was on top of the Raw Fish Eater before anyone realized he was there. The bear seized the warrior by the neck and shoulder, shook him vigorously, and flung him to the side. The goat carcass tumbled forward. The great bear rose to his full height, taller than two men. The Least High Druid felt a cold chill in his middle shoot up his back.

The warrior from the Cloud Men leaped between the great bear and the goat carcass. His hand automatically reached for his longbow and came up empty. He whipped the bola around above his head and secured a few seconds' hesitation from the bear. "Take the goat."

Those were the first words the druid had heard him speak. Least High glanced at the Raw Fish Eater's lifeless body sprawled against the base of a boulder. For an instant the druid considered conceding the goat carcass in hope of rescuing the young warrior who stood between him and the bear. In the time it took for a single revolution of the bola, the druid determined he would not jettison the original plan. "You heard him."

Rock Feet seized the goat, and they took off. The three remaining hunters flipped the carcass back and forth as they raced through the rocky terrain behind the druid.

Two lives lost. So far. What kept me from sensing the presence of that bear? Least High had no idea how close the beast might be. It was clear they would not be able to outrun a great bear. A picture flashed through the druid's mind of the next time he would face their parents and grandparents. What could he say? That it was an honor to be taken by the great bear? He shook his head and erased the image. *They knew what they were getting into. If they'd paid better attention, they wouldn't have put me in this position.*

The druid's lungs were near bursting. He signaled for them to drop the goat. He closed his eyes and tried to catch his breath, as he mumbled incantations at high speed. He dumped the mix onto the carcass and rubbed it in furiously. The druid and the three remaining hunters scrambled behind nearby boulders, leaving the sacrificial offering in the open.

Before long the great bear loped up the trail and went straight for the goat. They ducked and listened as the sacred beast tore into the carcass. When the crunching and tearing ceased, they glanced at each other. The druid felt cold. He hazarded a peek. The bear sat back on its haunches, teetering slightly.

It was time for the show. The druid had second thoughts. Third thoughts. Surely there were other ways to create the diversion they needed. It seemed like a good idea before he found out exactly how big the bear was. Before he saw how easily he batted away the wolf. Before he heard the thwap of a strong young warrior against a boulder. But now three sets of eyes were studying him. Too late to back out. No way to know how much the bear consumed, how long his concoction would work. He'd have to wing it.

The Least High Druid stood tall and grand, his back arched, arms folded. He was conscious of the Qrudd warriors watching him. He strode up to the great bear. The beast blocked out half the sky. The druid felt every hair on his neck and beard rise a fraction of an inch. The bear swayed more violently now. He snapped his head forward and sloshed the druid with a spray of bear slobber. The druid caught a flash of alertness in the bear's eyes. *Better get on with it, and fast.*

He spread his arms wide. He mumbled nonsense and pointed west. Least High looked to the sky once more and turned around slowly. The bear let out a disturbed moan. The druid ambled back to the hunters, trying to make his arms swing casually. The warriors looked up expectantly. Least High gestured with a nod farther down the trail and jogged away. When they caught up, he leaned close to Rock Feet's ear as they ran. "We need to put as much distance as we can between us and the bear. Or we risk contaminating the spell."

The group hurried away at a swift trot, leaping occasionally as they worked their way down. Now the real gamble began, waiting and hoping the bear headed off in the right direction. The druid lengthened his stride, throwing himself recklessly down the slope.

The warriors kept pace. "How long will he be under, Least High?"

"Not long enough."

Chapter Ten

BEST PLAN

THUNDERSQUAT HAD QUITE enough of the forest. It wore him out trying to keep track of hiding places that might conceal a potential predator. He and the silver stallion paused often at unfamiliar noises that so far had turned out to be birds or small rodents. His eyes adapted well enough to the shadows, but he didn't feel right. The air draped over him like a heavy blanket. In the morning and late afternoon, beams of light punctured the canopy and threaded through the trees. He pictured himself out in the open, wrapped in the sun's warmth, blessing him with strength. How could anyone keep from growing weak in here, when all you received were broken pieces of sunlight?

At night, he was cut off from the stars that linked him to home and had to be content with what he could see in tiny patches of sky. As he locked onto that handful of stars, he wondered through the night how Grandfather let himself be taken in by a vague story about the world coming to an end, and how a stupid stone could stop it. And where was he now?

Meanwhile, whether Grandfather was in front of him or behind him, he'd left his village defenseless. Not that anything ever happened there. Who from the outside would want what they had? Nobody had anything. They'd survived a long time before he ever came along. The village was probably on the move again. That's a lot of work. They could do without him for a while.

The twisted mountain loomed before him that morning. A single black tower rose from an outcrop that jutted out near the top. He left Bolstrus at the edge of the forest. The spiral path that encircled the mountain was worn smooth, gray and black rock mixed with red clay. Tufts of grass and low growth sprouted on either edge. The dew sparkled on the grasses and leaves that faced the sun. He was surprised at the toll the path exacted on his calves and thighs. Still no sign of Grandfather. Most likely he went back to the village. Thundersquat had come this far. Might as well see this sorcerer king.

The barbarian hesitated at a gate that opened into a garden. A low wall, almost waist high, framed the outside edge of the outcrop. At the far end of the garden was the palace, constructed of shiny onyx stone. A tower rose in the middle above the entrance, as tall as three or four men. The lower half of the palace was attached to the mountainside on the left. Two shoulder-wide openings had been placed midway up, between the entrance and the mountain. A wide path, outlined with decorative stones, led from the palace entrance to the gate. On either side of the path were well-manicured arrangements of bushes. Surely they didn't grow that way naturally.

Thundersquat slipped into the garden on the mountain side and made his way to the palace entrance. He pounded on the heavy doors.

The doors opened a crack and slammed shut. Thunder-squat bashed his fist against the door.

Footsteps charged in from several directions behind him. A dozen soldiers formed a semicircle around Thunder-squat, the front row armed with spears and daggers. Archers fell in behind them and strung their bows. Thunder-squat slid to the side, putting a wall to his back. He sized up the warriors and decided which ones he'd have to take out first.

The door opened again, and an oily pink man appeared. "What are you supposed to be?"

The man's slightly upturned nose reminded him of UncleCousin Sumac. He wore a fine tunic with an embroidered hem. Detailed beadwork graced his belt and sandals. He waited half-turned in the doorway, eyebrows raised, eyelids half-closed, giving the impression that he had something else to do that was far more important. Like clean his fingernails. The barbarian had never seen fingernails that trim, clean, and shiny. Thundersquat tried not to stare. "Here to talk to the sorcerer king."

"You're a barbarian, aren't you? From the Badlands?" The man pressed his thumbs and fingertips together in an arch. His elbows rested on a shelf of flab that jutted out on either side of his torso. "Are they all like you?"

"What do you mean?" *Half my size and looking down his nose at me. How is that even possible?*

The pink man sent a knowing glance to the ring of soldiers, several of whom snickered. "You have the honor of speaking with Jermbog, Chief Magistrate of All Things Pertaining and Otherwise. What do you wish to meet with His Eminence about?"

"Between me and him."

"His Eminence is engaged in a project of utmost importance, critical to the welfare of the kingdom. Why should he interrupt this vital mission to talk to something like you?"

"Maybe he'll tell you when we're done."

"You're being impertinent. His Eminence has granted me complete authority over his schedule. How can I arrange a meeting with him unless he can consider the matter beforehand?"

"Save you the trouble." Thundersquat stepped toward the door. The soldiers closed in.

Jermbog blocked his path. "Anything a barbarian would have to say is trivial compared to what His Eminence is working on."

"Maybe not."

"Wait." The magistrate waved the soldiers off; they stepped back. He cocked his head back and pursed his lips while he eyed the barbarian. Jermbog sniffed and slowly exhaled. He tapped his fingertips together in a rolling pattern. "I'm not without influence. Perhaps if you were to take care of a small problem, His Eminence may look kindly upon whatever you will ask him to do for you."

"Running out of time."

"We received news of a great bear on a rampage up north. It may be too much for you, but if you take care of the bear, I'll set up a meeting." Jermbog started to close the door, pausing with a sideways look back. "It's only time, my friend, not the end of the world."

"Might be surprised. Seen any old barbarians around here?"

"No. Why? Are there more of you?"

Thundersquat pushed through the ring of soldiers and jogged out of the courtyard.

"Come back! I haven't told you where to look for the great bear."

Not much of a rampage if I can't find him.

A few hours later, Thundersquat rode into the clearing between the old tree and the magic fountain. It was a little out of the way, but still north. The spotted lion napped near the tree, facing the other direction. His mane twitched. Smidgel leaned the rake against the old tree and wiped his hands on his tunic.

Thundersquat slid off the stallion. "Grandfather make his way back here?"

"We haven't seen him."

The barbarian looked west. Grandfather had cooked this whole scheme up to get him started on his quest. Probably safe home in the village by now. He'd come this far. A little longer wouldn't hurt. Plus, if he found the Stone, he might be able to use it to get a clue about what had happened to his father. "Quick question."

"I'm happy to help," Smidgel said.

"What do you know about great bears?"

"Ooh. You want to give them plenty of room. They're a lot bigger than the grizzlies you might be used to. Moodier. Cantankerous, actually. You know how crotchety the grizzlies are when they first wake up from hibernation?"

"Yeah."

"That would be a good day around a great bear. Why?"

"Trouble up north."

"I can't take off on an adventure just like that, without any advance notice. The work doesn't go away. It piles up while you're gone."

"Not asking."

"All the planning you'd have to do... What do you bring? How long will we be gone? I need to start a list."

Thundersquat shrugged. "World doesn't wait till you're ready. Still, not asking."

The troll looked back at the old tree. "You can't just run off and fight a great bear without thinking it through. You never know what you'll run up against."

The spotted lion jolted upright and blew out a series of staccato huffs.

"Your point is well taken," the troll said. "He's never even seen a great bear. But that's exactly why he might need us."

The lion snarled.

"Well, I may have implied that I would," Smidgel said. "Could use somebody who can speak with animals. But don't need anybody tagging along. Used to going alone."

The spotted lion shook his mane.

"I'm not hard of hearing," the troll said to the lion. "But he can't do this by himself. You don't have to go. We should be back in a couple of weeks."

The spotted lion dragged himself to his feet.

"Hold on," Thundersquat said. The lion could probably take care of himself. But he'd have to worry about the troll. If he didn't let him get too close to the bear, it may not be a complete disaster. "Shouldn't rush out on an empty stomach. Might have time for some of those pancakes, if you're not too busy."

"You're right, we should eat first. Get some wood. I'll whip up the batter. I'll make extra for the trip. You eat, while I pack."

A couple of days later, they approached abandoned hovels and torn fences that put them on high alert, the red-haired troll in particular. "We still don't have a plan."

"Think of something when we get there," Thundersquat said.

"But what if we don't? Don't you think it would be better to think about it now, while we have time?"

Bolstrus froze. The barbarian shrugged and kept walking.

"What happens next?" the troll called after him. "Do we wait until the bear charges to consider our options?"

"Keeps things simple."

"I don't know why I came with you." The troll planted his feet and dropped his pack on the ground. "I'm not taking another step until we figure out what we're going to do when we find him."

The barbarian stopped. "You're right."

The troll relaxed. "Thank you."

"By the way, there he is. Up ahead."

Chapter Eleven

BAD TASTE

TWO SHEEP SCOOTED back and forth, hugging the far side of the tiny corral. The bear slammed a paw down on the top railing, shattering it. He wound his immense paw up again and snapped the next railing in two. As he climbed in toward the sheep, one of them dashed to the bear's right. The other pressed itself into the corner on the bear's left. The great bear blocked the escape and closed in. He extended his neck and roared.

"What did he say?" Thundersquat asked.

"He's quite profane," the troll answered.

The sheep in the corner stumbled through the opening and fled.

Animals have to eat. But the barbarian went cold at the bleating and thrashing of the sheep in the corner, crushed beneath the great bear's paws. The bear ripped a chunk of flesh from the live sheep's shoulder. It was not any easier to listen to the agony of the other sheep, watching from the safety of the wood line. Thundersquat glanced at the troll next to him. Smidgel's eyes were clamped shut, both fists pressed into his beard. The troll cringed with each wail from the sheep in the woods, which showed no sign of letting up, even after the other one went silent.

"I'll take care of that," Thundersquat said.

The troll lifted his head. "Wait."

Thundersquat did a double take at Smidgel's commanding tone. The spotted lion drew his head back as well.

"Get the bear's attention. Draw him away."

Thundersquat and the lion stared at the troll.

"Now!" The red-haired troll dashed off into the woods.

Thundersquat shrugged and ran toward the giant bear. The beast reared up. A tingle shot down the barbarian's back. He feinted toward the carcass and scooted back a couple of paces. As the bear lumbered toward the barbarian, Bolstrus leaped over the fence and darted past him. The bear lunged at the stallion and swatted. All he got was a few strands of hair from the stallion's tail.

The barbarian, light on his feet, sprang forward just out of the bear's reach. "Hey!"

The bear chased him for a few paces before returning quickly to the carcass.

Bolstrus galloped up to the fence and reared. The bear rocked back and forth, watching them both. The spotted lion stalked in from the side, as close as he could get, head low to the ground.

Thundersquat continued to dart in and out, until he aggravated the bear to the point of frenzy. The bear lost all control. The barbarian fled. The spotted lion swooped in and swiped the bear's rear leg. The bear stumbled. He took off after the lion. The lion zigzagged. The stallion galloped between the bear and the lion.

Thundersquat jogged behind the bear at a safer distance.

Whenever the bear drew close to the lion or the horse, the barbarian pelted the bear with rocks. The three of them distracted the bear in turn. The bear's fury and frustration mounted.

From the corner of his eyes, Thundersquat saw the troll reappear at the carcass, toting an armful of leaves. He shredded the leaves and rubbed handfuls between his hands, grinding them down and sprinkling them over the sheep.

The giant bear panted, clearly exhausted. The trio closed in. The bear spotted the troll and froze. Thundersquat bounced a rock off the bear's snout, but he took no notice. The bear coughed and lumbered in the direction of the troll and the carcass, gathering speed.

The lion took off after the bear. Thundersquat swung up onto the stallion. The barbarian's heart raced. They weren't going to catch the bear before he got to the troll. "Get out of there!"

Smidgel kept his eyes fixed on the bear as he continued to grind the last of the shredded leaves. When the bear charged into the corral, Smidgel scampered over the fence. The bear crashed into the fence and stood with both paws leaning on the top as the troll fled into the woods. The great bear plopped down on his haunches, chest heaving, resting a heavy paw on the carcass.

The three pursuers veered off into the trees and circled around. They found the troll moving through the trees and undergrowth.

"What did you think you were doing?" the barbarian asked. "That bear wasn't playing."

"Just watch the bear. I think it'll work. But we may not know for a day or two."

The spotted lion took a couple of steps toward home and looked back. He growled.

"You don't have to check your schedule," the troll said. "You've never had any appointments as long as I've known you."

Smidgel found the remaining sheep, still bleating softly, at the edge of the tree line and placed his arm around it. He gently led it away. "It won't do you any good to watch this."

The great bear feasted for hours. The barbarian paced. The bear doubled over. He weaved back and forth and staggered off into the woods. Now and then he doubled over again, clearly in pain. Eventually the bear toppled over and lay still.

"Poisoned him," the barbarian said. "Good thinking."

"Not exactly," said the troll. "Just keep watching. We have to make sure."

Early the next morning the great bear began to stir. When he struggled to his feet, they followed.

Late that afternoon the great bear spotted another fence with several sheep penned inside. Just like before, he approached the fence. But this time, the bear doubled over. He stood up and roared before he spun around twice. He took another half step toward the fence and bent over again. The bear lunged back and loped off toward the east, headed for home.

"I don't think he'll bother sheep anymore," the troll said. "Ever."

"Whatever you did, it worked," the barbarian said.

"I couldn't stand what he was doing to the sheep. But I really didn't want to hurt the bear either."

"Well, looks like we're done here." Thundersquat and the stallion turned south.

"Where are you going?" the troll asked.

"Palace. Sorcerer king."

"We need to go back and repair the fence first."

"Can't. Need to find that Stone, so I can get back home."

"We can't leave that defenseless sheep wandering around in the wild. Not when we can do something about it."

"Gonna get eaten anyway. Cost me half a day there and back." Thundersquat glanced at the stallion, who joined him as they walked away.

The lion growled.

"I don't care how long it's been since you had mutton," the troll said to the lion. "You're not allowed to touch it."

"I wouldn't expect you to drop everything just because I asked," the troll called. "You don't owe me a thing."

Bolstrus stopped and turned to the side. Thundersquat looked back over his shoulder.

The red-haired troll stared at him, hands on his hips. "I have to try. Do what you think is right."

The red-haired troll headed toward the site of the previous day's attack. The spotted lion shook his head and trotted to catch up.

Thundersquat made eye contact with the stallion, who hadn't budged. The barbarian rubbed the back of his neck. He didn't have time for this. Not like anything was going to happen, one way or the other. He just wanted to get all this over with. *Get out of this forest. Get my life back.*

Chapter Twelve

THE FROG KING

THEY FOUND THE SHEEP huddled in the corner of the corral. A day and a half later, after the troll talked them into repairing the fence and laying out a week's worth of food and water for the sheep, they headed south.

Through the trees, Thundersquat caught a glimpse of movement off to the left. He concealed himself behind a tree and waved the others off. Smidgel crept up and peered around from behind the barbarian's waist.

A man with a well-trimmed gray beard sat in a puddle, wearing a muddy robe and a helmet crowned with a set of long, thin, twisted horns.

"It's the sorcerer king," Smidgel said.

"You sure?"

"No question," the troll said. "What's he doing out here?"

"Don't know. But it's critical to the welfare of the kingdom."

The sorcerer king appeared to be alone. His eyes darted around in sync with a hovering dragonfly. He snagged it with his tongue.

Thundersquat approached him with caution. "Eaten a few bugs myself. Never on purpose, though."

The sorcerer king flinched as the barbarian spoke. He looked around, disoriented. He waded out of the puddle and tried to smooth his robe, pasted to his legs. The sorcerer king regarded the barbarian standing before him. "Greetings."

"Need to talk to you," Thundersquat said.

The sorcerer king grabbed the hem of his robe and wrung it out. "I met a barbarian once, years ago. He was not much of a conversationalist, but he helped me on an important matter. Is it critical?"

"Only if you're alive and want to stay that way."

"Alas, I'm not able to speak with you at the moment. I'm not quite myself."

"When then?" the barbarian asked.

"My daughter…"

"What about her?"

The sorcerer king clapped his hands over his ears and gritted his teeth. He scrunched up his face, tilted his head, and squinted at the barbarian. "Bats. Wolf."

"What?"

The sorcerer king dropped into a squat, eyes bugged out, and scanned the air around him in random patterns.

The barbarian exchanged looks with the troll. This hadn't gone quite like he thought it would. "Think he fell on his head or something?"

"He's clearly not well," the troll said.

The sorcerer king seemed oblivious to their presence. He snagged another bug out of the air.

The lion released a yawn that morphed into a protracted grumble.

"He wouldn't make a dent in the number of bugs around

here," the troll said. "You know we can't leave him like this. What if he's sick?"

The lion rolled onto his side.

"Really? You're taking a nap now?"

The spotted lion muttered.

"There's no plague, and you don't have to save your strength to fight it."

Thundersquat poked the sorcerer king, to no effect. "What was that about his daughter?"

"He's not making a lot of sense," Smidgel said.

"Could wait for him to wake up." He knew that was a dumb idea as soon as he spoke it. Any plan with the word "wait" in it was probably not worth doing.

The troll tapped the sorcerer king on the shoulder. "Your Eminence."

Nothing.

"Can't talk to him like this," Thundersquat said. "Any ideas?"

"We have to find out what's wrong," Smidgel said. "Or we become partly responsible for what happens."

"So how are we gonna get him to talk?"

"Maybe we should take him back to the palace. Find out if anybody there knows anything."

"Need to find out what he knows about the Stone." Thundersquat scooped up the sorcerer king and plopped him on top of Bolstrus. He hesitated. "We gonna catch what he's got?"

"I don't know. I suppose we'll find out."

"Kinda late for us, then, isn't it?"

"Too soon to know. It's probably nothing. But let's keep it quiet for now," the troll said. "No need to risk sending the entire countryside into a panic."

Good idea, thought the barbarian. *Wait till they find out the world's gonna end.*

Outside the courtyard of the Onyx Palace Jermbog held the gate open a crack. "I haven't summoned you, barbarian. Or your nefarious cronies."

Thundersquat stopped the closing gate with a stiff arm. "Two things. Set up the meeting like you promised."

"I sent you on some urgent business, didn't I?"

"Oh yeah, the bear? Taken care of. Second, my, uh...friend here has something to say."

The red-haired troll stepped around him. "We found the sorcerer king sitting in a pool of water. I have some serious concerns."

Jermbog addressed the barbarian. "Since when do you let a troll get close to the sorcerer king? You tell him he's not to say a word of this to anyone. His Eminence has been involved in an urgent and highly secret project."

"Sitting in the mud?" Thundersquat asked. "Eating bugs?"

Bolstrus moved into the magistrate's view, the sorcerer king on his back.

"Your Eminence!"

"I know this is a sensitive issue," the troll said. "If I had to guess, I'd say the sorcerer king thinks he's a frog. I think it would be a mistake if we didn't consider that."

Jermbog sneered at the troll and addressed the barbarian. "I've never heard a troll say anything worth hearing. They create problems, but they don't ever try to solve them. You better hope there's nothing wrong."

Wolfmini leaped into the gate, causing the magistrate to

stumble back. The sorcerer king hopped into the courtyard. He sprang at Jermbog, slapped his hands on the magistrate's shoulders, and vaulted over him. Jermbog jumped to his feet and threw himself at the gate, shoulders first, and slammed it shut. "You're all to blame!"

Thundersquat pounded once. "Set up a meeting!"

He stepped away and stared at the gate.

"You're wasting your time," the troll said. "And we can't talk to him anyway, as long as he thinks he's a frog."

"Ever run into anything like this?"

"I was afraid to say it before," Smidgel said, "but the sorcerer king may not be ill. I can think of two other ways to explain his strange behavior."

The spotted lion growled.

"We haven't seen any evidence that he's crazy."

The lion growled again.

"Point taken. We won't rule it out just yet."

"If he's not sick or crazy, what else?" the barbarian asked.

"Sorcery," the troll said. "If he's under a spell, who has that kind of ability? We need to make a list. Who'd have a reason to do such a thing?"

"Could've done it to himself."

"We'd still need to call on someone to tell us what to do now. Someone who knows the old ways."

"Anybody come to mind?"

"I can think of two," Smidgel said. "One of them is the Least High Druid."

The spotted lion huffed. The red-haired troll and the lion stared knowingly at each other.

"Something we need to know about that druid?" the barbarian asked.

"Unless he wants to be found, we may never find him,"

Smidgel said. "But there is someone else. The mystic witch, Caprice."

"Easier to find? Sounds like the better choice," Thunder-squat said.

"Not necessarily."

Chapter Thirteen

LOOSE CHANGE

THE THREE TRAVELERS headed northwest along a shallow, winding creek. The trail opened to the right, revealing a set of roughly hewn steps. At the top they found a tiny cottage set back in a clearing, surrounded by a garden and neatly trimmed bushes. The troll and the spotted lion waited at the top of the stairs while Thundersquat jogged up to the door and pounded three times. The whole cottage shook.

The door opened to reveal a tall, gangly man, slightly stooped, his face well-lined and his hair dark and slightly unkempt. He seemed genuinely pleased to see them.

A loud screech blasted from one of the back rooms. "Assistant! Who is it? Is it the sorcerer king? Tell him I'm not speaking to him!"

The assistant led them into the kitchen. "We have guests. Smidgel, the red-haired troll, and two of his friends—a barbarian fellow and a spotted lion."

"Marvelous." The mystic witch, short and almost as wide as she was tall, stood in a dramatic pose holding a large spoon. Several pots steamed before her on top of the fire. Her hair was wrong: a spiked mess with streaks of sky blue and intense orange that Thundersquat had only seen in sunsets. She whirled around like she was dancing. "You must be starving."

"No, no, please, I'm fine," the troll said, a little too quickly.

The spotted lion backpedaled, turned, and slipped outside.

"How about you?" Her green eyes bored into the barbarian's, demanding an answer.

He understood that there was one, and only one, correct answer. Thundersquat ignored the troll's warning headshake. "Can always eat."

The mystic witch held the spoon high and swooped it into the pot in front of her. She scooped up some of the brew and tasted it, eyes closed, face toward the ceiling. Her lips smacked. "Something's missing. Get me the thing."

The assistant almost tripped in his rush to the cabinet. He rummaged through jars on the shelf, stuffing them in the crook of his arm, dismissing each in turn. The jars started to slip. The assistant juggled them, tossing a few back on the shelf until he got the remainder under control. He shoved the jars on the shelf to the side and knocked several others over. He stared at the back row with confused panic on his face.

"Hurry! You're ruining it."

The assistant scanned the jars on the shelf and looked lost. He grabbed a jar from under his arm and handed it to the mystic witch. She snatched it out of his hand and dumped half of its contents into the pot. She stirred, scooped, and sniffed the steaming brew.

"That's not it." Her tone left no doubt that the assistant didn't know what he was doing.

The assistant rearranged the remaining jars. He held his hands up and wavered for a few seconds. He selected another and held it out toward her.

"No, wait." She sniffed another spoonful. "It's just right."

The assistant collapsed on the stool and blew out a long breath.

The mystic witch ladled the slop into a bowl for the barbarian and handed it to the assistant to carry to the table. She waltzed over and slid onto the bench across from Thundersquat. Her unbroken gaze was discomforting. He shifted position and looked at the troll. "You had something you wanted to say?"

Smidgel edged into a seat and once again politely declined the offer of food. "We'd be grateful for a bit of advice. We're not sure how to proceed, and we'd like to run the problem by someone with more skill and experience in such matters."

"I don't follow recipes. That's for amateurs."

"This doesn't involve cooking, although clearly, you're in a class all by yourself. No, this has to do with sorcery."

"Ah." She leaned forward and rested on her elbows. She turned her unsettling gaze onto the troll. "As long as it's not trivial. I never do anything trivial."

The troll swallowed. He summed up the situation for the mystic witch. "We believe the sorcerer king thinks he's a frog. We don't know how it happened, and we're trying to figure out what to do."

"Of course he thinks he's a frog." She spoke loudly off to the side.

Thundersquat paused with his spoon near his open mouth. He glanced up at the corner of the ceiling where the mystic witch was staring. They waited; she held her pose.

The barbarian got up and filled his bowl again. They waited some more.

Caprice batted her eyes at her assistant. "Tell them what happened, back at the thing."

On cue, the assistant began the story. "When they were young, Wolfmini and the lady Caprice were in love. He was the prince then."

"He was mad about me, as you might imagine." Her lips curled inward, and her eyes watered. "It didn't last."

"He never had time for her," the assistant said. "She never knew why. He always said he was busy with his studies. Someday he would be king of Blisteria."

"But then he married someone else." She slapped her hands down on the table. "The scum. What do you think he was studying?"

"They had a daughter," the assistant said.

"I remember," the red-haired troll said. "His wife vanished without a trace. The princess was just a toddler."

Thundersquat broke eye contact with the mystic witch and looked at the assistant. "Sorcerer king's wife...what happened?"

The assistant swallowed. "No one ever found out."

The red-haired troll looked with compassion at the mystic witch and spoke softly. "I hope I don't touch on an uncomfortable subject. What do you remember about what happened back then?"

Silence. Her eyelids narrowed, and she pivoted toward the troll. Her words rolled out in a low growl. "I could've had my pick of anybody in the kingdom. But he needed me."

The assistant reached over and patted her on the hand. "When Wolfmini lost his wife, Caprice paid him a proper visit. After all, they'd been in love once."

"He was beside himself with grief," she said. "I tried to

help him. It was a very noble thing to do, in spite of what he did to me."

"But he had her dragged away," the assistant said.

She leaned toward the barbarian and spoke through clenched teeth. "In front of everybody."

Thundersquat raised the bowl to his face. He kept his eyes on the bottom of the bowl.

The assistant tapped his gruel with the back of his spoon. "She turned him into a frog."

Thundersquat lowered the bowl slightly, looking directly into the still unblinking eyes of the mystic witch. The troll stared at her in stunned silence.

"Amphibians are kind of my specialty," she confided to the barbarian. She held the back of her hand to her forehead and spoke to the ceiling. "I was miserable."

Thundersquat filled his spoon, stared at it for a second, and dropped it back in the bowl.

The troll turned to the assistant. "Then what happened?"

"Well, for a while that's how he lived, as a frog."

"He wouldn't let me help him," the mystic witch said. "Completely selfish to the end."

"But Wolfmini had a brother," the assistant said, "who was also skilled in the old ways. He prepared a changing mix and fed it to his brother, the frog. Then the frog turned back into the sorcerer king."

"The brother solved the problem, then?" the troll said.

"Yes," the assistant said.

"So why now, after all these years, does the sorcerer king suddenly think that he's a frog again?"

The barbarian felt an odd churning in his stomach. "Food's not right."

"Yes," the troll said. "That's it! What if the brother's

changing mix was off a bit? Too weak? The effect now wearing off?"

"He did it on purpose," the mystic witch said. "He hated his brother."

"Regardless, what do we do now to set things right?" Smidgel asked.

The mystic witch leaped to her feet and screeched at the assistant. "Get me the stuff from the thing!"

The assistant jumped up. The pair became whirlwinds of frenetic activity. The mystic witch slapped another pot on the stove. The assistant seized jar after jar.

"Yes! No! The other one!" She tossed a jar over her shoulder and sent two skidding across the floor. She dumped the contents of several into the pot. Snatching another jar from the assistant, she sprinkled the contents in and stirred. She sniffed the spoon. "That's it."

The assistant poured the mix into a jar and handed it to the red-haired troll. "This will undo the damage done by his brother."

"What'll we do if it doesn't work?" the troll asked.

Caprice glared at the troll. She flicked a pinkie at the assistant. He dropped to the ground and contorted. His face, while it was recognizable as a face, strained. Suddenly, in the assistant's place was a human-sized salamander, dark brown with lime-green spots, wearing the assistant's tunic. If the expression on a giant salamander were readable, he looked resigned.

Thundersquat studied the mystic witch, mindful of that pinkie finger, wondering what she could do if she put her weight into it. He plotted the distance to the exit. They'd never be able to get out in time.

The mystic witch straddled the salamander behind his

shoulders. She seized his open jaws. "Pour in half of the changing mix."

As the salamander squirmed, the barbarian dumped half the contents into the gaping jaws. The mystic witch stepped off; the assistant's jaws snapped shut. She wiped the drool on her hand against the barbarian's buckskin vest, gave a little squeeze, and casually returned to her seat.

The salamander twisted and rolled. Lumps emerged and spread across his skin in a popping fashion as he trans- formed back into the assistant, propped up on his elbows. The assistant stood and brushed himself off. He smacked his lips and worked his tongue, as though he had just tasted something awful. "She's never wrong."

"I have to lie down now," Caprice said. She gave the troll a dirty look. "I'm getting a terrible migraine."

The assistant scrambled over to assist her.

Smidgel stepped forward. "Is there anything we can do to help?"

Thundersquat clamped a hand on the troll's shoulder and steered him to the door. "Let's get the rest of this mix to the palace."

Jermbog met Thundersquat, Smidgel, and Mudcat at the gate to the courtyard of the Onyx Palace. He glanced briefly at the troll and addressed Thundersquat. "Barbarian. I hope you and your worthless minions have some news worth hearing."

"We have a special potion," the troll said. "A cure."

Jermbog was hesitant. He spoke to the barbarian. "Will you tell that ignorant troll nothing's wrong?"

"I know His Eminence looks human on the outside, but

he's not on the inside." said the troll. "This potion won't hurt him. It will change him back into what he was before."

"If it hurts him, you'll pay. Dearly." Jermbog escorted them to the palace. He stopped and eyed the spotted lion.

Mudcat growled.

"It might be better if you wait here," Smidgel suggested.

Jermbog glared at the troll and nodded. The rest of them followed the magistrate through the entryway, past a room on the left, and into a large hall with smaller rooms off to the right. They turned left and went up a flight of crude wooden stairs that led to a walkway outside two closed doors. At the door to the far room, Jermbog deigned to speak to the barbarian. "This is merely a precaution. Superstitious, really."

They entered, and Jermbog closed the door quickly behind them. Across the room, the sorcerer king faced the wall in his characteristic squat.

"Your Eminence," Jermbog said. "We offer you this gift. Medical experts believe it will restore things to how they're supposed to be."

The sorcerer king turned his head slightly toward them, his eyelids half shut and his eyes unfocused. The red-haired troll approached the sorcerer king with the jar of the changing mix. Wolfmini leaped to the side. Thundersquat dove and caught him in midair and managed to twist around and cushion the fall before they crashed to the floor. He restrained the squirming sorcerer king while they force-fed him the mix. After Wolfmini swallowed the last bit, the barbarian released him.

The sorcerer king blinked at them indifferently. He smacked his lips.

"How long does this take?" Thundersquat asked.

"How long does what take?" a female voice asked from the doorway.

Thundersquat turned. It had to be the daughter. She wore a fancy faded-blue dress, like dusk. Much thinner than animal skins. It would likely tear easily. It wouldn't be much use when the winter winds swept across the plains, he thought.

"Your Highness," Jermbog said.

Wolfmini stood up and smoothed his robe. He tilted his head, surveyed the visitors, and smiled. "We met in the forest. The troll. I recall the red hair. And the barbarian."

"Time we finally talked," Thundersquat said.

"I didn't realize we had guests, Father."

"I was about to introduce her, Your Eminence," said Jermbog.

"My daughter, Princess Blundren." The sorcerer king's eyes shifted suddenly, out of focus. He dropped into a squat and searched the ceiling randomly.

A brief period of awkward silence ensued.

Jermbog was the first to speak. "Clearly you failed, barbarian. As I expected. What are we supposed to do now?"

"Hate to say it, but maybe another visit to the mystic witch," Thundersquat said.

"What do you mean, another visit?" Blundren asked.

"You saw what she did the last time," the troll said. "Are you sure you want to risk it?"

The barbarian shrugged. "Maybe she didn't get it right the first time. Doesn't mean she can't do it."

"Can't do what?" Blundren asked.

Thundersquat moved to escort her out the door. "Explain as we go."

Blundren tried to squeeze past the barbarian. "I need to talk to my father."

"Not the only one." The barbarian scooped her up, threw her over his shoulder, and headed for the door.

"Get your hands off me! What do you think you're doing?"

The sorcerer king leaped and reached out to her. Blundren grabbed his hand. He snapped his hand back and sneezed violently. The troll and the magistrate scurried out of the room. Jermbog slammed the door on the sorcerer king. They heard the sorcerer king sneeze again.

Blundren pushed free from the barbarian and stumbled back a few steps. The barbarian caught her at the edge of the runway. She thrust her head close to his, her face and neck red. "Is that how you handle women where you're from? Sling them over your shoulder and carry them into the next room, without asking?"

"Don't have rooms."

"That's not the point. Just stay away from me."

"Don't want to be here any longer than I have to. Running out of time."

"Why? What's wrong with my father? Is he sick?"

Thundersquat shrugged. "Something's wrong."

"More than usual?"

"Maybe. From long ago. Gonna find out."

"I'm going with you." She stalked off down the stairs, the barbarian and troll trailing behind. As she exited the palace, she called back without turning her head. "Where to?"

"West." Thundersquat followed her into the courtyard. She showed no sign of slowing down. The troll and the lion trotted behind them.

"Now—tell me who you are and what you're doing here," Blundren said. "And don't ever lay a hand on me again."

Thundersquat picked up the pace, brushing past her without a word. Smidgel trotted up and explained to Blundren what they had learned about her father. He interrupted himself occasionally to redirect the barbarian.

"Does he even know where he's going?" Blundren asked.

"Yes," the troll said. "But not necessarily how to get there."

"So you think it's a good idea for us to keep following him?"

"More or less. He might get close."

Blundren finally slowed down. "I can see where the loss of my mother could've been too much. Maybe he retreats into the belief that he's a frog when he can't handle it. How is this formula from the mystic witch supposed to fix that? What'll we do if she can't fix the problem?"

Smidgel gave his head a shake. "Good questions. We'd just have to consider other options."

"Sounds a lot like we're lost," Blundren said, "with no clue where to go next."

"Been there," Thundersquat said.

"We still have the Least High Druid," the troll said.

"Illusions can't fix delusions," Blundren said. "After this mission fails to pan out, we're going to rethink this whole thing."

At the cottage of the mystic witch, the barbarian jogged up to the door. His stomach growled. Before he knocked, the assistant opened the door a crack and gestured for him to be quiet. The assistant glanced behind him, slipped outside, and silently closed the door. He grabbed Thundersquat by the arm and led him away from the cottage. The others gathered around. The assistant's smile disappeared when he laid eyes on the princess. He looked like he'd just seen a ghost.

"May I introduce you to Her Highness, Princess Blundren?" the red-haired troll said.

The assistant stared dumbly at her. After an awkward pause, he nodded. "Highness."

"Changing mix didn't work," Thundersquat said.

"It should've worked. We were very careful with it."

The red-haired troll took the lead. "We're missing something."

"I don't see how," the assistant said. "We considered every spice in the cabinet. Some of them twice, I think. She has her own system."

"No, we're missing some information. Can you recall anything else about what happened back then?"

"It was a long time ago." The assistant stared at the top of the trees. "The mystic witch didn't want a frog around. That's why we took the sorcerer king to his brother."

"My father had a brother?" Blundren asked.

"Of course," the assistant said.

"You didn't know?" the troll asked.

"Someone mentioned him once," she said. "You knew him?"

"I knew him, yes. He hated your father," the assistant said. "I think he was jealous."

"What did the brother do?" Thundersquat asked.

"Nobody knows," the assistant said. "He was always hard to deal with. Made up his own batch of changing mix and refused to let us look over what he did. No telling what he put in it."

"Do you think he added something to the mix?" Smidgel asked.

"Who else could've done it? Nobody else had access to the sorcerer king, even when he got loose."

"What do you mean, got loose?" the troll asked.

The assistant shrugged. "Just for a short while. We found him in a pond."

"Wait a minute." Blundren put her hands out like she was trying to slow everybody down. "After it seemed that my father was turned into a frog...but before he presumably changed back...the frog you thought was my father got loose?"

"Caprice couldn't have a frog in the house."

"You let him escape?" Thundersquat asked.

"I don't think she would've let him loose on purpose," the assistant said.

"Then what happened?" the troll asked.

"We tracked him to a pond. That's where he went to join the other frogs. Hundreds, maybe thousands. You couldn't hear yourself think."

"Could anyone else have gotten to him?" Blundren asked.

The assistant smiled. "They wouldn't have known what he looked like. I waded in and retrieved him myself."

"You're sure it was him?" The red-haired troll exchanged glances with the princess. "Is there is any chance at all, no matter how remote, that you picked the wrong frog?"

"We might've picked the right one."

Chapter Fourteen

REVERSE SHIFT

"I MEAN, IT WAS getting dark," the assistant said. "Caprice was in such a hurry…"

Blundren's heart rate quickened, but she calmed herself down. "My father might've thought he was a frog. Everyone could have thought it. But that doesn't make it so. It doesn't matter which frog they pulled out of the pond."

"Where's the pond?" Thundersquat asked.

The red-haired troll turned toward the princess. "If we're going to figure out what's wrong with your father, we need to examine all of the possibilities."

"Ridiculous, but let's get it over with. While we're at it, you can tell me about my uncle, who everyone else seems to know about."

"Can you find the pond again?" Smidgel asked the assistant.

"I think it was this way." The assistant slid a leg forward and stopped. He looked back the other way and squinted. He looked like he was about to reverse course, but he pushed off in the original direction and led them into the forest. "It was such a long time ago."

Several hours and a few dozen hesitations later, they heard distant croaking. Blundren and Thundersquat rushed past the assistant. Smidgel and the spotted lion followed.

When they arrived, the sun had already dipped below the top of the trees, and shadows blanketed more than half of the pond. Reeds rustled all along the edges. The pond was wide where they stood and narrowed to a bend on the other side. The surface of the pond seemed alive, in constant motion, ripples everywhere, as thousands of frogs jockeyed for position on lily pads. No shoving match lasted longer than a few seconds, as the edge of the pad collapsed when they shifted their weight and dislodged the previous tenant. Each frog that wasn't diving and reemerging belted out its own tune, out of sync and off key with respect to the others. It was deafening.

The assistant surveyed the pond, scratching his head. "This might be it."

Blundren could hardly hear him. She didn't care if anyone heard her. "Might be the right pond. Or maybe he's in some other pond. Or maybe he was never a frog at all."

"Can't take them all back to the palace," Thundersquat yelled.

"Why not? We could change them all into my father. See which one we like best." *Maybe they can find one who'll be there when I need him.*

"You know what to do," a voice whispered from behind.

The princess whirled around. Hovering Herb. Outside and around people. *It's true. I'm crazy. Like my father.*

In the corner of her eye, she caught the barbarian scanning the area for what she was alarmed about. "Do you see anything unusual?"

"Like what?" Thundersquat asked.

"They can't see me or hear me," Herb said.

"I just thought I heard something." Blundren faced the pond without really focusing on anything. She tried to conceal her rising panic.

"You already know how to find your father," Herb informed her.

She ignored him. "It's hard to hear anything over all this croaking, isn't it?"

"I know you're still listening," Herb said.

Maybe her mind superimposed patterns over the noise. She wasn't actually hearing voices.

"But you can see me as well as hear me. How do you explain that?"

He's reading my thoughts. But he's a product of my mind, so why not?

"Yes, I can read your thoughts, although I rarely do. I try to respect your privacy. I usually have too much on my mind anyway." Herb hovered on her left. "But forget about me and think about what's been happening to you."

Not much to tell. Unless you count being kidnapped by bats, traveling with a wolf, or seeing and hearing things that aren't there.

"What else?" Herb asked.

She glanced at the others. The barbarian, troll, and assistant looked out over the pond, none of them saying anything. The spotted lion sat off by himself, curled up. He rubbed his eyes with the back of his paw. His eyes itched. She tilted her head.

"Yes!" Herb disappeared.

His tone seemed to imply something more. Apparently, he wanted her to work it out herself. She reviewed the recent past. The ideas fell together in a sudden realization. "Of course."

They all turned toward her. "Animals. They're allergic to me."

The others stared, with no change in expression. The barbarian and troll exchanged glances.

"It's obvious. The birds, the bats. And the wolf. Back at the palace, my father sneezed."

As if on cue, the spotted lion sneezed.

"See, that's exactly what I'm talking about!"

Thundersquat looked back at the pond.

"My father is an animal!" The princess hurried over to the edge of the water. "If the story is true, then I was raised in the palace by a frog who looked like my father. And my real father may be somewhere out there."

Blundren for a second had been ready to suspend her disbelief, even for a short while. But when you start to consider all the possibilities, this story could spiral way out of control. *No way my father's out there.*

She started to turn back, but paused. She sensed something from the water, softer than a whisper, lighter than the touch of an insect. If she had to label it, she would describe it as the pull of an intriguing question. She shook her head at the absurdity of it all and quashed for now whatever doubts that made her hesitate. It wouldn't take much time to check out this ridiculous notion. *Stop arguing with yourself and just test it already.*

She held her hand out to the barbarian. "Walk me through the pond."

Thundersquat stared at her outstretched hand. "Told me not to touch you."

She fluttered her hand impatiently. "We need to start eliminating possibilities. Quickly."

"Gonna get wet."

Blundren rolled her eyes and stretched her hand out again. "Come on. I might need you if there's something lurking under the surface. Think teeth. Lots of sharp teeth."

Thundersquat took her hand between his thumb and forefinger as they waded in. She thought the pond would be colder than it was. Frogs parted before them, sneezing as they leaped to the side. The barbarian scanned the surface nonstop. At its deepest, the water was waist high. When they reached the grasses and full-leafed plants that poked out of the water within the reeds on the far side, it was knee deep. She considered the curve that disappeared to the left. It can wait.

"Walk me back through." She tugged Thundersquat's thumb, aiming the two of them at another angle through the pond. He wrapped his hand entirely around hers. His hand was rough, but with an unexpected warmth and gentleness. Again, frogs leaped aside, sneezing. Her confidence started to droop. Even if the story were true, they might not even be in the right pond.

"Take me through again." She ignored the look the barbarian gave her. This time a large frog waited patiently for them to approach. Its eyes held hers. "Father?"

The frog nodded. Or dipped, to be precise, since he didn't have a neck. She lifted him up and held his squishy wet leathery body aloft. His forelegs and hind legs dangled while he gazed at her intently.

I can't believe I'm doing this.

She laid him on her shoulder and carried him toward shore; he didn't struggle. Unlike the others, the old frog didn't sneeze. Could she have failed to detect this—that the man who raised her has been a frog the whole time? *Clearly not possible. For a dozen or more years? No way I was that blind. Absurd.*

The assistant approached. His face was all aglow, as if he'd just run into a long-lost friend.

"Wait," Blundren said. "Turn around."

The assistant did as she commanded.

She motioned to Thundersquat. "Go collect three or four others, the same size as this one."

Blundren set the old frog down. She dodged a frog that sprinkled her ear as it flew past. She batted another with her forearm as a third splatted against her thigh and dropped. The princess glared at Thundersquat. His eyes looked innocent, but his smirk suggested otherwise. "What's wrong with you?"

Smidgel and the princess herded the four frogs together. She stepped back next to the assistant. "Take a close look."

The assistant got down on all fours and peered into their eyes. He shoved two aside and looked back and forth between the two remaining. The assistant shook his head. "So hard to tell. I'm going to go with this one."

He selected the younger one.

"And you believe this is my father."

"Yes. I'm quite sure we have the right frog this time."

She smiled, knowing it was not the one she'd selected. It didn't matter which one he picked—not now, and not back then.

"We need to take him to the mystic witch," the troll said. "She might be able to change him back."

"The changing mix will work," the assistant said.

"As well as it always did, I'm sure. Let's go back to the cottage." Blundren lifted the frog the assistant selected. The older one bellowed and leaped at her thigh. The frog in her hands sneezed violently. He gathered his hind legs against her shoulder and shot away, tearing himself from her grip. The older frog leaped at her face. Her hands flew up in self-defense and caught him. He blasted her with a raucous belch but made no effort to escape. She tilted her head.

"It's him," the troll said. "He's desperate. You can't leave him. He can't go through this again."

"Okay. If you say so."

The frog's back legs dangled over Blundren's shoulder, his forelegs pressed tightly around her neck. She felt his heart quicken when they arrived at the cottage.

The assistant slipped inside. He emerged with a jar and a blanket. He eased the door shut behind him and gestured toward the steps. The group tiptoed away and gathered at the creek bed below. Blundren set the frog on the ground and offered it the jar. The frog nodded and swallowed its contents.

The frog rolled onto its side and kicked. One leg twitched, like an involuntary cramp. Then the other leg did the same. He groaned. Both forelegs shot out. The assistant draped the blanket over the frog. The bulges that represented the legs lengthened underneath the blanket. A pair of human feet poked from the edge. Other mounds lengthened and widened into the shape of a human torso. A hand reached out from underneath and grabbed the edge of the blanket. From the other side, a hand pushed against the ground, and the body sat up. The blanket slipped to his lap. Wolfmini grinned at his daughter.

Blundren did not smile in return. No question, when it came to illusions, her father was the best. *And thanks to the assistant for that blanket.* But she didn't like being played.

Wolfmini wrapped the blanket around himself in a makeshift toga before he stepped back and gazed at his daughter, his eyes moist. "The fool almost chose my great-great-great-great grandson."

Then he snagged a dragonfly out of the air with his tongue.

Silence.

"Sorry, old habits." He winced and swallowed. "A little salty."

Wolfmini glanced up at the cottage. "We need to get out of here. Fast."

Blundren strolled with her father up the spiral incline to the Onyx Palace. The others hung back. She was grateful for the privacy. Frog or not, she hadn't spent this much time talking with her father in years. If ever.

"How did you do it?" Blundren asked. "And more importantly, why?"

"What you saw was exactly what it seemed."

"Yes, I know. You had us believe that you were a frog, in order to set up this elaborate scheme. Really, where did you put the frog? I missed it entirely."

"As I said, all of it was what it seemed to be. Thirteen years ago, a few moments changed my whole life. I've replayed them every day since, clearly as the day it happened."

Wolfmini stared off in the distance. "The mystic witch screeched at the assistant. I couldn't make out what she was saying. The pond was jam-packed. The cacophony of sound was maddening. I didn't want to go back, but I didn't want to be left out there either. The assistant looked rattled. They were sure to make a serious mistake."

The sorcerer king exhaled. "The assistant scooped up armfuls of frogs that squirmed out of his grasp as fast as he could grab them. I swam, jostled, and hauled myself over. It was like slow motion. Tumbled over two, got dunked by a third. I screamed."

He hesitated. His face grew pale. When he resumed speaking, his voice was softer. "All my croaking got lost in all the clamor. Almost there. The assistant got a good hold on a thigh and pinned a frog to his shoulder. He turned and waded toward shore. I contemplated life as a frog and slipped below the surface of the water."

The sorcerer king's fists clenched. "Unacceptable. I kicked again. The mystic witch screeched nonstop at the frazzled assistant, who managed to hurry and hesitate at the same time. I kicked hard, drawing close, as time raced away. The assistant struggled to climb out of the muck near the edge. He reached the reeds. A single option presented itself— the only point of clarity and my last chance."

Wolfmini spoke faster. "He slipped. I leaped. I pivoted on a reed and flew at him. With the pads on my fingertips stretched full out, I linked souls with the frog in his grasp. I tried to hold on, but my arms had no strength. The assistant climbed out of the pond as I slid down his back and then his leg. He presented his catch to the mystic witch. She kicked the assistant and stormed off. The frog squirmed. For a second, I thought I had another chance. I raced forward. The assistant regained his grip on the frog and hurried after her. I was undone."

Her father stared at the ground. He brightened up. "With those leaps into my human body, I was able to keep track of you from the pond. I haven't missed a thing."

Except for almost every minute of every day. And the part about me hallucinating. "You may have more to catch up on than you think."

"I noticed how you eliminated all of the possibilities in the pond," Wolfmini said.

"I decided to rule out all the frogs that were not you. Since animals are apparently allergic to me now, I simply had to find the one that was not."

"Like your grandmother. You can't know what something is, but you can be pretty sure what it's not."

Blundren stopped. "You've never said a word about my grandmother."

"She was a Querion, you know." Her father gazed at her fondly. "By the way, what did hovering Herb have to say?"

Chapter Fifteen

AWAKENING

BLUNDREN WAS STILL in a fog as they climbed the spiral path that wound around the twisted mountain. She hadn't mentioned Herb to anyone, yet her father knew. They couldn't both be crazy, not about the same stuff. She hadn't been hallucinating. But she was at a loss to explain it.

Outside the gate to the courtyard surrounding the palace, Jermbog pleaded on his knees with a frog in a shallow pool. They were almost upon him before he noticed. The magistrate rose quickly and brushed off his robe. "Your Eminence, I didn't realize you slipped out for a walk. I was trying to keep this disgusting thing off the palace grounds."

Wolfmini paused. "He's an old one, is he not?"

"No doubt, Your Eminence. Check out the ugly bumps all over his head. The foul creature stinks of the marsh. Belches like a bloated bear."

"Qualities that would distinguish him among his own kind."

Jermbog was hesitant for a second. "I suppose so, Your Eminence."

"He must've been propelled here when we switched back to our original bodies."

"If you say so, Father. You want us to believe he's the same frog."

Wolfmini turned to the barbarian, just arriving with the troll and the lion. "This esteemed creature has been part of me for thirteen years. Will you see that he gets home?"

Thundersquat nodded. "Then we talk."

"Yes. Then we talk."

"About what?" Blundren asked. *They just met, and already Thundersquat gets a talk?*

"Tell you when I have time." The barbarian waded in and grabbed the frog. He balanced it against his shoulder and glanced at the princess. Thundersquat plunked her on the head with the frog as he jogged past.

"What's wrong with him?" Blundren asked.

"I haven't had a lot of experience with barbarians," Smidgel said. "But I think he spent a lot of time alone."

"I hope he got used to it," Blundren said.

"We'll be going too. Seems like you have a lot to catch up on." The troll and the lion headed down the spiral path.

As they entered the palace, Blundren turned to her father. "I still can't figure out how you switched places with that frog, right in front of me."

"There's nothing to explain."

"The mystic witch's assistant had to be part of the illusion. Probably the troll. Even the barbarian."

"Maybe it's better if you keep thinking of it as an illusion."

"What gave it away was the idea that the mystic witch turned you into a frog for rejecting her. That was just too much of a stretch."

"Agreed. That's hard to believe."

"You were already married to my mother at the time."

"Yes."

Blundren noted the sadness in his voice. "Do you ever think about her?"

"Every day."

"I wish I could remember her. There's just an empty place where she might have been. No specific memories to put there."

"She loved you."

"Why have you never told me more about her?"

"I haven't been here, except in short spurts."

That much was true enough. He was never there when he should've been. "And Herb, what is he? I thought I was crazy. Now I find that maybe we both are."

"Herb is what some might call a spirit from another dimension. He's not bound by space or time. He discovered how to pass through into our reality to train us in the mystical arts."

"That would explain how he comes and goes and hovers in the air. That idea's outside anything I've ever imagined." She leaned against the wall and gazed absently at the ceiling. "At least I'm not seeing things. And nothing about him suggests that magic is real, no matter what he says."

As if on cue, hovering Herb popped into the conversation. "Do you have to believe in magic in order to do it?"

"That question doesn't even make sense," she said. "If I don't believe in it, why would I ever try to use it?"

"Because evil forces are brewing, and your powers will be needed."

"What evil forces? When?"

"That I can't tell you. Some of it remains to be written. But you must be ready when needed."

"You think she'll be able to use the old ways effectively, in spite of her disbelief?" her father asked.

"She has already proven that to be true."

"Wait a minute," said Blundren. "You want me to learn how to use sorcery, even though you always taught me there was nothing to it and I don't believe in it and never will?"

"I may have held back a few things," Wolfmini said.

"I'd rather spend my time learning something worthwhile."

"Excellent," Herb said. "We start tomorrow."

The spirit vanished.

"I don't know what he thinks is going to happen."

Midmorning, as promised, Herb reappeared with an enthusiastic smile. "Are we ready?"

Princess Blundren looked at him blankly and did not answer.

"You're in for a pleasant surprise today."

"I can't promise the same."

"I've taught many the old ways, across ten generations. Even some whose minds were closed to what's possible, like your grandmother."

"I don't know much about her. Did she ever learn about magic?"

"She chose not to pursue the old ways. Yet she passed great powers to her two sons."

"You mentioned once before that my father had a brother."

"Has a brother."

"What can you tell me about him?"

"I can tell you a lot."

"Well?" Blundren asked.

"You'll learn when it's time."

"Why not now? What are you keeping from me?"

"Do I detect an eagerness to learn?" he asked.

"I want to know about my family. It has nothing to do with what you're here to teach me."

"On the contrary. What you wish to know has a great deal to do with the old ways."

"So the sooner I learn about your beliefs, the sooner you'll tell me what I want to know?" Blundren asked.

"If you truly grasp what's possible, then what you wish to know will be revealed at the proper time."

"And when do you consider the proper time to tell me?"

"I won't be the one to decide," Herb said.

"Again," Blundren said, "why not now?"

"So many things are beyond our control. You must learn to wait, to allow things to unfold. You can't force things to be revealed before they're ready to be known. In small ways, you can shape events in the direction you desire."

"I thought you were supposed to teach me special powers."

"The toughest lesson for you will be learning to wait."

"I don't even want to be here," the princess said. "This is a complete waste of time. The only thing I learned today is frustration."

"Excellent. And that concludes the first lesson."

With that, Blundren found herself alone. "I guess I made him disappear. That's something."

The next afternoon, the hovering spirit set a candle before the princess and moved back about ten feet. "You're still a bit frustrated, are you not?"

Blundren glanced at him but said nothing.

"Set your frustration aside for now. Think of nothing but the candle." Herb took a second to focus. He flicked a fore-finger at the candle. A flame appeared. He turned his thumb over and pressed it down in the air. The flame extinguished. He smiled at the princess. "Now you try."

"That's a special candle, right?" Blundren flicked her finger at it. Nothing happened. She looked sideways at the spirit. She forced herself to not look where he wanted her to look.

Herb flicked again and drew a flame. It disappeared with another downward movement of his thumb.

"How are you controlling that candle?"

"That frustration I asked you to set aside? Focus it now into a fiery sphere in the center of your being. Feel it burn. Let it explode down your arm, through your fingers into the candle."

The princess balled her hands into tight fists. This was the last place she wanted to be. How many afternoons were they planning to waste while she toyed with these unfounded beliefs? It amounted to nothing more than calculated misperception and showmanship. How long before Herb and her father tired of their foolish experimentation? *I can outlast their games.*

A tiny curl of smoke drew out a final gasp from the wick. The top surface of the candle still held its melted translucence. Blundren let the room fade. A ball of heat in her rib cage tightened into a fiery intensity. It shot up into her shoulder and down her arm. She flicked her finger and produced a flame.

"Excellent!"

She smiled for the first time. Regardless of what she felt sweep through her body, to fool her into thinking she caused it, Herb's timing was perfect. She flipped her hand and swept it downward, trying to mimic the spirit's movement from a few moments ago. She flattened the candle into a waxy heap.

"You're learning. Let's try again." Herb waved his hands in

a broad flourish, palms out. When he pulled his fists into his chest, both hands curled around sets of fresh candles. He tossed them into the air. They floated down and set themselves up, single file.

With a quick flick of her hand, Blundren lit the candles. And a pillow on a chair. She jerked backward and abruptly plopped both palms down. The pillow flames went out, but she demolished the chair. She laughed aloud.

At the same time, the ground started shaking. Her smile disappeared as the tremors persisted for a full minute.

Herb's face went pale, even for a spirit.

"How did you do that?" she asked.

"You did it, Princess. You just need a softer touch."

"Right."

"To be accurate, you can take credit for the chair—what's left of it. But that earthquake was caused by something else entirely."

"Like what?" she asked.

"I think it may signal the beginning of the end of times."

Chapter Sixteen

BLUGWERT'S BRIDGE

TWO TROLLS PEERED over the edge of Blugwert's Bridge. The simian creature leaned hard to the left, knuckle-walking toward them in a sideways, corkscrew fashion. Its gray simian frame was covered with sparse yellow hair. Flecks of green and blue spattered its scaly back and lighter-toned belly. Thick drool dripped from a mouth filled with razor-sharp daggers. Its arms stretched as long as two men laid end to end.

The trolls dropped down into the dry creek bed. Gimbel's heart pounded.

"The abysmal," Blugwert whispered.

"It looks drunk," Gimbel said.

"Don't make a sound. Maybe it'll just move on."

"You're not going to make him pay?" Gimbel asked.

"He gets a discount."

The creature poked at the bridge. It bit into the edge and peeled back the first two slats. Splintered pieces tumbled out of its mouth.

"Hey!" Gimbel immediately regretted how loudly he'd

spoken, not to mention his demanding tone—particularly when the abysmal became still. It was quite huge. Not that size should be a factor when it came to excusing rudeness. But the creature was enormous, just the same. Perhaps a soft whimper might be in order. "Sorry."

Blugwert grabbed the smaller troll up close, his face twisted, eyes bugging out. Gimbel opened his mouth to apologize. Blugwert flipped Gimbel around and clamped his hand over Gimbel's mouth.

The abysmal crawled out onto the bridge. Droplets of oil beaded on Gimbel's skin. He started to hyperventilate. Gimbel felt Blugwert lift him high, knocking his head against the underside of the bridge before dropping him to the ground. Gimbel looked around.

Blugwert was gone.

A deafening boom overhead made him jump. The bridge shuddered.

"What did you do? Oops. Sorry." Gimbel covered the lower half of his face with his arms and hugged himself tightly. He rocked from side to side, holding his breath. His skin was gushing oil. He heard the plop of goo as something warm dripped onto his arm from above.

"Hey! Mm-mm-mm-mmm... Sorry... Oooooo."

Gimbel scrambled to a respectful distance. He looked back. Waves of panic swept up and down through his body. The creature ripped into Blugwert with its razor-like teeth. It munched lazily with its mouth open. A thin flap of green skin swung from the corner of its mouth.

Gimbel never particularly liked Blugwert. As an apprentice, he thought maybe his boss could've done a better job of explaining things. And maybe not always look so annoyed. But that didn't mean he wanted to see the older troll devoured. Sloppily.

Gimbel couldn't move as the bog creature gobbled down most of the remaining traces of Blugwert. It picked up Blugwert's head and opened its mouth wide. Gimbel gagged. The abysmal looked around and set its eyes on the quaking troll.

"*No!* Oops, sorry. Sorry. No." Gimbel fled. "Sorry, sorry, sorry."

Chapter Seventeen

THE BLUE TIGER

JERMBOG BLOCKED Thundersquat's path at the palace entrance. He smiled and did that impossible thing again, looking down at him from below. "Barbarian. You're back."

"Need to see the sorcerer king."

"You'll have to wait."

"Already have."

"You can't demand to see him at a moment's notice."

"About to find out."

Jermbog pressed his fingertips together into a steeple. "Have you submitted a scroll to formally request a meeting?"

Thundersquat stared at him.

"There has to be a process. Can you read?"

"No."

Jermbog inhaled a lengthy victory sniff. "Then I would anticipate a delay."

Thundersquat pulled off his buckskin vest and tossed it at the magistrate, who caught it, or it caught him, as it wrapped around his fingers.

Jermbog turned his hands down and let the leather

unwrap. He held it aloft between his thumb and forefinger. "What's this?"

"Scroll. Set up the meeting."

"This is a vest," Jermbog said.

"Scroll. Wear it like a vest, easier to carry."

"It can't be a scroll. There's nothing written on it."

"Can't read that?" Thundersquat asked.

"It's blank."

"Been up north lately?"

"No. Why?"

"Bear blindness."

"I'm not blind."

"Sweeping through the country. Don't know you're blind till somebody points it out. Didn't think it would come this far, that fast."

"I'm not..." Jermbog threw the vest back at the barbarian. "Get this off me. No telling where it's been. Get out of here."

Thundersquat slipped the vest back on. "Can't let a blind man walk around bumping into things. Let me help you find the sorcerer king."

"Something that stupid might work in the Badlands, but... How long does this bear blindness last, anyway?"

"No more than a few days."

"No need to worry about it, then."

"Only if you survive the fever. You hot yet?"

Jermbog held his palm to his cheek.

Thundersquat pushed past him. "Not everybody died."

"Wait, you can't go in there."

Thundersquat kept walking. Jermbog circled around in front of him and scooted backward. "Follow me."

Jermbog entered the great hall and paused to wipe his hand across his forehead and glance at his fingertips. Thundersquat veered past him to a room on the right.

Jermbog hurried after him. "Wait here. I can still see, mostly. I'll let His Eminence know you're here. When he's ready, we'll send for you."

"Get some rest. Better chance of pulling through."

Jermbog broke into a run.

~

At the edge of the forest that overlooked the village, the Least High Druid waited at the foot of the twisted mountain. The young Qrudd warrior from the Cloud Men clan watched him without expression. The Cloud Men almost never spoke, and they were hard to read. Least High never knew if they understood or if they expected a reply to what they hadn't said aloud.

"We'll walk right through the village. It's Market Day. There's so much for them to look at, they'll never see us. Not so much invisible, just unnoticed. I've done it many times and I've never failed. But don't look at anyone too long, especially if they look at you. Too much and they'll notice; but too little, they'll see that too."

The warrior gestured toward the half of his face painted blue. He reached out and lifted the tip of the druid's beard.

"True, we're not actually invisible and they're not blind. Even so, they won't see us. Sounds crazy, but they won't see what they don't expect. Do nothing out of the ordinary. Nothing, not even the tiniest bit."

Clad in loincloths and sandals, the bearded old man and the young warrior with the half-blue face strolled into the moving throng. The druid forced himself to think of nothing at all. Like tiny interior gusts, now and then he felt like all eyes were upon him. He forced himself to ignore the sensation. He fought off the worry that the young warrior at his side would give them away. He had to trust him, or he'd give it away himself. He gave the people just enough passage, so they only paid attention to how they'd squeeze through.

Not one individual in the mindless horde appeared to detect their presence. They climbed the spiral path and crossed the courtyard that surrounded the Onyx Palace. The pair stopped below a palace window. The Least High Druid shot both arms upward.

Just as quickly, he resumed his unassuming lack of focus. The warrior and the druid left the courtyard and threaded through the market as before.

Thundersquat stepped out into the great hall. He'd been waiting for hours. Some time in the past, somebody somewhere forgot where he hid the Stone. Here, they forget when you come to ask about it.

Light flickered from the two rooms at the top of the stairs. Thundersquat took the steps three at a time. In the first room Blundren flicked her fingers at a row of candles. One of them lit. She seemed to be talking to herself. He'd spent enough time alone; he knew it was bound to happen sooner or later.

Thundersquat crept past and, from the shadows, peered through the open doorway beyond. Wolfmini stood parallel to a row of candles. With a flick of his hand, they lit up. He pressed his palm downward. The flames went out. *Firestarters. Both of them.*

Behind the sorcerer king, Jermbog leaned close. A swirl of blue gases formed beyond the candles. The sorcerer king jumped back and crashed into Jermbog. They stumbled. The ball of gas took the shape of a translucent tiger covered in blue flames.

Thundersquat heard a muffled scream next door. In a few strides Thundersquat was at Blundren's side. They faced a luminous, fiery blue tiger identical to the one next door. The barbarian slid in front of the princess. *Fire-starters and tiger-makers.*

The tiger roared. It bounded to the window and leaped out. Thundersquat rushed to the window. Before the tiger reached the ground, it merged with its mirror image that hurtled through the air from the adjacent room. The tiger landed with noiseless grace in a single solid form and loped out of the courtyard.

The princess was pale.

"This happen often?" Thundersquat asked.

"Barbarian." Jermbog stood in the doorway, hands on his hips. "I told you to wait."

The sorcerer king rushed past the magistrate to his daughter and placed his hands on her shoulders. "Are you okay?"

"Yes. No. I don't know. It just… I was trying to light some candles. I know we can't really control that kind of thing, but then this tiger… "

"Same thing happened in my room," Wolfmini said.

"You saw it too, then?" she asked.

"This can't be a mistake." Wolfmini locked his hands together behind his back and strolled over to the window. "There's somebody out there. Somebody clever enough to be very close but remain unseen."

"Who, Father? Is he dangerous?"

"Need to talk," Thundersquat cut in.

Wolfmini looked up at him. "I need to protect my daughter. My kingdom."

"How dangerous, Father?" Blundren asked.

Thundersquat glanced over at Blundren and then at the sorcerer king. "Came a long way. Running out of time."

"Barbarian, it's a lot to ask, but if you could wait a little bit longer. I need to discover who's behind this. His plans. We can start by finding that tiger. I'm not sure what that would tell us, but I don't know where else to look. I'd be very grateful if you could help."

The sorcerer king didn't know what he was asking of him. The barbarian pictured his village, at least the way it looked the last he saw it. Now nobody was watching over it. Chances are they've moved a time or two since he's been gone. And he still didn't know if Grandfather made it back there.

Thundersquat formed a fist on the windowsill. He glanced back at Blundren once more. She was staring at the place where the tiger had formed. *Not my problem. Need to find that Stone and get out of here.*

"I can take care of myself," Blundren said. "You don't have to do anything."

Thundersquat pounded his fist on the sill, and with a final glance at the princess, he leaped out the window. He tumbled a few times but came up running. He shook his head as he ran. *Stupid.*

The red-haired troll and the spotted lion stepped out of the old tree. The smell of smoke was unmistakable, though not yet thick enough to see. "I can't tell how close it is or what direction it's coming from."

The lion held his nose up in the air. "Hang back. There's something else out there."

"What could be scarier than the forest burning?"

"The barbarian's coming, for one, but that's not what I'm talking about. A tiger, I think."

Thundersquat abruptly stepped into the clearing. "Tiger come through here?"

"Mudcat was just talking about it. We smelled something burning and came out to see what it was."

"How long ago?"

"A few minutes," Smidgel said.

"Close." Thundersquat ran ahead.

The red-haired troll hesitated, felt a chill, then scampered after him, followed by the spotted lion. The trail curved back, toward the Onyx Palace. The barbarian picked up the pace. After a few hours, the smoldering footprints came to a dead end where they met the previous trail.

Thundersquat stooped down and felt the ground within the footprints in both directions. When he touched the paw prints that headed back toward the old tree, he jerked his fingers back. "He's going in a circle."

They headed up the trail again, slower this time. Smidgel smelled smoke. Suddenly he heard crashing in the under-brush. He wheeled around. The tiger appeared, low to the ground in the shadows, its face lined by a thin blue flame.

"Get behind me," Thundersquat commanded.

The tiger slid a forepaw forward. Thundersquat took two steps toward the tiger. The tiger shuffled back. The blue tiger slowly lowered his head and shoulders into a crouch. The tiger's upper lip curled up to reveal the gums above two gleaming daggers. Smidgel glanced at Mudcat. The spotted lion nodded and moved next to the barbarian.

A high-pitched shriek startled them all. Bolstrus exploded out of the woods, hooves thundering, branches cracking. The stallion reared and settled next to the barbarian, his ferocity simmering a mere twitch away.

"Glad you finally showed up," Thundersquat said. "Now it won't be so hard for him to make up his mind who to eat first."

Bolstrus shifted his weight and bumped a hip against the barbarian.

Thundersquat glanced back at the lion. "Take the troll back to the old tree."

"What about you?" Smidgel asked.

"Go. Now."

Smidgel didn't argue. He couldn't be much help here. When they reached the top of the ridge, the troll and the lion paused to catch their breath. They heard an angry shriek, followed by a blast of pain, mixed with the crash of bodies and branches blown apart.

Smidgel and Mudcat plunged through the underbrush until they reached the glen below. Sounds of pursuit behind them spurred them on. At the top of the second ridge, the troll's lungs were near bursting. He dared to hazard a look behind him. The blue tiger reached the valley below and began to climb.

The spotted lion shoved Smidgel over the ridge. The troll tumbled down the ravine and got snagged in the underbrush. He ripped himself out of the bush and found he was alone. The spotted lion looked on from ridge above. Mudcat tossed his head in the direction of the third ridge. He turned and disappeared from view.

The red-haired troll shimmied up the third and final ridge. Fierce roars behind him drove him on. He slipped often. His legs were rubbery, his forearms numb. Nearly to the top, Smidgel fell and lay there. His head was spinning.

His lungs tried desperately to process enough air. The roaring suddenly ceased.

He summoned enough courage to lift his head and glance back. The fiery blue tiger stared at him from across the ravine. The tiger roared, and blue flames surged above him. Smidgel screamed and leaped out beyond the steep ridge. He flew ten or more feet before he crashed into branches and rolled through low bushes until the ground leveled out. He dashed through the trees and broke into the clearing. The troll wobbled with each stride as he raced toward the old tree. His legs locked up and it seemed like he was running in slow motion. He was on the verge of blacking out.

The fiery blue tiger bore down on the troll. Smidgel felt the beast's hot breath upon his back. He veered sharply toward the magic fountain. The blue tiger lost a step making the turn but gained it back. The tiger lunged. Smidgel dove. Just short of the fountain, the troll smacked the ground and rolled to the left. He felt a wave of heat pass above him as the tiger twisted and swiped at him. The tiger rolled within its flames, skipped twice, and slammed into the fountain's surface. Its paws floundered in the churning water. Bubbles crackled and fizzled. The magic fountain became still. A blue vapor lingered above the water and dissipated.

Smidgel lay there, trapped in the quiet. He listened. Waiting, hoping for sounds of the two he left behind. An unforgiving heaviness pressed the troll deep into the soggy ground. His red hair sopped up the dampness. The filtered rays that filled the forest normally brought with them a comforting stillness. Today they taunted him. What of his friends? Time no doubt continued into the night, but without the troll. Another night like this would have been cold. He listened.

The spotted lion dragged himself with one final step to

the top of the ridge. His lungs burned. He collapsed and dropped his head over the edge. He lay there, panting, straining to see into the clearing below. His ribs stabbed at him. In the splintered moonlight that reflected off the magic fountain, something lay still, a lump the size of the red-haired troll. Adrenaline surged, and the lion's pain retreated. Gravity hurled him forward to the lifeless lump that was his one and only friend.

Mudcat stood over Smidgel, hoping. Not believing. Fearing what might propel him into the next moment. His paw hovered close to the troll's shoulder, the thickness of a leaf apart. To push any further might confirm a reality he couldn't handle. How long to let him lie there before he knew? How much would the troll need to move before one could trust in the hope that he still breathed?

Gingerly, Mudcat let his paw graze the troll's shoulder and then hover once more. The pain started to creep back. He waited. Smidgel's chest moved. *Maybe.*

Again. He hadn't imagined it.

A tap of relief was crushed by pain that trampled the lion from within. He toppled over next to the troll. Smidgel reached over and laid his hand on the spotted lion's paw. They listened.

Chapter Eighteen

SHAKEN

THUNDERSQUAT ROLLED onto his side and propped himself up on an elbow while he tried to get his bearings. As he stood up, he clutched his head and spun around, struggling to keep his balance as he hit the ground hard. He vomited. Bolstrus limped over to him, legs spread wide, wavering slightly.

"Help him, Least High," a voice said.

The stallion reared and shrieked. Thundersquat collapsed into his vomit and rolled into a crouch on one knee. He squinted at two silhouettes swaying within a blinding haze.

"It would not hinder the plan." The second voice was calm; it sounded older. "Lower your bow."

Thundersquat wiped his forearm across his mouth and chin and calculated the distance between them. The shorter one was armed. He'd have to take him out first.

The older one spoke again. "We mean you no harm. I have a potion here that will help the pain."

"Help it do what?" Thundersquat leaned against the stallion's foreleg. He could not summon enough breath to say more. The pressure inside his skull threatened to blast it wide open. It took everything he had to maintain his composure and ready himself for the attack.

After a few minutes, the taller one slowly approached, extended a gourd and pressed it into the barbarian's outstretched hand. Thundersquat watched the tall one back away. He sniffed the top of the gourd and jiggled the liquid inside. *Could be poison. Might be something to ease the pain. Only one way to find out.* He sipped until it was gone.

He allowed himself slow, shallow breaths. The rocking motion slowed, and the bright light dimmed. The pair of silhouettes ripened into blurred images of a bearded old man in a loincloth and a young warrior with wild, wavy hair, his face painted blue. As the pain began to subside, the barbarian nodded his thanks. Then a wave of nausea struck when he moved his head. He waited for his eyes to focus again.

"Find your way to the troll," the old man suggested to Thundersquat. "He'll make more of the same potion. Drink some each day for half a moon." With that, old man and warrior disappeared into the forest.

Eyes still closed, Thundersquat struggled to his feet and laid an arm over the stallion's back. Bolstrus emitted a low groan. With labored steps, he guided the barbarian up and over the next two ridges.

It was well into the night when the barbarian stumbled to the base of the old tree. Thundersquat pounded once on the door. The door flew open and smashed into his knee.

"Sorry!" the red-haired troll said. "Did that hurt?"

Thundersquat rubbed his knee. "Compared to what?"

Smidgel helped his friend down the spiral staircase. Thundersquat rolled into an empty space on the floor and slammed his shoulder against the wall.

The spotted lion lifted his head as the barbarian settled

nearby. He dragged his battered body over to the barbarian and placed his head on his lap. Jagged scars showed along his ribs, still oozing. Thundersquat held his hand over the dingy mane and lowered his fingers, like he was about to dig through garbage. He stroked the lion's neck. The spotted lion purred softly and drifted off to sleep. The barbarian's head slowly fell forward.

When the barbarian woke, he grabbed his head. Smidgel was ready with a potion. Thundersquat drained the cup and handed it back. "Drank this before. Forest. Old man."

"What old man?"

"Don't know. Maybe not real."

"The beating you took was real enough."

Thundersquat cocked his head and squinted through one eye. "Tiger…circled back… Should've known."

"You saved my life. Just rest now. I have something to put on those burns."

Two weeks passed. Thundersquat made a complete recovery, except for the constant dull headache and the sharp pain in his ribs when he breathed. If he held his head still, the world didn't spin as much. The skin on his arms had mostly grown back. The gashes on his ribs didn't ooze terribly. His legs were in good shape, though, if he held them about shoulder length apart and didn't try to move laterally. Or at all. He was ready to resume the search for the Half-Forgotten Stone.

Thundersquat had given a lot of thought to his village while he lay there doing nothing those two weeks. He kept telling himself they'd be okay, that they didn't need him watching over them. Grandfather surely made it back; there was no sign of him out here. Maybe a quick look, he argued, would satisfy his worry; then he could continue this fruitless quest for the Stone. They wouldn't allow him to meet with the sorcerer king anyway—one excuse after another. Grandfather wouldn't have to know. Just a quick look. They'd never see him, and he could be on his way.

"I'd feel better if you took Mudcat with you," Smidgel said.

The spotted lion twitched an ear in the troll's direction and grumbled.

Thundersquat scowled. "He'll have to scale back some of that enthusiasm."

Chapter Nineteen

GRISMAL THE ABYSMAL

THE ABYSMAL'S MOUTH watered. As he knuckle-walked over the ridge, he found several dozen of the little-creature-places. They hid inside. *Fast. Good to eat.*

The abysmal leveled the first two creature-places. He could hardly hear the creatures' screams over the howling wind that battered his face. They fled, some of them bleeding. He turned toward one of the creatures who limped away. An old one stepped between them. An old one with a pointed stick.

The old one was quick. The abysmal swung; the skinny creature rolled under his fist. The creature poked the abysmal with the stick and dodged. *Ouch.* The abysmal looked around for easier prey. The old one stayed close, just out of reach. *Ouch.* The abysmal charged. The old one feinted left and dove right. *Ouch.*

The abysmal whirled around and leaped at the wiry creature. The old one ducked and thrust upward. The abysmal roared at the stick now protruding from its upper abdomen.

The creature snapped the stick with one fist and caught the old one with a backhanded blow.

The old one rolled and climbed to his feet. He leaned to one side. The abysmal charged again. The old one dove, but the abysmal crushed him with a downward blow to his upper back. He dropped both fists once more, and the old one lay still.

The abysmal delivered yet another smashing blow, followed by another, and another. The old one's body bounced and flopped with each bash. The other creatures cried out. He pummeled him again.

A handful of the others huddled together, watching. He released a discordant wail that sent them hobbling in all directions. The monster paused to crunch the old one's bones.

Before he was through, half of the creatures had seen their final sunrise. The abysmal feasted on their remains.

Thundersquat spread his fingers and reached for the endless sky. He let the warmth fold in around him, and he felt free for the first time since he'd left. When he opened his eyes, he surveyed the nothingness that stretched as far as he could see in all directions. "World gives you little out here," he said to the lion, "but it's enough."

Bolstrus trotted like a young colt. They both needed this, more than he had realized. All he had to do now was find the village. You could bet it wasn't where it was before, if he could even figure out where that was. Still, he usually got where he was going. Eventually.

UncleCousin Sumac was bound to say something about it. Sumac always said Thundersquat was just like his father.

Navigationally challenged, Grandfather liked to say. Once he overheard Sumac joke about Father after they called off the search. Maybe nothing happened, he said. Might still be out there somewhere, trying to find his way home. Never said that in front of him or Grandfather.

Buzzards circled, floating in the distant sky. The spotted lion sniffed the air and seemed rattled.

Thundersquat smiled. "Sign of a good hunt. Buzzards are hoping for some leftovers. Village should be nearby. Wouldn't have gone far—too much work to do. Preparing the skins. Getting the meat ready."

Thundersquat slipped off the silver stallion and headed up the last rise. Even if it was his village, they still had a long way to go. "No smoke yet. Might make it in time for the feast."

He nudged the lion. "Wait till you meet Grandfather. Probably could outrun us both."

At the top of the rise he stopped, and so did his heart. The disarray was apparent even from this far away. The barbarian leaped onto the stallion and goaded him into a gallop that seemed far too much like slow motion. The stench hit him like he had crashed into a wall.

When he arrived at what was left of the village, several buzzards hopped to the side and took to the air. Thunder-squat rolled off his mount and searched the ground.

The carnage was scattered as far as he could see. An arm here, half a leg there. Pieces. Pieces of the people he grew up with. The sight clutched at his soul, clawed at the back of his eyes. All over, signs of something huge, heavy, some kind of monster.

Maybe there were survivors, hiding somewhere, still in danger. The barbarian narrowed his vision into a tight box and blackened everything outside it. He began to disentangle the threads, one at a time. He would feel nothing until he found them.

Two days later, the trail led the barbarian over a shallow ridge. A tiny grove of trees stuck out like a blotch on the landscape in the distance. Something moved, almost as large as the tree it closed in on. At the base of the tree, more movement, obscured by shadows.

Thundersquat bellowed and charged ahead. Bolstrus caught up to him, and the barbarian swung up on the stallion. In seconds they were at a full gallop. The spotted lion streaked beside them.

Chapter Twenty

BATTLE

"LOST IN THOUGHT, girl?"

"Not really. Well, Father… I was thinking about when you believed you were a frog in the swamp. You mentioned something about remote viewing. Do you ever wonder if it's really possible?"

They both turned at a muffled *poof*. "Aha! I've been waiting for you to ask!"

"Herb." Her enthusiasm was but a distant echo of his.

"There are two ways," the spirit said. "You can use the chemical mirror in the stone, like your father does. Or you can borrow the eyes of an animal for a time."

"I'm not—"

"I can teach you to seek out an animal in the area where you wish to search. Then you can join with it long enough to observe remotely."

"I don't see how that—"

"I wouldn't expect much success at first. This skill takes years of practice."

"I wouldn't expect any success at all," she said. "And I don't want to wait years."

"Some have been able to hold an image for a few seconds after their first few attempts. Are you ready to try?"

"I was just curious. I'm not committing to learn about impossible things." Blundren started to turn and paused. She had asked for a reason, not out of idle curiosity. "Suppose we don't know exactly where to search?"

"For that to work, you'd have to have a special connection to the person you want to view. You wouldn't have to know where."

"Well...what about that barbarian, Thundersquat, for example? Just to see if he's okay. I don't have any special connection, but he helped rescue my father before he took off after the blue tiger. We haven't heard from him since."

"Close your eyes. Imagine him as you last saw him."

"What harm can it do?"

"Empty your mind of all other thoughts."

A blackish purple void appeared. Random thoughts jerked her away from it. She let them drift away and settled into the void. She tilted her head.

"What do you see?" Herb asked.

"Well, I know this can't be real." The image faded. "It was like I was circling, far above the ground."

"Try again," Herb said.

She cleared her mind again and entered the purple void. The same image took shape. "Something's moving, far below... It has to be him—there's the silver stallion...and the spotted lion... They're at the top of a ridge. They're looking at a grove of trees."

"What you're doing is extraordinary," Herb said.

Her heart pounded. Her voice took on a new urgency. "They need to stop, go back the other way."

"Just relax and watch."

Blundren shook her head. "I lost it again. It switched to the forest. I think I saw Qrudd warriors, painted yellow."

"That happens sometimes. Rest a minute and we'll try again."

The images seized control; the barbarian stood far below. Her heart raced. "They're running toward a grove of trees. Some kind of monster! Huge! That's crazy!"

"Easy, daughter."

"I'm surprised that you're still holding the image," Herb said, "pleasantly surprised. But there's nothing you can do."

"No! Stop!"

The abysmal turned and clambered in a rush toward the invaders. The simian creature paused and leaned on its knuckles, then rose and extended its arms wide. A broken stick protruded from its upper abdomen. Crusted blood covered its gut and trailed down one leg. The monster thrust its head forward into a roar that shook the landscape.

In the roar Thundersquat heard tones of agony, of outrage, of unforgivable grievance. "Feel your pain. You're about to feel mine."

Bolstrus's body dropped a notch as he lengthened his stride.

Pinned against the tree was UncleCousin Sumac.

"Scoot around the tree," Thundersquat yelled to him. "Then run."

"Can't run. Leg's hurt."

Thundersquat slid from Bolstrus's back, hit the ground, and rolled to the right. Bolstrus veered to the left at a full gallop. The creature drew back and swung at the barbarian.

Thundersquat hurdled sideways above the arm, hammered a fist into the creature's ribs, and dove.

The abysmal wheeled around. Bolstrus leaped and twisted, planting both rear hooves into the creature's back. The monster stumbled forward. As it turned, the spotted lion swiped the back of its knees and drew blood. The abysmal dipped to one knee. The barbarian leapfrogged over the abysmal's head.

The three of them goaded the beast in sequence, hitting it wherever it was not looking. The abysmal roared its frustration. They kept up the onslaught for hours, until they all gasped for breath. The creature's counterpunches took a little longer to unwind. It staggered with each follow-through. The monster paused and sat, staring at nothing.

Bolstrus delivered a powerful kick to the creature's back, which nudged it forward. The abysmal rocked back, turned his head slowly, and spotted Sumac, still pressed against the tree.

Thundersquat inserted himself between the creature and Sumac. "Told you to run."

"Can't."

"Can you crawl, or hop, or something?"

"You didn't say anything about that."

"Well, pick one and do it!" Thundersquat waited in a diagonal stance, light on his feet. The creature reached an arm back to swing. The barbarian hurled himself into the abysmal's midsection. It was like tackling a tree. Thundersquat drove his legs relentlessly and won scant inches for his efforts. The abysmal raised both fists.

Mudcat and Bolstrus made desperate passes over and around the abysmal. The monster swatted at them, wavering from the effort. Thundersquat summoned what strength he had left and pounded his legs into the ground with fury, pushing in the direction the creature swayed. The abysmal pushed back and roared, wreaking havoc on the barbarian's eardrums. The beast lifted its fists once again.

A sudden explosion resounded through the valley. Grismal the abysmal toppled over on top of the barbarian. Thundersquat's vision went black.

At the Onyx Palace, Wolfmini recoiled at the sight of his daughter, lying in a crumpled heap, eyes open and staring.

"Herb! What happened? Do something!"

"I don't... How...? It's not possible..."

"What's not possible? Do something!" Wolfmini commanded.

"Not possible. I don't..."

Her father rushed to Blundren's side. "We can't just stand here and watch!"

"But I don't... You can't... She saw through its eyes, but how could she make a raptor plunge to its death?"

"Its death?"

"Yes."

"Then what will happen to my daughter?"

"I don't know. This has never happened. It's impossible."

Chapter Twenty-One

IMPACT

"WHERE DID THAT raptor come from?" Sumac asked. "Killed itself and the monster too."

Beneath the weight of the abysmal, Thundersquat struggled to breathe, unable to get any leverage. His arms were pinned. One foot was free, but there was nothing to push against. He couldn't feel his other leg.

"Probably crushed Thundersquat. Need our help under there?"

Can't sneak anything past UncleCousin Sumac.

"He's not answering. Think he's okay?"

A few choice words came to mind, but they were difficult to articulate against the putrid slime that was pasted across the barbarian's face and mouth. With each shallow intake of air, his rib skewered him. *Not worth the effort. Council used to say I never knew when to keep my big mouth shut. All I needed was the right amount of pain. Could almost pass as good judgment.*

"Never gonna get that thing off him," Sumac observed. "Good as dead."

Thundersquat scraped the ground with his heel. The spotted lion attacked the dirt to the barbarian's right.

"Not gonna work," Sumac said. "If you dig a hole underneath him, that monster will just slide down on top of him. Never gonna get him out."

Thundersquat watched the lion's paws tear at the earth. He felt the ground shake as the stallion charged toward him and leaped over. Through a tiny sliver he could make out Bolstrus's hooves as he bolted into the thicket. The stallion then backed out and circled Sumac with a woody vine. He whipped around and pulled the older barbarian to the ground.

"What are you doing, you stupid animal?" Sumac stood back up.

Bolstrus repeated his maneuver.

"Have you gone stark raving crazy?" Sumac hopped into the thicket. "Goes to show you about horses. No more sense than the fool who tries to train them. Put a stop to this right now."

Sumac hacked away at the vine, grumbling nonstop about how in his day they walked everywhere on their own two feet. Hauled everything themselves. Didn't waste all their time trying to get somewhere faster.

Bolstrus snatched up the freed vine and leaped over the abysmal. Mudcat stopped digging, grabbed the creature's left forearm in his jaws, and lifted it. Bolstrus dropped the vine underneath the arm. He circled around and tightened it.

"We can use that vine to pull the creature off him," Sumac announced, inspired.

Way to keep up, UncleCousin Sumac.

The stallion and lion grabbed the ends of the vine and threw their shoulders into it. The abysmal started to slide. Soon Thundersquat's head and torso were free. Sumac dragged Thundersquat the rest of the way out from under the abysmal.

Breathing was a little easier, but Thundersquat's damaged rib made itself known. His leg suddenly felt like it was covered with angry hornets.

"Are you all right?" Sumac asked.

"Yeah." Thundersquat rolled to his side and climbed to his feet. He stamped the ground until his leg felt right. The remains of the raptor were still laid out across the abysmal's back. Thundersquat coughed and winced. "Must've been one hungry bird."

"Good thing I was here to pull you out," Sumac said. "Don't know how I did it, hurt leg and all."

"Don't know what we'd do without you." Each breath caught a little before Thundersquat's ribs fully expanded. "Anybody else make it?"

"A few. You'll find them farther up in that batch of trees. Wouldn't wait for me."

"Grandfather?"

"First to fall. Stood alone and fought to give the rest of us time to escape."

Thundersquat combed both hands through his mane. "Never should've left."

"Got that right. Half of the village is dead. Thanks to you."

Thundersquat grabbed Sumac. His arms shook as heat rushed to his head. He hurled the older man to the ground.

Sumac's head whacked when he collided with the dirt, and his whole body bounced. He grabbed his head and squinched his cheeks. "Your fault. Your grandfather's bones, laying out in the sun. Buzzards picking them clean. All because you weren't there."

Thundersquat clenched his fists and walked away.

Sumac kept railing away at him. "Never should've

happened. Nothing but trouble since the day you were born. If we hadn't been out looking for you back then, we might've found your father!"

Thundersquat tried to suppress those words, but they were all he heard. If anything, the echoes became louder. His stride was brisk, spurred on by the images and smells he batted away.

Cool sprinkles in swirling gusts of wind awakened the barbarian, still walking at a lively pace. Bolstrus and Mudcat trotted alongside. The stallion was lathered up, and the spotted lion's tongue hung out. Thundersquat slowed and scanned the surrounding vista.

As far as he could tell, they had just entered the ridgelands at the eastern edge of the Badlands. They must've been walking for days. The rain drops started to fall heavier. Thundersquat headed toward a large tree and leaned back against it. He sank to the ground.

The spotted lion grumbled at him and waited for a scant minute before taking off into the forest.

Bolstrus trotted past. Thundersquat was aware that the stallion was staring at him. He passed by again, closer. The stallion charged the barbarian and reared. Then he planted his feet, stepped forward, and nudged the barbarian.

"Go away, horse."

The silver stallion raced away. The rain fell in a steady patter.

The barbarian's gloom pressed him into the tree. *Should've been there. Never should've left. That Stone's never gonna be found anyway.*

Chapter Twenty-Two

VENGEANCE

THE MOSTLY WHITE WOLF watched intently from his predatory crouch, low in the undergrowth. Yellow-painted warriors from the Jackal clan closed in around the old tree. The wolf had been tracking them for a day. The red-haired troll emerged and proceeded to sweep around the entrance, a losing cause in the swirling wind. One warrior emerged near the magic fountain and approached the troll.

"Can I help you?" Smidgel asked.

A second warrior slipped behind, positioning himself between the troll and the old tree. Two or three others waited in the bushes.

"You keep this place clean," the first warrior said.

"Thank you. I don't believe in falling behind."

"Too ashamed to show that you've been here?"

"No, I—"

"You'll pay for what you did to the great bear."

"I didn't hurt—"

"You wanna poison us?"

"Why would I—"

"Shut up!"

The Qrudd warriors closed in on the red-haired troll. The mostly white wolf eased forward. He crouched, ready to spring. The warriors attacked the troll. The wolf leaped. Like a meteor from above, something dealt the wolf a crushing blow. He collapsed.

The red-haired troll drifted in and out of consciousness and places in between. Braided leather straps sliced into his wrists and ankles. His arms were stretched taut, just short of ripping him apart. His light-green skin was stretched cherry white across his shoulders. There was not enough flex to fully expand his chest, so he had to ratchet in mere thimblefuls of air. A stone the size of his fist plopped onto his lower belly. Another hoarded pocket of air whooshed free. A few rocks rested on his chest and abdomen. Others bounced into mounds that hemmed him in on both sides.

Yellow-painted figures danced and cheered. Their shouts sounded far away. A warrior thrust his face close to the red-haired troll. Smidgel focused on the warrior's face, searching for any sign of empathy. His tormentor grinned. The Qrudd warrior snatched a rock from the troll's chest and lifted it high. Abruptly he jerked his head to the side; he screamed. The rock slipped out of his hand and bounced off the troll's shoulder.

The Qrudds scrambled, disappearing into the forest.

Something cold pressed against the troll's chest. He peeked through the eye that was not swollen shut. The mostly white wolf assured him that his agony was over.

The wolf pawed away the surrounding mounds and nudged the rocks from the troll's body. He gnawed through the leather straps. The troll lay fused with the ground, arms extended. He felt no need to move if it meant he would unleash the pain that lurked in his limbs. Razor teeth clamped down on his shoulder. Searing, blinding light seized the back of his eyeballs, wrenched, and squeezed. The troll was dimly aware of being dragged.

The wolf released the troll's shoulder. He gently lifted one of the troll's forearms and dipped it into water. The wolf pivoted the arm and let the water drip onto the troll's forehead. A trickle of water trailed across his face.

Smidgel's eyes fluttered. He began to breathe more regularly. The troll pushed up with one arm and uttered a soft moan as he flopped over onto his stomach. Smidgel cupped his hands and poured the healing fluid from the magic fountain over the back of his head.

Chapter Twenty-Three

RECOVERY

WOLFMINI HADN'T SLEPT since his daughter's collapse three days ago, nor did he feel the need. He'd driven himself past the point of sleep many times before when necessary. This time he couldn't have slept if he wanted to. He tenderly observed Blundren, asleep in her bed.

From the corner of his eye, he caught a movement and turned his head toward the doorway. He saw Dekatria waiting there and beckoned to her to enter. "You received our message."

"I've beseeched the gods to intervene and bring her back to us in good health."

"We're grateful."

"Fate has something different in store for her, I'm sure of it." The priestess leaned over the side of the bed. "How did she get the bruises?"

"We don't know. Her fall couldn't have caused all that. She was learning to view remotely, and she was doing well. But something terrified her. Then her eyes filled with an intense anger. We called to her, but she couldn't hear us. She dropped to the floor. No. She threw herself into it."

"She'll wake up," Dekatria said.

"I wanted to share the old ways with her, to make up for lost time. It blinded me, made me careless." The sorcerer king rubbed his forehead. "I did this. I pushed her too far."

Jermbog entered. "Your Eminence, a storm approaches."

"Do you think we care what's happening out there?" Wolfmini snarled.

Dekatria pulled her head back slightly and stared at him.

The magistrate's face colored slightly, but otherwise he gave no indication that the sorcerer king was out of line. "I believe you should see this, Your Eminence. I've never witnessed anything like it."

Why all the melodrama over a storm? With my daughter in the shape she's in. Still, I need to show some support for his subordinates. Regardless of what I feel. That's what leaders do. He spoke through his teeth in a deep guttural voice. "Forgive me, Jermbog. I know you must think it's worth my attention."

Wolfmini searched his daughter's form for any sign of movement.

"I'll watch over her," Dekatria said.

"If she awakens, tell her I'll be right back." Wolfmini couldn't filter out the grumbling tone. The lack of sleep was catching up to him. His worry for his daughter—his guilt— no doubt contributed. He allowed some space behind Jermbog as he followed him through the hall and took a moment to rein in his irritability.

As he stepped down into the great hall, a subtle heaviness in the air wrapped around him and pushed against his lungs. Walking required more effort. Until now, he'd tossed the weakness off as a sign of fatigue. But it was getting worse, happening more often. Through the palace entryway, he noticed the constant flickering and heard rolling thunder that hinted at the power headed in their direction. The prophecy foretold in the stars crossed his mind. *Maybe I pushed her too fast, before she was ready. But what about what's coming? Will my fear for her cause me to hold back when I shouldn't?*

Jermbog and Wolfmini stepped into the open courtyard. Large drops fell sporadically. Wind gusts bent the trees at right angles before they snapped upright again. Suddenly, lightning struck the outer wall. A thunderclap knocked them both off their feet and shook the palace. They scurried back inside as a torrent of rain slammed into the courtyard.

They looked out from the protection of the great hall, partly soaked, looking like someone had tossed a bucket of water over them. Wolfmini couldn't see more than a few strides into the courtyard. Jermbog was right. This storm was worse than usual, maybe the kind that arrived once in a generation. But something more was brewing.

Indigestion and nausea pulsed within the sorcerer king's rib cage, rising into his throat. The pressure he'd noted earlier swelled and squeezed his torso in a vise-like grip that brought him to his knees. A stench unlike anything he'd ever encountered assailed his nostrils. It enveloped him, swirled through his gut and wrung it out. He nearly gagged. He couldn't breathe. The crushing pressure seized his soul and tried to wrench it free. He was alone and tiny in a vast nothingness between light and dark, the acrid taste of the diabolic filling his mouth.

And then it was gone. He was intact. A wave of exhaustion rolled up from his feet. Wolfmini tottered over to the wall and leaned against it before he slumped to the floor. Not since he'd done distant magic from the pond had he felt so groggy. He just needed to close his eyes for a few moments. No more than…just a…

Blundren awoke on all fours, facing the wall. Her neck and shoulders were tight, heavy. The smell of sweat was thick, and her mouth tasted of salt. She leaned forward to drink but bumped her head. Her fingers ran down the cold stone that wasn't supposed to be there. Her right hand felt like it was dripping wet up past the wrist, but it was completely dry. Every thought seemed to have to claw its way free, as if through a crusty loaf of bread. She surveyed the room. Dekatria, wide-eyed, was pinned to the opposite wall.

"Where's the troll?" Blundren asked.

"What are you talking about?" Dekatria asked.

Blundren grimaced. "When did you get here?"

"This afternoon."

"What am I doing down here?"

"You jumped out of bed, like a wild animal. It startled me. Then you crawled over to the wall. Like you were dragging something heavy with your teeth."

Blundren sat on the bed. "Weird. Have you seen my father?"

"He just left. I'm sure he'll be right back."

"You don't have to cover for him."

"I'm not. He went to check out the storm."

Blundren cocked her head. The rolling booms followed one after the other, some loud enough to rattle the whole palace. "Sounds like you'll be staying here for a while."

"Or you could do something to slow down the rain. Disperse the clouds, maybe?"

Blundren would've scoffed at the idea a few weeks ago. "If I tried something like that, it might make things worse."

"Well, if you won't do anything about the weather, then I should probably stay."

Blundren nodded. She gazed at the floor, her eyes unfocused.

"You were fuzzy back there. What happened to you?" Dekatria asked.

"I don't know. I feel weak. Still not fully awake."

"Not surprising. You slept for three days."

"Are you kidding?"

"Your father doesn't know what happened to you."

"Me either." Blundren stretched her neck and rolled her shoulders. "Everything hurts."

"Why did you hit the floor like you did?"

"I don't know. All I can see are little snippets. Visions, or dreams, whatever. Strange."

"What about?"

"Random things. I don't know…a monster, the barbarian. Qrudds with yellow spots, the red-haired troll. None of it makes any sense." She rubbed her shoulder. "In the dream, I was flying. I streaked down from above, like an arrow, trying to crash into a monster. He was about to kill the barbarian. I felt angry. I was afraid I might not get there in time—or worse, that I might miss."

"That must be when you crashed into the floor. Did you hit the monster?"

"I don't know. I had a quick flash of another scene. I had four legs this time. The Qrudds were approaching the troll. It didn't smell right. Then they attacked him, and something smashed into me. I don't know. I never saw it. Later I chased them away, and dragged the troll to the water…"

"Do you think any of it really happened?"

Blundren felt her heart race. "I don't see how. It means we'd have to believe in monsters. Symbols, more likely. Just a dream. Could mean anything. Maybe I'm more afraid about what happened to the barbarian than I realized. The last we heard of him, he took off after a tiger."

"What if he's hurt somewhere out there, and you detected it somehow?"

"I doubt if we'll ever hear from him again," Blundren answered.

"Didn't you say he wanted to talk with your father?"

"Good luck with that."

"What if I told you I saw him?"

"The barbarian?" Blundren's heart pounded again. "What do you mean?"

"On the edge of the woods outside the village. We've all heard about that gray stallion of his. I'm sure it was him."

"So, he's alive. That would prove the visions can't be true."

"Unless he was seriously hurt and came here for help."

"It's so unlikely. The only way to test it would be to talk to him ourselves." Blundren considered the effort involved. Her eyes met Dekatria's. "We're going."

"You have feelings for him, don't you?"

"Don't be ridiculous. He's a barbarian. How could that ever work?"

"Then you've thought about it?" Dekatria teased.

"You're my only friend. Don't blow it."

"That storm's worse than you think. How are we ever going to get to your boyfriend?"

"It'll be okay. Let me throw something on to travel in. And he's not my boyfriend."

"We'll never get past your father."

"We just have to toss out a little misdirection. I was taught by the best. Follow my lead."

They encountered the sorcerer king pacing in the great hall, rubbing his temples. Jermbog stood off to the side.

Wolfmini rushed over and threw his arms around her. "You're awake!"

"I'm fine. Father, if this rain keeps up, the valley might flood. Dekatria should stay with us until it's over."

"No question. She's most welcome."

"First we need to pick up some of her things."

"You can't go out in this storm," he said. "I'll send one of the soldiers."

"I wish we could," Dekatria said. "But some of the items are holy. Only I can touch them."

The sorcerer king nodded. "I can appreciate your dedication to the old ways. But is it worth the risk?"

"It looks worse than it is," Dekatria said.

"I can see myself how bad it is. And my daughter needs to rest. I still don't know what happened to her."

"We'll be okay," Blundren said.

"You're not going." His voice was loud. "Someone's out there. Remember the bats. We still can't explain the tiger. Look at your face! There's no reason in the world for you to leave this palace."

"Nobody's going to be out in this weather," Blundren said. "You can't be swayed by your fears about what happened before."

"If everybody else has the good judgment to stay indoors, how are you different? I'm telling you, something evil is happening."

"We're not going near the woods, just to the village," Dekatria said. "I've never once felt unsafe there. I promise I'll take care of her."

"Go tomorrow. Take a contingent of soldiers."

Blundren hesitated. "That's probably not a bad idea. But we don't need anybody to come with us."

"Take the magistrate. You can send him to summon help if you run into any problems."

"True," Dekatria said. "But why disturb him? I'm sure he has a lot to do."

"I can assure you, it would be no imposition," Jermbog said.

"I suppose we could talk tonight, Father," Blundren said. "Go over whatever happened. Some of it's foggy. I'd like to get your take on it."

"Tomorrow's just as good to collect my things," Dekatria said.

"I'm so relieved. Rain'll likely slow down by then. You'll still be able to beat the flood. Wait for us in the dining room. Magistrate, get them some soup."

As soon as the pair had left the room, Blundren and Dekatria hurried out into the storm. The skies were dark; it was hard to see through the blinding rain. They leaned into the wind and headed down the spiral path toward the village below. In a couple of places, rushing water tore at their ankles. The market-place at the edge of the village had already begun to flood.

"I think we're being followed. Don't look back," Blundren said.

"It's Jermbog. I can smell him from here."

"He must have seen us leave."

Dekatria pointed. "Turn left into that alley."

They dipped into the alley between the market fronts and picked up speed. It was considerably darker in the alley. Ahead of them, two figures emerged. The women stopped and took a step back.

From behind them, Jermbog called, "Highness! Get back to the main road."

The young ladies walked quickly, just short of a run. They

stopped abruptly when three more figures appeared behind Jermbog. The magistrate faced the intruders, retreating until he backed into Blundren and Dekatria. The five cloaked figures casually circled them.

Blundren kept her voice steady. "Who are you? What do you want?"

The tallest figure stepped forward. "We need to get you across the river, Princess, while we still can."

Chapter Twenty-Four

CROSSING OVER

THAT FIRST NIGHT was the coldest Blundren had ever been through. Rain pelted the canopy above, rerouted into steady streams too numerous to escape. She pulled her cloak tighter and huddled next to Dekatria.

Jermbog splashed over and slid next to them. He blew into his hands and rubbed them together. The magistrate edged in with the air of one who is overly familiar.

Dekatria jerked away. "Keep your distance. Before the princess turns you into a slug."

"Magistrate," Blundren said, "It might be better if you stayed near our captors. Find out what you can."

"Of course, Highness. I was thinking the same thing." Jermbog leaned closer and whispered, "I caught a glimpse of one of their faces. They're Qrudd warriors."

"Qrudds—are you sure?" Blundren asked.

"Wait'll the rain stops. You'll be able to identify them by smell." The magistrate grinned. He pulled his cloak further over his head and traipsed off to a spot within hearing range of the Qrudd warriors and the tall leader.

Blundren looked at her friend, who stared darkly at the magistrate. "Dekatria. He's just as cold as we are."

"I don't need another lecture." Dekatria's teeth chattered. "It's bad enough I have to be in this weather. I don't need to put up with him too."

"You know I couldn't turn him into a slug."

"I know. Somebody beat you to it."

The next few days and nights the tempest showed no signs of letting up. If anything, the rain fell harder. If they'd waited till the next day, Blundren realized, they would never have gotten out of the palace. They wouldn't have ended up where they were now.

Water covered their feet on the path. They waded across wide creeks, swollen by the rain to waist high. Getting wetter meant nothing at that point. After one of the creek crossings, they paused to rest.

Jermbog now claimed a spot in the midst of the warriors. They all faced away from him. None of them responded to his attempts to start a conversation. The magistrate meandered over next to the tall one, staring into the woods in the direction they were headed. The two were near enough for Blundren to make out what they were saying.

"I'm sure you know that I'm one of Wolfmini's trusted advisors."

"I wouldn't have suspected."

"If the opportunity should arise, I can be useful to you."

"I hear that a lot. You have the trust of the sorcerer king?"

"Absolutely."

"And yet under the right circumstances you'd be willing to betray him?"

Jermbog shrugged. "Power changes, bounces around. I try to be useful to those I serve."

"I'll consider what you've said."

Jermbog retreated.

"You heard that?" Blundren whispered.

"Yes. Don't you feel safer now?" Dekatria asked.

"I guess it's better to know what we're up against."

"Be careful who you trust."

Above the pounding rain, a constant roar menaced from up ahead, louder than the gusts that ripped through the tree-tops. The tall one led them on a trail to the left that sloped gently upward. Through the breaks in the trees, they saw a raging river. The line of trees that marked the original boundaries of the river were under water, now halfway up their trunks.

The tall one stopped near the bank with one of the Qrudd warriors. He pulled back the hood of his cloak. He was bald on top, his long beard now becoming drenched.

"We're too late, Least High," the warrior said.

"Perhaps," the tall one said.

The Least High Druid! A chill swept through Blundren's core. She'd heard about him in the village. They spoke of him in hushed whispers, with more than a touch of fear. People argued whether he was more powerful than her father. When she asked him about it, if he answered, he'd just tell her not to believe everything she hears.

"The river's too wide, too angry," the warrior said.

"Perhaps."

Blundren spoke up. "Surely you're not thinking about crossing here, under these conditions."

"The conditions are formidable. Almost anyone else would turn back." The druid scanned the tops of the trees on both sides of the river. He reached within his cloak and removed an amulet, about the length of his forearm. The druid raised it high.

"Do you have a miracle for us?" Dekatria asked.

"That's what it would take to get across, no doubt." The druid rocked back on one leg. He stretched the hand holding the amulet behind him.

Blundren studied the hand not involved in the action. She was careful not to be pulled in the direction of his gaze. She failed to detect any telling movement in his legs or hands that might give away his intent. Nothing in the surroundings seemed out of the ordinary.

The druid slashed the amulet through the air. A jagged beam shot from the amulet to the base of a tree a few dozen paces away. The exposed roots exploded. He whipped the amulet back and snapped it forward. A taut line of light snared the tree about three-quarters up the trunk. He jerked right.

They heard a loud crack. The tree trunk split, and the upper length dropped toward the river. It lodged between two trees near the riverbank; the trunk stretched halfway across the river. The current brutally batted the branches back and forth.

The Least High Druid repeated the sequence on a tree across the river, wielding the amulet like a whip. When he snapped it again, the tree fell across the roiling river. The tops of the two trees meshed. The rushing water bent the trees at right angles. They sprang back, sending up a wall of white spray.

In rapid succession, he felled two more trees on each side, dropping them to fall diagonally into the first trees, bracing them against the current. He pulled down one more tree down river on each side, falling into the bridge for added support as it swayed back and forth. In the center, the tops of the trees slammed into each other and strained against the river's fury. Broken branches stabbed and lodged together in a lattice that slapped the river into a frothy morass.

The druid twirled the amulet in the air. He caught it without looking and stuffed it into his cloak in one motion. "That might work."

Blundren was breathless. It was impressive, and nothing he did tipped her off as to how. "You prepared those trees before we came here."

"That would've been one way to do it."

"But you're not going to tell me how you did it, are you?"

"Let's get across, while it still holds."

One of the warriors grabbed the roots of the fallen tree and swung around onto the trunk. "I'll try it first, Least High."

The Qrudd warrior moved in sync with the trees as they whipped back and forth and up and down. The white water in the middle of the bridge tore at his legs. He leaned into it. As the bridge bounced, the foam obscured him from ankle to midthigh. The warrior carefully negotiated his way across to the far side of the bridge.

"See how he moves with the trees?" the druid said. "Whether the trunk moves up, down, or sideways, it then rebounds the other way. Bend your knees, go with the movement, and be ready when the trunk bounces back."

A second Qrudd warrior started to scoot across the bridge, followed by Dekatria. Blundren wiped her eyes. She stepped up onto the trunk. Both feet slid a little on the slippery surface. With first one foot and then the other, she anchored the outside edge of her foot into a crease in the bark to keep from being swept off as it rocked back and forth. The princess eased further out onto the bridge. She found her balance as the tree swayed with the current. Behind her, she heard the druid.

"Not you."

She glanced back.

The Least High Druid leaned over and whispered in Jermbog's ear. The warriors watched them closely. The magistrate hastened away and disappeared into the underbrush.

No one was watching her. *There might not be a better opportunity.* She could slip away, and they'd never be able to trail her in this weather. Blundren caught Dekatria looking back at her. *No way would I leave her. We'll find a way to get out of this together.* She eased forward. The tree bounced higher the further she went out from the bank.

Back at the Onyx Palace, Wolfmini grasped the concave pedestal in the corner. Whenever he had leaped into his body from the pond, remote viewing had always left him exhausted. After that last time, he slept for half a day. He had yet to try it since he'd been restored. But there was no other choice. Squads of soldiers had returned without information about Blundren's whereabouts. In this tempest, that situation was not likely to change.

The sorcerer king cleared his mind. He retrieved the vials and poured them into the pedestal. The liquids swirled together and gave off a yellowish vapor. His breathing eased. After a sufficient amount of time, he let his eyelids drift open and gazed, unfocused, at the shimmering surface. An image gradually took shape.

Dekatria stood poised as the tree undulated above the raging river. She stepped calf deep through the turbulent foam in the middle of the makeshift bridge. A vertical branch impeded her path. She grasped the branch and swung her foot around to probe the foam. As she lowered her weight, the branch snapped. Her hand slipped. She teetered to the right, toward the waters below. The Qrudd warrior dove back and caught Dekatria by the forearm. He twirled her around and tossed her back onto the tree. She grabbed at the vertical branch, wobbled, and dropped to all fours, regaining her balance.

The warrior's momentum spun him out over the river. As he fell, he tried to grab one of the trees below. He slammed into the trunk and bounced off. The waters swallowed him and swept his body away.

Dekatria made it the rest of the way without incident.

Blundren approached the frothy middle. The sorcerer king clutched the pedestal. Abruptly, he lost the signal. He tried desperately to still the sloshing fluid in the pedestal. Failing, he pounded the edge of the pedestal and flung it against the wall.

Chapter Twenty-Five

HEART SLAPS

THE SPOTTED LION approached the clearing with the old tree. He had been on the move since he left the barbarian. The smell of all that carnage had awakened memories of his time before the troll. Fresh meat. Good memories, that made him feel fully alive. He had given up a huge part of himself in order to live with the troll. But it was worth it. His body relaxed. He felt what he always felt here, something that he was not quite willing to label joy, but a clear notch above comfortable.

The lion slid to a sloshing stop. The red-haired troll lay prone, drinking from the magic fountain in the heavy downpour. A few feet behind the troll, a white wolf stretched his neck and watched the troll intently. The spotted lion approached with caution and looked the wolf over. "You're not moving in, I hope."

The wolf stared back at the lion without expression. The red-haired troll lay there without turning around.

The spotted lion sidled over to the wolf. "He'll make you eat vegetables."

The wolf snarled and slipped into the forest.

Mudcat leaned toward the troll. "He has a problem with your cooking."

No lecture followed. No admonishment.

Smidgel drew handfuls of liquid and washed himself slowly and deliberately. Every breath seemed to catch. Then Smidgel rolled over onto his back, in obvious pain. His lips were chapped and swollen; bruises covered his face.

The spotted lion drew back. "What happened?"

The troll swallowed. He snatched a few measured breaths. "Qrudds."

The spotted lion rocked left, then right. He tried to restrain a looping growl, but his rage unraveled in a sustained roar. Smidgel scooted away and winced from the pain. Mudcat roared again, unable to contain it. He trotted aggressively over to the old tree and sniffed the ground.

"Whatever you're thinking," Smidgel gasped, "don't. I need you."

The lion jumped forward and thrust his face into the troll's. "I'm going after them."

"You'll only make it worse. Let them go."

"Where's the justice in that?"

"Revenge is a poor form of justice."

The lion dashed about in frenzied circles around the magic fountain and the old tree. He roared again and again, for what seemed like hours, until the roars tapered off into a pathetic rasp. Then he rasped until there was no sound whatsoever. He stared at one of his big paws with wild eyes and extended his claws. He reached toward his other foreleg, ready to dig deep and dredge across.

"Enough!" Smidgel propped himself up on his elbow. "Hurting yourself won't change anything."

The troll's eyes lost focus, and he dropped to the ground. The spotted lion sat in the clearing, shaking.

The red-haired troll slept in snatches, when exhaustion overrode the pain. With each passing night, his pain subsided a little more. He awoke less often, but his struggle to return to sleep intensified. Like the rain outside, his worries pounded without mercy. "How hurt was the barbarian?"

"He didn't say," the lion said.

"What if he needs our help?"

"He didn't look like he wanted help from anybody."

"That's his way," the troll said. "Doesn't mean it's the best way. He's out there somewhere in pain. Alone. You said he lost everybody?"

"Most everybody."

"He shouldn't have to fend for himself. But I don't know what we can do." Anytime there was nothing else he could do, Smidgel cleaned. Since he kept the place in pristine condition, it didn't take long. He tore everything out, spread it all over, and put it back where it was before. He paced like a caged animal, frustrated. Exhausted. His eyes burned.

He stopped and stared at the spiral staircase. He had a sudden urge to tear the place to pieces. Smidgel screamed. He tore his cloak from its hook and rushed headlong into the storm. Without a plan. The rain hammered at him sideways. He lowered his head and pushed toward the west.

The spotted lion caught up. "Couldn't wait for good weather to have your breakdown?"

"Go back to the old tree, if you want. No reason for both of us to be out here."

"I'll take you part of the way. Till you come to your senses."

"I appreciate it."

"No problem. Life's absurd. I was afraid you'd never notice."

Thundersquat hadn't moved from the tree. The stallion, sides heaving, belched and coughed into the barbarian's face. Steam rose from the steed's back under the pelting rain.

"Thought I told you to leave me alone."

Bolstrus shook his mane. He wheeled and faced the woods to the barbarian's right. Footsteps splashed toward them. Thundersquat never turned his head.

The red-haired troll jogged up to the tree. "I wasn't sure we'd ever find you!"

Thundersquat didn't lift his head. "Didn't ask to be found."

"Are you okay?"

"Why wouldn't I be?"

"Well, I think you know the answer to that better than I do."

"Did I pick the one public gathering tree in this part of the world? Go somewhere else."

The spotted lion shoved his face in and poked the barbarian with his nose.

"No, he's right," Smidgel said. "I was wrong to come out here. Let's go back."

The spotted lion stared blankly at the troll. He curled up next to the barbarian, crossed his paws, and draped his head over the barbarian's lap.

"Looks like you're stuck with us for a while," Smidgel said. He cleared out a spot on the other side of the barbarian and settled back against the tree, legs crossed.

Thundersquat continued to stare ahead as if they weren't there.

Smidgel fidgeted, tapped his feet together. "How long do you plan to sit here?"

"Long as it takes."

"To do what?" the troll asked.

"Nothing."

"If you're not doing anything, then how will you know when you're done?"

"You just know."

Smidgel's feet were in constant motion. He uncrossed his legs and crossed them again the other way. "I don't think I'll ever get the hang of it."

"Well, nobody asked—" Thundersquat noticed the bruises across the troll's face. He weighed his curiosity and walled-off empathy against the prospect of prolonging the conversation. It was a toss-up. "What happened to you?"

The red-haired troll hesitated. He took a deep breath. "Nothing. It's…nothing. You don't want our help. I shouldn't have bothered you."

"Good. Maybe get some peace and quiet for a change."

The troll sighed. Thundersquat looked at him from the corner of his eye. Smidgel sighed again.

So much for peace and quiet. "Came all this way. Might as well tell me what happened."

"What good is that going to do?"

"Just come out with it."

"You don't have to sound so exasperated." The troll blew out slowly. His eyes widened, and he stared off into the distance. He winced.

Thundersquat continued to stare ahead, his curiosity and concern rising.

Smidgel swallowed and coughed out a single word, "Qrudds..."

After a minute, Thundersquat glanced at the troll. "What did they do?"

Smidgel sucked in a huge gasp of air and blew out again. "They...I... Nothing I could do..."

"What happened?"

"Nothing. Stop... Just stop."

"Okay. Won't ask anymore." Thundersquat listened to the pounding rain. He looked right. The troll glared at him. "What?"

"Don't you care?" Smidgel asked. "Don't you want to know what happened?"

"Told me not to ask."

"You just kept pushing."

"Not going to ask. Don't worry about it."

"All right, all right—just leave me alone. I'll tell you." Smidgel swallowed. His fingers rubbed against his thighs. He rocked as he talked. "They beat me...tortured me. Threw rocks. Couldn't breathe. Thought I was going to be buried alive. There! Satisfied?"

Thundersquat let the words sink in. "You okay?"

The troll rubbed his neck. "I'm better than I was."

"Why you?" Thundersquat asked.

"Because of what we did to the great bear."

"Didn't do anything. Made him a little sick, that's all."

"I know," the troll said. "But the great bear is sacred to them. They thought they were right to punish me."

The spotted lion growled.

"I'm not making excuses for them. I just think it's impor-tant to understand their point of view. I mean, it's nothing I haven't run into before. All my life."

"Been tortured before?" Thundersquat asked.

"No, just bullied. The other trolls. Not all of them. Maybe I did something to deserve it. Maybe I haven't done enough. I don't know. They always find me."

Thundersquat digested this last piece of information. "Shouldn't have to put up with that. Can't let them get to you."

"Easy to say, hard to do," Smidgel said.

"Good enough like you are."

"You can always do more."

The barbarian looked down at his hands. "Tried to do the right thing once in my life. Got everybody killed."

"Sorry. I heard."

Thundersquat pushed the lion away and stood. He stretched before he ambled over to a nearby tree. He stomped an exposed tree root with his heel. Thundersquat opened his mouth. He closed his eyes and swallowed. "Half the village… Grandfather…"

"He was a good man."

"Liked your pancakes." Thundersquat pounded the tree and turned his face to the rain. He swallowed. "Not the worst part."

"What could be worse?"

Thundersquat squatted and stared at the ground. He slid forward onto his hands and knees. His eyebrows dug deep; his eyes could have bored a hole through granite. He gripped the vines in front of him. When he spoke, it was in a barely audible whisper. "Pieces…scattered all over…"

He heaved, losing what little remained in his gut. The vomit trickled away among the ground cover. He wiped his mouth with his forearm. He panted. "Buzzards…the abysmal…ate them."

Smidgel pressed his hands into his forehead to where his hairline had receded and combed through his remaining hair. His hands cradled the back of his neck.

Thundersquat swiped the back of his hand across his eyes, filling with tears. "Stupid rain. Can't see a thing out here." He continued to breathe heavily. "Could've been there. Never should've left."

"There's no way you could have known what was going to happen."

"That dream. It was trying to warn me." Thundersquat shook his head. "Didn't want to leave. Watched over them till they told me to leave. Stupid to leave. Now they're gone. My fault."

"You didn't know that monster was out there. Nobody did."

The barbarian stood up and started pacing. "Could've stopped it."

"You don't know that," the troll said. "You might've died too."

"Should've been there to try. Even if I died with them."

"What purpose would that serve?"

"Purpose? What purpose was served by me being away all the time?" The barbarian was shouting now, not looking at the troll. "Ten years! What was the point? Never looked that hard for my father. Wouldn't matter if I did. Never part of my life."

He slapped the tree with the back of his hand. Blood beaded on his knuckles. His lower lip trembled. "When I was a kid…if they hadn't had to look for me, might've found him. My fault from the beginning."

With his visibly shaking thumb and forefinger, the barbarian massaged his forehead. "Never wanted anybody else to go through what I went through. Watched over them all the time. Never knew I was there. Outsider. Always thought someday I'd be more a part of the village. Missed what I had right in front of me. Missed it completely. Nowhere to go back to. Lost it all."

"What about those who are left?"

"Only cause them more suffering," Thundersquat mumbled.

"Why should they lose you too?"

"Think they'd want me around, after what I did?"

"You don't really know what they're thinking," the troll said softly.

"Doesn't matter. Grandfather raised me, always there for me. One time he needed me. Wasn't there."

"You couldn't have known."

"Wasted my whole life, for nothing."

"I don't know what to say," Smidgel said.

"Finally." Thundersquat couldn't dislodge the images seared into his brain. *Why couldn't he have run out of words a little sooner?*

"I'd never say life was a complete waste," the troll said. "But what if it was? You have a life to live now."

Thundersquat knew it was too good to last. "Heard anything I said?"

"What about what brought you here to begin with? Weren't you here to speak with the sorcerer king?"

"Don't really care. Doesn't matter anymore. Not to me, anyway."

"Are you the only one you ought to be thinking about? What would your grandfather have wanted you to do?"

"You don't know what he wanted! You don't have any right to talk about him." The barbarian pressed hard on both sides of his head. If he had to crush his own skull to stop from thinking, he would. He slammed his back against the tree and slid down. He buried his face in his arms propped across his knees. The rain hammered at the leaves on the ground cover.

Chapter Twenty-Six

RESET

FENESTRAL SMOGEN SHIFTED in her seat, roughly chiseled from the cavern wall. She poked at the fire with her cane. She was a seer who no longer wanted to see anything. Not in that way. Not anymore. Not for a long time. *It's all about to end, so what difference does it make?*

In her training years, her mentors spoke of a state of oneness with all existence, which would bring inner peace. She'd settle for a disconnected lack of focus and to not feel terribly uncomfortable. *Enlightenment's a joke. Near oblivion is the reality.*

A brown cloud hissed from the fire and expanded. It faded to reveal Axiom Punctilio, with his comb-over ponytail and gold earrings, sitting across from her. If she remembered her mythology, he was single.

"Dost thou know who I am?" he asked.

"I did not summon thee." She brushed an errant strand of hair from her face. "But thou art welcome."

"Noted." He cleared his throat. "I'm here to work out a deal."

"What kind of deal?"

"First, let us set the pertinent facts before us. Thou wert requested, wert thou not, by the Braider of Time to oversee the progress made by one barbarian, who goeth by the name of Thundersquat?"

"What's he done now?"

"Nothing. That's the point. Thou art fully aware, art thou not, of the shortage of time remaining in thy present circumstances? And of what one might reasonably conclude regarding thy imminent demise?"

"Big whoop. Expect me to go after him? With these knees?"

Axiom Punctilio pressed his forefingers together against his lips and leaned toward the fire. He snorted. "The Braider of Time made my life a living hell. I know it's her. She put me on every committee thou can think of. I'm on a committee about committees. Meetings. Rules of order. Hidden agendas. Meetings cancelled, rescheduled. Filling spreadsheets for reports that no one reads. They count everything! But things that count don't really matter. Things that matter don't count. It's too much. I want my life back."

She hadn't known that gods perspired. "Can't help you. Thee. Too much of a head start."

"I can place thee in the vicinity of the barbarian long enough for a brief conversation and return thee to the cavern. I don't even care what thou might say to him. We just need to make it look like we've satisfied the intent."

A cold shiver traveled down her spine. "Forgive me, but isn't teleportation of humans forbidden?" *Not that it stopped the Braider of Time. But this one follows the rules.*

"I've already filed an OCRAP. Official Corollary for Revision of Antiquated Policies. It would authorize thee to speak with him for a few minutes."

"When would you w—" A wave of knots crawled across the muscles in her back. A gray blur whipped around her and seized her breath, wrapped her in a veil of frigid air, and squeezed. She felt her bones crunch into splinters. The blur cleared. Her legs tingled and burned with the touch of a thousand frozen needles as a flash flood of sensations returned. She held her hands out to steady herself. The seer caught her breath and blinked. "Dramblunkit," she muttered, "he never said a word about rain."

Thundersquat slumped on the ground before her, his back to a tree. His eyes connected with hers, held for a bit, and returned to the ground cover. A red-haired troll stared at her, mouth agape, eyebrows raised. Off to the side was the silver stallion, restless as ever, and a spotted lion, stunned.

She poked the barbarian with the cane. "Don't you have something to do?"

The troll held a hand up. "I think if we give him a little time…"

"A little time? That's all we have left."

"If you knew what he just—"

"I don't care what he just. Got to move *now*." She felt the acid back up in her chest. She stepped forward. "Get up. Get up!"

She caught herself. *This isn't going anywhere. Need to think it through.* She surged forward, standing almost nose to nose with the barbarian, and turned up the volume. "Get up!"

The troll laid a hand on her shoulder. "You're not accompl—"

She swatted his hand away and raised her cane to strike him. Smidgel threw both arms up and peeked through under where his wrists crossed.

"Leave him alone," Thundersquat said, rolling to a knee and inserting an arm in front of the troll.

Fenestral Smogen noticed the old bruises on the troll's face and lowered her cane. She faced the barbarian. "You're worried about a little love tap? When you know what's coming? What's going to happen to him then?"

She yelled as the wave of knots rolled over her back again. The gray blur descended, and her legs disintegrated. She reconstituted near the mouth of the cave. She shuffled into the cavern, her feet impelled by jumbled orders from a distant command. Water pooled around her feet as the seer watched the embers' last flicker. If she poked at them, she could still get a fire going. *Whoop-de-freakin'-do.*

Chapter Twenty-Seven

INERTIA

THE RAIN CLEARED the swirling dust and peppered the four of them with mud. Smidgel stared wide-eyed at the spot where Fenestral Smogen had stood a moment ago. "Was she real?"

"Real enough." Thundersquat was beyond exhausted from the previous conversation. The last thing he needed right now was something more to talk about.

"What did she mean, what's coming?" the troll asked.

"Nothing," Thundersquat said. "Just some crazy old woman living in a cave."

"She seemed like she knew you."

Thundersquat shrugged. "At least she doesn't stay long."

The barbarian became conscious of the troll staring at him, waiting, as if he expected him to break down and say something worth hearing.

"The sorcerer king owes you a conversation," the troll said.

"You talk to him."

"Do what you came here to do," Smidgel said.

"Can sit here till the end of time if I have to." Which he guessed was around the corner.

"Okay." Smidgel stood. "It's starting to look like a pattern. When you wouldn't go the first time, your grandfather set out to do your quest for you. He's not here, so now maybe it's up to me."

"What're you gonna do?" Now the troll was talking nonsense.

The red-haired troll walked away with the spotted lion. Bolstrus followed.

"Stupid horse. Should've let the gods take you." *Won't last a week. Probably drown on the way to the palace.*

The Stone.

Last thing Grandfather asked me to do.

If I started when he was told, might've gotten back in time.

Failed him.

Never did anything anybody expected.

"Come back a new man, or not at all."

Do this one thing.

Don't fail him in this. After that, it doesn't matter.

The barbarian rose as if laden with sacks of rocks slung across his back. He straightened and stretched every muscle. Through the torrential rain, he dragged the invisible weights toward the Onyx Palace.

Thundersquat could barely make out the stallion, picking his way a few strides ahead in the downpour. The mounted troll slumped forward with the horse's rocking motion and seemed to be sleeping. They hadn't spoken a word since the barbarian had caught up to them. It was just as well; they couldn't hear each other above the torrent anyway.

They maneuvered up the spiral path leading to the palace like they were skating on peanut butter. When they reached the palace garden, the red-haired troll slipped off the horse.

Thundersquat dove and caught him. He slid in the muck and almost went down. He realized the troll was blazing hot. The barbarian slung Smidgel across his shoulder, rushed to the palace, and pounded on the door.

Jermbog opened the door a crack. "Barbarian. I am not aware of an appointment."

The spotted lion crashed into the door, and Jermbog went flying. Thundersquat surged past the administrator. The magistrate trailed behind them. They found the sorcerer king in the great hall. Wolfmini glanced at the unconscious troll.

"We can't have animals in here." Jermbog looked pointedly at the troll. "Or lions."

Wolfmini fixed a stern look on Jermbog. "Bring blankets."

"But... Yes, Your Eminence."

"Follow me," Wolfmini said.

They hurried into an adjacent room. The sorcerer king replaced the troll's wet clothes with a loose smock. He set him in the bed and covered him with blankets. Mudcat hovered near the troll.

"Anything you can give him?" Thundersquat asked.

"Yes, if he wakes up. For now, we wait." Wolfmini walked to the doorway. "You don't look well yourself."

Thundersquat shrugged. "Still vertical."

"Tell me what you learned about the blue tiger."

"Ancient history." Thundersquat told him of the battle with the tiger, of the old man and the young warrior who helped him afterward. He described how the troll took care of him at the old tree.

His mind jumped to the quick visit home afterward. He tried to fend off a barrage of images: the buzzards picking at flesh from pieces of bodies strewn about, the putrid smell. Lying crushed beneath the stinking creature. Imagining

Grandfather, standing alone against the abysmal. Sumac blaming him for not finding his father.

"Barbarian, are you okay?"

"Yeah."

"What was it you wished to discuss with me?"

Grandfather would've expected him to do this. "On a quest. Supposed to find a stone that somebody lost."

"The Half-Forgotten Stone?"

"Heard of it?"

"I can't help you." Wolfmini abruptly turned and exited.

Thundersquat seethed as he listened to the sorcerer king's footsteps echo in the great hall. *Waited all this time, lost everything that matters, and the sorcerer king decides to walk away without saying a word? No.*

Early the next morning, the troll awoke. Smidgel looked weak, and he still ran hot to the touch, but he was awake.

Jermbog appeared with a warm brew. "His Eminence prepared this for the fever."

"Where's the sorcerer king?" Thundersquat asked.

"He's not to be disturbed."

"We'll see." *Could've told him all about the Stone, wouldn't have cared. But don't lie to me.*

Thundersquat and Smidgel stared at each other without speaking. The silence was good while it lasted.

"Why did you follow me?" the troll asked. "I thought you didn't care about the Stone."

"Who said I did?"

"Then why did you come?"

"If I didn't, you'd be lying out there in the mud until you floated away."

"Well, I appreciate your help. Even if you don't care," Smidgel said. "So, about the Stone—have you decided to go after it, or not?"

"Tell you what I am gonna do. Find out what the sorcerer king knows about it."

"I suppose that's a start."

"Wouldn't count on it. Might be the finish. Just want to know what he won't say."

"What's going to happen if you don't find the Stone?"

Thundersquat ran his hand across his face. "Stupid Stone. Ruined my life. About to ruin everybody else's."

"Is that what you want to happen? For everyone to feel like you?"

"Don't worry about it. Won't last long."

A couple of nights later, the five of them gathered around the table for dinner. Wolfmini finally made an appearance and sat at the head of the table. Jermbog sat to his right, then Thundersquat. Smidgel, well enough to join them for the first time, sat on Wolfmini's left, next to the spotted lion. Conversation was stilted. Between pauses they touched on the troll's health and how long it had been since anyone could recall so much rain.

Thundersquat took a swig of the mead provided by the sorcerer king. He slammed the mug on the table. He had their attention now. "Came here for a reason. Time after time, turned away."

"Impertinent fool," Jermbog said. "Have you noticed anybody missing the last few days?"

"Jermbog," the sorcerer king said.

"My apologies, Your Eminence," the magistrate said. "My patience is wearing thin."

The moment hit Thundersquat like a plunge into an icy spring. Wolfmini wore the same look Grandfather had the day his father disappeared. His outrage, which he'd worn like a suit of armor, crinkled like a dry leaf. "Where is she?"

Wolfmini toyed with his food. "She was taken."

"Why didn't you say something?"

"What you have to do may be more important." The sorcerer king sat back and pushed his plate away. "I was wrong to put you off earlier. I let my own pain, my guilt, get in the way. Those are not easy times to remember. But I've decided to tell you all I can recall."

"It can wait," Thundersquat said.

"Kind of you, but we have time now while we wait for the weather to clear."

"What weather?"

"You can't go out in this. You'll never get through."

"Where did they take her?" Thundersquat asked.

"Snartglobber's castle, I believe. That's what they told Jermbog. Southeast of here, across the river, in Qrudd territory."

"What do they want her for?"

"Probably to demand some concessions from me. We have to wait until the storm passes for them to contact us. Nobody will be able to cross that river until then."

"Then they wouldn't expect a rescue before it clears up." Thundersquat slid his stool back and stood. Wolfmini was right, of course. But he'd made up his mind the instant he saw the look on the sorcerer king's face. "Back as soon as I can. With your daughter."

"I'm going with you," Smidgel said.

"Not going anywhere."

"Maybe you don't realize it, but you can't tell me what to do or not to do."

"Don't need you. Don't need anybody. Especially somebody I have to watch out for. Can't do what I have to do and worry about you too."

The lion leaned toward the troll and growled.

Smidgel gazed at the spotted lion and then studied his plate. "Seems it's unanimous."

"No one should go out in this," Wolfmini said. "Especially in your case. It's important for you to heal. We'll need you later."

"Thank you, but you don't need to console me. He's right. I'm a liability."

"For now, perhaps," Wolfmini said. "As a fighter."

Smidgel regarded the barbarian. "Be safe."

Thundersquat looked at the sullen troll. A kind word would probably go a long way. Smidgel wasn't demanding; not whining. Just expecting him to say or do the right thing. *Can't do both.*

He turned and left.

Chapter Twenty-Eight

THE WEATHER TURNS

THE QRUDDS, THE LEAST HIGH DRUID, and the two captives were pelted by rain as they trudged through water up to their armpits. The druid scrambled up a steep incline onto an apparent bank and stood over them, in ankle-deep water. Blundren tried to follow, but her feet slipped repeatedly in the soft loam. The Least High Druid knelt and offered his hand. She hesitated. As she slid down once again, she grabbed his hand and climbed out of the muck. The others followed. The druid signaled for them to sit and rest.

Blundren watched the rain wash away the mud that coated her legs and forearms. She forced her mind to dwell elsewhere: she imagined a butterfly, newly emerged, opening its wings to drink in the sun for the first time. The rain abated. A light sprinkle left tiny ripples that nudged against each other and disappeared. The princess scanned the sky. She felt a flicker of warmth—and, with it, hope. She closed her eyes and let her body relax, intent on making the most out of the respite that was offered.

The wolf eased forward to the middle of the tree bridge. The entangled tops of the trees whipped back and forth. He crouched, weighed the distance beyond, and leaped over the churning froth. He snagged the tree with his forelegs and hung on. Paws slipping, he struggled to rock with the oscillating tree. The tree bobbed below the surface and then shot him upward. Onrushing water tugged at his paws. When the tree settled, he took a step. The bridge tore itself apart. The wolf scrambled to climb onto the rolling tree, but the current dragged him under.

Suddenly Blundren felt her lungs lock. She clutched her throat and tried to suck in air. She flopped down in the shallow water and splashed frantically.

The Least High Druid placed a hand on Blundren's shoulder. "Relax. Look around. See where you are."

Her lungs released the trapped air within, and she inhaled the fresh air in gulps. She jumped to her knees; her head was spinning. A moment ago, she'd been certain that she was drowning in the river, trees slamming into her. It was a relief to realize she was a captive once again.

She pressed her palms together and focused on the light touch of her fingertips. The cool drizzle tapped steadily on her shoulders. She noted the softness of the soggy ground against her knees, the feel of the water slapping against the back of her legs. Her panic subsided.

Blundren ignored the others' stares. She took a seat next to Dekatria. Her friend did not give her so much as a glance. "I'm fine, if you're wondering."

Dekatria held a fierce stare off in the distance.

"I know you don't want to be here," Blundren said.

Dekatria fingered the tear in her dress.

"Are you okay?" Blundren asked.

"What do you think?"

Blundren placed a hand on one of Dekatria's. "I've been insensitive. You're thinking about that warrior who went into the river."

"He was a fool."

Blundren shivered. "He saved your life."

"No one asked him to."

"There's nothing you could've done. You can't blame yourself."

"I don't. I blame you."

"That doesn't even make sense," Blundren said. "I wasn't anywhere close."

"You were born with such a gift and you don't even try to use it. What a waste."

Blundren pulled her thoughts together. "I know how such beliefs can give us comfort, make us think we have more control over—"

"Go away and let me enjoy this break. Ever since you brought on that storm on Market Day, the weather's gotten worse. Take a good look around. See what you started."

"I didn't do anything. I just flicked my hands in the air like this."

The skies released a thundering waterfall.

Just great.

The unrelenting chill of the night kept Blundren from sleep. Dawn brought no relief, just the realization of another day without end. Blundren was determined to work the problem. Their chance would come.

A heavy fog rolled in and hugged the ground. She and Dekatria could probably escape and stay hidden. But they could step off into something worse. The druid gathered the group together. The group held hands and were quickly on the move again.

By midafternoon the flood was thigh high. They had

moved into a grassland, and the tips of the grass waved above her waist. As evening set in, she noticed a small rise in the distance. Atop the rise was a crude stone wall surrounding a single-story structure. They headed in that direction.

Before the last light of dusk disappeared, the waters had risen above the high grass. In the darkness the water level reached her neck. Occasional flashes of lightning kept them on course, spurring hope that they were closer and fear that they wouldn't get there in time. By the time they arrived at the high ground, the waters had risen well up the sides of the walls. They waded in waist deep to where the waters receded at the entry to the castle. Another flash showed that it was not much more than a pile of rocks.

The inside was drab and empty, the stone floor uneven. The Least High Druid escorted the girls to a sparsely furnished room in the back. Sopping wet, they shivered in the drafty room.

"Wait here," the druid said.

"Where are we?" Blundren asked.

The Least High Druid closed the door without answering. She heard something snap into place with a thud on the other side of the door. Blundren rattled the door and pushed against it with her shoulder. "We're trapped."

Dekatria held the edge of her dress and waved it. "Don't make it rain in here. I'm ready to be dry for a change."

"The way the druid treats us, I don't think he means us any harm."

"What do you think they want then?" Dekatria asked.

"Ransom, perhaps. I don't know. Maybe they want to force my father to do something."

"You think they'll let us go free after they get what they want?"

"Let's hope so. But keep your eyes open for any chance to escape, just in case."

"You've seen the druid's magic," Dekatria said. "Can you beat him?"

"If you mean with magic, no. But I don't believe he has any more power than I do. Than any of us has."

"If you say so." Dekatria shivered. "It's cold in here. I'm tired of it."

Footsteps approached. Blundren heard something scrape against the door and the stone door frame. Likely, a heavy wooden post had been laid across the door and set in brackets to lock them in. The door swung open. The Least High Druid entered, followed by several warriors, the Qrudds' head chieftain, and his entourage.

Snartglobber thrust his chin in the air and viewed the prisoners with a smile. He glanced over at the three dancing girls and back at the two captives. "Which of you is the daughter of the sorcerer king?"

"I am."

"Can you dance?"

"Not particularly," the princess said.

He looked over at Dekatria. "Maybe we'll start with you then." He signaled to the warriors. "Bring her to me."

"Leave her alone!" Blundren said.

The room went quiet. Snartglobber's eyes widened; his jaw clenched. When he spoke, the soft monotone belied the volcanic threat his face promised. "Bring. The. Dark-haired. Beauty. To me."

Blundren moved in front of Dekatria, holding the stare of the Qrudd head chieftain.

Two warriors stepped around the princess and took Dekatria by each arm. They escorted her to the smoldering Snartglobber.

His arrogant smile returned. "Well done, daughter."

They embraced.

Chapter Twenty-Nine

SPELLING ERRORS

LEAST HIGH EXAMINED the gruel crusted over in Blundren's bowl. "You must eat, Princess."

"She planned this from the beginning, didn't she?"

"If you knew the answer to that, what difference would it make?"

"Perhaps none," she said. "Maybe I like to learn answers."

"The plan has been in place for almost a year. The day the two of you met, I brought her to the marketplace. We were there a few times before, but you never saw us."

"Is she really training to be a priestess?"

"Yes."

"Then how could she deceive me like that?"

"She was cleansed of this wrongdoing in a sacred rite before the plan began. Now that she's back, she'll undergo purification."

"What do you intend to do with me?" the princess asked.

"The goal is strictly political, as far as I know. You won't be harmed."

"They lied to me. How do you know they didn't lie to you?"

The Least High Druid paused. "I can't rule out that possibility. But I'll do all in my power to make sure you're not harmed."

The druid approached. The intensity of his eyes was disarming. It seemed like he was scouring the pores on her face. He extended his fingers until he almost touched the bruises still evident on her cheek.

She drew back. "What are you doing?"

"Just sit still."

A pulsating warmth enveloped her face. He withdrew his hand. Her skin in her cheeks and across her forehead tingled.

"It was healing nicely. But that should speed it up a bit." The Least High Druid abruptly left the room.

Blundren gritted her teeth and clenched her fists. *She betrayed me. My friend. And now this druid comes in, acting like he cares, then turns around and leaves me a prisoner.*

Heat rose to her head and neck. She zeroed in on the wooden door. The princess relaxed her grip and calmed her breath. She flicked a forefinger at the door, intending to set it ablaze, then to freedom.

Nothing happened.

Some power. I can't count on it when I need it. If I really have any at all.

On the third day, Dekatria entered the cell. Snartglobber marched in, followed by his entourage. The Least High Druid squeezed in behind them.

Blundren stood. She visualized sinking her teeth into

Dekatria's throat, then blinked the image away. "How could you do this to me? We were friends!"

"Oh, please," Dekatria said.

"Were you this cold the whole time? Did nothing mean anything to you?"

"You think you know everything. I'm glad I don't have to listen to your useless babble anymore."

"Useless babble? What about all your sacred devotion to the old ways? You were just deceiving me the whole time."

"Watch how you speak to my daughter, Princess." The Qrudds' head chieftain puffed up his chest and drew closer.

"Why? Can't I go through some magical purification and make like it never happened?"

"Your people need to be destroyed," Snartglobber said. "You have no respect."

"And you have no truth. You twist your fables to support whatever you want to do."

"When we finish with your people, there will be no king-dom! And you'll no longer be a princess, except in memory."

"Being a princess has brought me to this tiny cell, facing you! Do you think I'll miss it?" Face-to-face with her enemy and flush with power, chemicals raged through her body. Blundren felt she had clearly won that round.

The head chieftain of the Qrudds searched wildly about the room. His eyes found the druid, blending with the back wall. "Least High! Turn her to stone! I command you!"

The holy man hesitated and regarded the princess. Blun-dren saw uncertainty in his eyes. A chill shot down her spine. Her breath was shallow. She forced herself to stay calm. *It's not possible. He knows he can't do it. The druid must be stalling for time.*

Snartglobber stepped aside. "Do it. Now!"

The Least High Druid raised his arms high and wide. He stood there, motionless, eyes still locked with hers.

He doesn't want to do it. He can't. No one can.

"Least High!" Snartglobber yelled.

The druid shot his arms forward, all his fingers pointing at her. A flash and fizzle shot around the room. The six hangers-on and the three dancing girls looked down at their feet and tugged. None of them could move. The stone crept up their calves. They writhed and screamed.

"Stop it!" Blundren yelled.

In less than ten seconds it was over. Beneath the tallest statue was a pool of liquid.

Blundren stared open-mouthed at the nine statues.

Snartglobber's head swiveled erratically as he took in what had happened. He faced the druid, his eyes livid. "Wha...?"

The head chieftain's face twisted into expressions hitherto unseen. Snartglobber hopped and skipped about the room, snorting, unable to find words. He grabbed the tallest statue and pivoted it around until it fell. One arm broke off. He snatched up the limb and pounded away at the statue until there was no piece left larger than a fist. The chieftain flew at the remaining entourage. The more he swung, the faster he went. Dust filled the room and coated the sweat-covered chieftain. He seized additional limbs to use as battering rams, until the six hangers-on were pulverized.

Snartglobber gasped for breath. He tossed aside the last limb and placed his hands on his knees. The chieftain arched his back and looked at the druid. He pointed at the dancing girls. He coughed. "These I like. Move them into the courtyard."

He gestured to the pile of rubble that had once formed his

entourage, strewn about the room. "Spread that around, like they meant something to us."

The Qrudd chieftain stormed out of the room.

Dekatria stepped toward the druid. "What happened?"

"What did you do?" Blundren asked.

"I might ask the same of you, Princess." The druid looked at her with a questioning expression mixed with disgust. "Nine people. You saw fit to end the lives of nine people?"

"I didn't do anything! And you know they're fine. You switched them somehow."

"What a liar," Dekatria said. "You blocked his spell and deflected it onto these nine innocents."

"I didn't do a thing," Blundren said. "You don't know what you're talking about."

"You're trying to pass this off as an accident?" the druid asked.

"I don't know what it was!" Blundren shouted. "What exactly did you do?"

"I called up the powers I needed," the druid said, "but I hadn't set them loose."

"Then she acted first." Dekatria said. "Without provocation."

Blundren looked at the Least High Druid. "Don't make them think I'd hurt nine innocent people. Please."

"I never imagined you to be capable of something so evil."

"I didn't do anything!"

"Why did you hesitate, druid?" Dekatria asked.

"I underestimated her. I promise you; it won't happen again." The Least High Druid turned to the three statues. With both palms up, he gave a short upward lift, followed by a broad swishing movement toward the doorway. The dancing girl statues hovered just above the surface of the floor and vibrated out of the room, into the hallway. The druid stretched his arms wide and closed them in a broad circle. The rubble trembled and scraped together into a large pile in the middle of the room. The druid made a broad, forceful sweeping gesture, and the rubble trailed out the door in a low cloud of dust. The Least High Druid followed.

Dekatria paused at the door.

"Please, I didn't do this," Blundren said. "I don't know how he did what it looked like he did, but he's trying to put it all on me."

"The druid would never do such a thing. Who's left?" Dekatria slammed the door behind her.

Blundren stared at the door. *Surely, he didn't just turn nine people into stone and let six of them get destroyed. Where did they go? What's the druid's game? There's no way I could have done it myself, without feeling anything, without knowing how I could have done it. Surely not.*

Chapter Thirty

THUNDERSQUAT

THE STORM ABATED. The river below surged like a wild stampede.

In the soft drizzle, Thundersquat rested his hand on the stallion's shoulder. Washout from upstream and the surrounding land would likely feed the river for a few days, maybe more. It'd get worse before it got better. Maybe the sorcerer king knew what he was talking about. They might have to wait for a while after all.

"Race you across," the barbarian said.

Bolstrus gave him a long sideways glance and snorted. He gathered himself and leaped far out into the churning water.

"No, wait, I—" Thundersquat dove in after him. "Now he listens?" he thought just before he smacked into the maelstrom.

The current seized him and whipped him around. He nearly crashed into the stallion spinning in the opposite direction. Thundersquat grabbed the stallion's mane as they twisted and rolled. They bobbed up briefly. He snatched half a breath before they were sucked under again. The stallion kicked toward the surface. Thundersquat locked an arm around the steed's neck. Their heads barely above water, the river swept them along, battered by branches and other debris. The river held them in its iron grip for hours before it began to slow down. The barbarian could no longer feel his arms or hands. His fingers started to slip. He yelled in the stallion's ear.

The mighty steed responded. Driving toward the other shore, Bolstrus pitched against the current, hammering his powerful legs against the ruthless whitewater. He won the battle in increments. Thundersquat squeezed with his legs and forearms, yet still felt himself slipping as the current surged across the stallion's shoulders. The stallion plunged out of the deep water and staggered through the rushing shallows onto the bank. His hooves slipped in the soft mud, and he collapsed, tossing the barbarian over his head. Thundersquat dropped with a hard splash and rolled.

Thundersquat lay in a few inches of water, on mud and soft grass. Half of his body was numb, the other half in pain. If he moved, he was pretty sure he'd feel worse. He rolled onto his elbow and sat up. *Hate being right.*

Thundersquat unwound his aching body into a standing position with a slight lean forward and to the side. The silver stallion stood flat-footed; his back sagged and his sides heaved.

He had to find the princess and return her to her father. She was out there somewhere, probably headed to Snartglobber's castle, roughly southeast from the Onyx Palace. The river had taken them south, but there was no way to know how far. Fortunately, he had a lot of experience with not knowing exactly where he was. Away from the river seemed like a good enough choice for now. Then northeast and look for signs.

Thundersquat leaned forward and trusted his feet to catch up. After a while his joints loosened up, and his walk was a closer approximation to a creature this side of the grave. Being lost and in pain shoved the memories of the abysmal into the background. Until he made that realization. The surge of returning pain was welcome.

Night and day, he fought the weariness and pain. When he couldn't keep his eyes open any longer, he napped on the stallion's back. When Bolstrus slowed to a halt and fell asleep on his feet, Thundersquat slid off and kept moving. He trusted the stallion to find him again later, like he always had before. The barbarian didn't worry about drifting off course. He knew exactly where they were headed. Just a little fuzzy on where he was now and how to get there from here.

Sometime during the night he noticed he was bumping into fewer trees. The forest opened into a waist-high grassland. The waters had receded but still reached his knees, and the muck sucked his foot down with each step.

The sun had not yet peeked over the horizon when he spotted a rock castle, surrounded by a wall, on a rise in the distance. He couldn't imagine why anybody would live where their enemies would always know where they were. They'd have to lug their food into the castle all the time, no matter how far they had to go to hunt. If they had any sense, they'd move with the food and keep their enemies guessing.

To draw the attention of any possible sentries, Thundersquat sent Bolstrus away on a run to the north. The barbarian squatted below the tall grass and picked up the pace.

The moon was a mere sliver when he arrived at the rise below the fortress. The flood was only ankle-deep. The crude stone wall would provide plenty of footholds. The grass between him and the wall was shorter and patchy.

Thundersquat sniffed the air. The stink of damp refuse was too strong to detect any sentries, if any were watching. He slipped over the outer wall and crouched in the shadows. The layout of the bushes around him suggested he was in a courtyard. He stepped carefully across the sodden ground toward the stone castle.

The stench diminished as he moved away from the outer wall. The muggy air held a hint of human sweat, that failed to conceal a faint scent that was unmistakable. He recalled how she smelled when he first threw her over his shoulder, when he stood by her in the face of the fiery blue tiger, and when she held his hand in the pond. Blundren was here.

As he crept past a hedge, he encountered a dark figure, its arms raised. The barbarian threw up a forearm and drove his fist into the attacker's throat. He jerked his hand back, now throbbing. He'd punched a statue of a dancing girl.

Chapter *Thirty-One*

ESCAPE

BLUNDREN SAT CALMLY, her arms folded. Her shock and outrage over her friend's betrayal had transformed in the wee hours of the night. In its place was a cool, simmering determination to escape. The sudden reappearance of the hovering spirit guide barely registered.

"I sense a shift in your motivation," Herb said.

Blundren responded mechanically, without so much as a glance in his direction. "I need to get out of here. Any ideas?"

"Getting out of here is nothing compared to what lies ahead."

"Until I get out of here, it doesn't matter what lies ahead."

"Time is short, Princess."

She made no attempt to hide her annoyance. "Do you plan to tell me what you came here to say?"

"The future dangers are beyond anything you've seen or considered before now. You must be ready when the time comes."

"First, I'm going to escape. After that, who knows what'll happen?"

"The details are yet to be written," Herb said. "But the signs all point to something dreadful, perhaps even the end of the world as we know it."

"If you're not sure, then the signs are unclear. That leaves us open to believe whatever we want."

"The world cannot afford your skepticism, Princess. We need you to master the old ways, the sooner the better."

"I'll rely on what I can count on for certain—my wits, not false hopes for impossible things."

"We may fall short of what we hope for, my lady, but they're not false hopes."

The princess looked away. "How could I have been so easily fooled?"

"A question worth asking. What did you want so badly that you ignored the signs?"

Blundren turned on the spirit. "I can't believe she did this to me!"

"And yet she did. What did you fail to consider?"

"Nothing. It felt good to have a friend, that's all. How was I to know you can't trust anyone?"

"This time, agreed. And it's hard to know what people want from you when you're close to the sorcerer king."

"Close? For all practical purposes, I've been alone all my life. I don't need anybody."

"I suspect the opposite is true."

"Are you done?"

"This isn't about lighting candles anymore, Princess. We haven't even scratched the surface of what you have yet to learn, and we're running out of time. Trust what I've taught you so far." The spirit guide disappeared.

～

The wooden beam that stretched across the door and locked it from the outside scraped upward. Something slammed into the door, again, and a third time. The door broke open into splinters. Stone crumbled around the frame. Thunder-squat stood in the doorway. He let the beam drop.

Blundren's eyes started to well. She fought the tears back. "You're alive."

"Mostly." The barbarian rubbed his shoulder.

She looked at what was left of the shattered door. "You do know how to make an entrance. Did you know the door pulls open toward the hallway?"

"Oh."

"You came for me."

"Not my first choice."

Blundren heard footsteps running toward them. "Just get me out of here. I won't trouble you any more after that."

The pair dashed through the door and skimmed over the hallway floor. They turned a corner and raced to the end. The barbarian pointed right; she pushed past him to the left. That hallway ended in a right turn. As they burst around the corner, they froze.

The Least High Druid blocked their way. He glanced at the barbarian and the princess in turn. "Your escape plan isn't going so well, is it?"

Gesturing to an open doorway, he said, "This way. You have very little time."

Blundren hesitated. The approaching footsteps were louder. She nodded. They darted into the room and pressed against the wall. The footsteps ran past.

The druid scanned the walls. "I used to know a little about how they make castles."

On the far side of the room, a roughly hewn stone slab jutted from a wall; it likely served as a bed. He ran his fingers along the underside of the edge. The holy man grunted as he dropped down on one knee and examined the supporting stones. He reached in and popped out a small triangular stone. The druid looked back at them, stuck his hand in deeper, and tugged. He grimaced. They heard a click. The lower end of the slab pivoted up at a 45-degree angle.

The Least High Druid crawled through the opening and headed down a set of stairs into the darkness. The staccato footsteps were returning. The barbarian set his eyes on the doorway. Blundren tapped him on the arm and hurried into the passage. Thundersquat followed. Above them, the slab lowered.

The trio huddled together in the darkness, broken only by a few pinholes of light around the edges of the slab overhead. Footsteps overhead shook the ceiling and sprinkled them with dust. They heard the footsteps leave the room. Thundersquat moved toward the slab. The druid hooked a hand over the barbarian's shoulder and held him back. After a while, several more footsteps left the room. The druid guided the two of them deeper into a tunnel.

"Where does this go?" the barbarian asked.

"It should reach most of the castle and come out somewhere on the outside," the Least High Druid said.

"Why did you help us?" Blundren asked.

"I'll explain when I can," the druid said. "Let's get out of here."

The Least High Druid placed a hand on their shoulders and guided them slowly through the blackness. At times, they could see nothing. No one spoke. They stopped at a wall, an apparent dead end. A tiny sliver of light traced the uneven edges of the stones on all three walls. It was impossible to determine where the light was coming from.

The druid explored the rocks comprising the base of the

wall. "We have to presume there's more to this than meets the eye."

Again, he encountered a lever. He tugged, and a block of stone pivoted open to the outside. They found themselves in the garden with the statues of the dancing girls. It was dusk.

"This way," Thundersquat said. They turned the corner around a wall of shrubs. A squad of blue-faced archers, their stretched bows aimed at the three fugitives, froze them in their tracks.

The Least High Druid patted the barbarian on the shoulder as he slipped past him and through the row of archers. He took his place just behind and to the left of Snartglobber.

The chieftain grinned. "Well done, holy man."

"What kind of game are you playing?" Blundren growled.

Chapter Thirty-Two

A SIMPLE SOLUTION

THE BARBARIAN MOVED in front of her, shielding Blundren from the archers. She peered around him.

Snartglobber stepped forward. "Is this the barbarian that desecrated the great bear?"

Thundersquat pointed to the necklace of five bear claws. "Great bear gave you those out of the goodness of his heart?"

"Sacrilege! You'll pay for what you've done." The chieftain glanced at the princess; his nostrils flared. "And you, daughter of the sorcerer king. I missed my dancing girls this morning."

"I'm not to blame for that," Blundren said.

"I decide who to blame. And I decide who'll dance for me next."

"Have you considered the barbarian?" she asked.

"Oh, I'm going to enjoy taming you, Princess," Snartglobber said.

"Have to go through me," Thundersquat said.

"You don't speak, barbarian."

"Don't dance, either."

Snartglobber raised his voice. "Least High! Should I marry the princess and kill her father? Or kill them both, and take the land anyway?"

The druid looked uncomfortable. "I believe we should consult the entrails of a hummingbird. The birds will return in a month or two."

"Least High's slow to make up his mind again, daughter. What do you think we should do with her?"

"She thinks she knows everything," Dekatria said. "I wish we could wipe her mind clean, so we don't have to listen to her nonsense anymore."

"Done. Least High! Make her simple."

"Have to go through me," the barbarian said again.

"Out of the way, barbarian scum." Snartglobber slipped behind his daughter and held a dagger to her throat. Dekatria held perfectly still.

"What are you doing?" Blundren asked. "She's your daughter!"

"She was your friend, and she betrayed you. Do you expect me to wait until she does the same to me?"

Blundren searched Dekatria's face and saw only haughty disgust. Not one iota of compassion. *How could she come to hate me that much?*

Snartglobber locked eyes with Thundersquat. "Now, barbarian. Move. Or this deceitful wench will breathe her last."

"Up to you."

The Qrudd chieftain tightened his grip on his daughter and pressed the blade into her skin, drawing tiny droplets of blood.

Blundren touched Thundersquat's arm. He flinched. She removed her hand and spoke softly. "I can't let him hurt her, no matter what she's done. Please, step aside."

Thundersquat didn't move.

"I don't think the druid can actually do anything to me without me playing along," Blundren said.

Thundersquat slid left, a stride away, maintaining eye contact with the Qrudd chieftain.

"Least High!" Snartglobber yelled.

The druid shuffled forward, as if he had to consider each step. "What you ask is difficult."

"Do it. Now."

Blundren looked at the druid's expression, apologetic, almost pleading. He's lost control of the situation. Or so he wants us to believe. "You look out of practice, Least High. Don't miss."

The Qrudd warriors slowly scooted back.

The Least High Druid began to mutter unintelligibly, as proscribed by tradition. He held both hands behind him, low and to the side, fingers stretched. His rhythmic chant rose in volume as he swept his hands forward into a full overhead stretch. He howled at her, eyes rolled back and popping white.

The princess felt warm dampness on her face. No question, he puts on a good show.

The holy man shot his arms forward.

Thundersquat leaped in front of Blundren. A crackle and fizzle exploded in a bright flash before the barbarian crashed to the floor. Her heart pounded like drums.

Snartglobber released Dekatria and rushed toward the barbarian. The cadre of warriors surrounded him, bows drawn.

Thundersquat pushed up on his elbows. He rose on his knees and then dropped, curled up on his side in a fetal position, cradling his forehead in both hands. After a while he rolled over and sat up. His face slipped up through his hands until his fingers held his lower lip down; he stared at the surrounding circle of arrows. He reached out and touched one of the points. The blue feathers in the Qrudd chieftain's hair caught his attention, and his hand reached toward them. Snartglobber slapped the barbarian's wrist down with the flat end of a bone dagger. The barbarian cocked his head and stared at his wrist.

Dekatria stepped forward. "This turned out better than I thought. How do you like your boyfriend now?"

"He's not my…"

The barbarian turned to the princess with a befuddled look on his face.

"Lock them up again," Snartglobber said. The head chieftain exited with Dekatria. "You know I wouldn't hurt you, daughter."

"Of course not. Why would you?"

The druid's shoulders hunched over. His face was haggard. "I'm sorry, Princess. It was the least bad choice I could think of at the time."

The barbarian rubbed the sides of his head. He scanned the garden in an idle, undirected manner.

"How long will he be this way?" Blundren asked.

"I don't know. I acted in haste."

"His mind can't really be that simple. But for now, I suppose he believes it to be true."

"I'm sorry, Princess."

She looked at the barbarian, playing with his fingers. *First person to be there for me, and he's not all there.*

Chapter Thirty-Three

FIRED UP

THE LEAST HIGH DRUID followed two warriors down the narrow corridor. In the lead was the crazy peacock, matched stride for stride by his daughter. Two more warriors trailed the druid, blocking any escape.

They passed the cell with the damaged door.

Snartglobber stopped outside Blundren's new cell. Two warriors rushed forward to lift the beam outside the door and scooted back out of his way. The chieftain threw open the door and barged through, followed by Dekatria. Least High hovered near the door. The four warriors remained behind in the hallway and shoved him forward.

To the left, the barbarian squatted against the wall, playing with his fingers. Blundren stood facing them from the far side of the room. The room was devoid of furniture except for a crude bench behind Blundren.

The druid was discombobulated by the events of the past few days. He was unable to get a good read on the flow of energy in the room. Forces swirled, ripped high and low, and crashed in tiny disturbances that popped and crackled, though no one else seemed to notice. Least High tried to maintain his focus on Blundren. After what the princess did to the dancing girls and advisors, no telling what she might do next.

The barbarian seemed entranced by the feathers in Snartglobber's hair. The head chieftain looked at the barbarian with amusement. He plucked a feather and handed it to him. Thundersquat glanced at the princess, a hint of a smile trying to burst through.

Snartglobber sneered at the princess. "I have a place for him among my advisors."

"Don't be cruel," Blundren said.

"If it weren't for you, witch, I wouldn't have to replace them."

"I've done nothing to them or to you."

"No one wants to hear your rubbish," Dekatria said. "We saw it all."

"Oh, please. You'll probably find all of them in a hidden chamber below the cell we were in."

Dekatria scoffed. "I was raised in this castle. There are no hidden rooms."

"Say what you will. I know better."

The Least High Druid rested a forefinger over his moustache and stroked the underside of his beard with his thumb. The princess nearly had him convinced. But nobody can see through a good liar. It all came back to the evidence. *What is she up to?*

Snartglobber extended his arms. "Enough. I leave tomorrow. My warriors will crush your father's army. I'll drag the sorcerer king back here and put him in a cage for all to see. I'll come up with new ways for you to watch each other suffer. Then one of you will watch the other die."

Blundren's eyes pleaded with the Least High Druid. "Do you plan to stand by and watch all this happen?"

"The sorcerer king and I have unfinished business, Princess. From long ago."

"You know I didn't do it," Blundren said. "Tell them what you did, please."

The druid's forehead knotted up. "They saw what I saw, Princess."

Blundren looked at Dekatria. "I truly thought we were friends."

"You act so skeptical, so above everybody," Dekatria replied. "Truth is, you'll believe anything."

Snartglobber's skin glistened. He paced. "I'll drag your worthless father through the streets. Tie him to a post in the courtyard." The Qrudd chieftain's voice became louder, faster, his pacing more animated. "Chain you between two teams of horses. Make your father watch. Burn him alive while he sees you being ripped in two!"

Blundren's face was red. "Don't get so overheated. You might burst into flames yourself."

"Show some respect for my father," Dekatria shouted.

"I'll find a way to stop you both," Blundren said.

"I'd like to see you try, Princess." The enraged head chieftain stood panting, triumphant.

The forces were wild, chaotic, popping in an erratic spiral around the chieftain. Snartglobber burst into flames.

The druid leaped back. The princess and the barbarian pinned themselves against the wall. The warriors rushed in but were unable to get close. The chieftain shrieked and hopped wildly around the room. The flames shot up in a blinding white flash and fizzled. Dekatria stood frozen, eyes wide, mouth agape, arms close to her side, elbows back and fingers outstretched. The Least High Druid could not tear his eyes away from her.

The druid blinked as the room came back into focus. The energy in the room was now a dead silent calm. All that remained of Snartglobber was a pile of ashes and a curl of smoke. Only the old ways could've burned so hot, so intensely, and be over so quickly.

Several feathers stuck out of the ashes. The bear claw necklace, not even charred, lay partly buried in the ashes. Thundersquat scurried over and reached for one of the feathers.

Dekatria kicked him hard in the shoulder. "Get away!"

The barbarian rolled and scooted back against the wall. The Least High Druid inserted himself between the barbarian and the pile of ashes. He glanced back and forth between Dekatria and Blundren.

Dekatria lowered herself before her father's smoking remains. Still trying to catch her breath, she pulled out a feather and used it to retrieve the bear claw necklace.

The druid took a step closer. Good, he thought, keep that. Something to remember him.

Dekatria tapped the claws, and a tiny puff of ash rose and drifted to the floor. She stared, unfocused, at the sacred relic as she let it rest in the palms of her hands. She raised her eyes and let her gaze drift until it settled on Blundren. Her eyes narrowed and grew hard, cold, accusing. She transferred her accusing look to the holy man. Lips trembling, her eyes filled and overflowed.

"Feel what you need to feel, young lady." The druid dared to touch her lightly on her shoulder. *I'd hold you if I could.* "I'll see to his remains."

She nodded slowly. Trance-like, she climbed to her feet and headed for the doorway. The warriors placed themselves on either side of the ashes. Dekatria took one final look at the ashes and left the room.

As he knelt before the ashes, the Least High Druid shot an angry glance at the princess. Her face was pale. She stared at the ashes without expression. He focused his attention within the area framed by his hands, shaped as if he were lifting something round. An urn materialized, modest in design. He placed it next to the head chieftain's ashes. He felt free. Finally. Never again would he have to fear what spewed from that disordered mind.

With a twinge of guilt, he waved his hands over the urn and made it more ornate. As he scraped the ashes together, he hazarded another glance at the princess. She looked distraught, drained of life. "Second thoughts, Princess? Not good enough."

"Very realistic," she said. Her voice was softer, a little less certain. "I was completely caught up in it. Is he in the same hidden chamber as the others?"

"Not now," the druid said through clenched teeth.

The next morning the Least High Druid shuffled toward Dekatria's quarters. The hallway seemed twice as long, but he was getting there far too fast. He'd seen death before and sat with many in its aftermath as they pieced their lives together. But he couldn't dislodge the image of her face, her eyes, as she watched her father engulfed in flames. Rarely had he felt this inadequate. He hated her father, still, but she'd done nothing to deserve it, not the way it happened.

The look she always gave him pulled him in and made him feel for a moment like he was the only other person in the room, as if something remarkable were happening. He acknowledged the twinge of resentment he felt when she gave the same look to others. It was a gift she had. He did not aspire to be more than a mentor, perhaps her chief advisor; their age differences were insurmountable.

Least High paused before he entered her chamber. Two warriors nearly collided with him as they came out. They fell back in terror and scrambled around him. He watched them scurry down the hall and out of sight.

Snartglobber's daughter stood in the middle of the room in a commanding pose. She wore full warrior's regalia—loincloth, buckskin boots, curved dagger, and a loose-fitting top that left her midriff exposed. Hanging from her neck was the sacred relic of five bear claws. She looked confident, infused with purpose. She turned her disarming gaze upon him. She was not exactly the lost soul he expected.

"Are you lost, druid?"

"I've come here to see how you are doing."

"I'm busy, if you must know."

"Perhaps I can come at another time," the druid said.

"As long as you're here, I have something for you to do."

"As you wish, Highness."

"I leave soon to take command of my father's warriors."

The Least High Druid nodded. "Forgive me, Highness, at such a time. But the five clans must meet to choose a successor."

"They'll follow me."

"According to custom—"

"It's time now for a new tradition."

The way she said it, the idea almost seemed intriguing. He respected traditions, but he was always ready for change. A druid might make a good leader, for instance, if the idea should ever come up. "You've made up your mind, then?"

"Am I going to have a problem with you?"

"No, Highness. What do you propose to do?"

"We'll destroy the Blisterians and capture the sorcerer king. We'll drag him back and parade him before the five clans. And then I'll fulfill my father's final wish."

"No one can truly grasp the depth of your loss, Highness. But is this the best time to pursue a war against the sorcerer king?"

"Any time is a good time for that."

"Many will die, on both sides."

"Blisterians have a weak-minded ruler who can't even control his own daughter. They are of no consequence."

"Well, to some—"

"And the Qrudds live to serve me, is that not so?"

He forced himself to forget how her eyes lured him in. *Something's not right.* "True. But perhaps we can find a more fitting way to pay tribute to your father's memory."

"Hah! This isn't for my father's memory. I'll do this because it's a good idea."

"A good idea..."

"A magnificent idea." She appeared amused. "Just picture the two of them, forced to watch as we torture one, then the other."

Her eyes narrowed, and the hint of a smile disappeared. "They'll see. Once they see what can happen, they'll all return to the true path."

"Highness, if you would permit—"

"I found nothing wrong with how you carried out my father's plans. Will I be able to count on you, now that he's gone?" Those eyelids closed just enough, and the trace of a smile at the edge of her mouth had the force of gravity.

"I'll serve you as I've served your father."

"I'll make up my own mind as to how much we need you."

Despite the alluring tone, her words made his spine run cold. "As you wish, Highness."

"When I return with the sorcerer king in a cage, I want to see the prisoner's face. Have her in the courtyard when we arrive."

The druid nodded and withdrew. His mind raced. Two young women, very disturbed. One stirring up a war to avenge her father. The other a heartless killer with immense power. Both of whom he'd sworn to protect. *And what of those I must protect from them? And for that matter, from what's coming?*

Chapter Thirty-Four
A WAR UNNECESSARY

THE LEAST HIGH DRUID entered Blundren's cell. She slouched back on the bench. The princess glanced away and developed a sudden interest in the stones on the wall across from her. The barbarian crouched in the corner, running his fingers across the head chieftain's feather. The druid stooped and gazed hard into the barbarian's eyes. "There has been no change?"

"No," Blundren said, still averting his gaze. "Did you expect any?"

"I was hopeful, yes."

"Why?"

"I held back. I was only trying to stun, enough to make them think your mind had been nullified, without causing permanent damage. Should've worn off by now, especially considering his size."

"Can't find it," Thundersquat said.

"What?" the druid asked.

The barbarian winced and stared at the ground. "Don't know. Something."

"Clearly, it hasn't worn off," Blundren said.

"I'm not sure what could've gone wrong," Least High said. "I deeply regret what hap—"

"Save your regrets. Whatever you did, change him back."

"Let's wait for this to clear up," the druid said. "I don't want to do worse damage."

"That could've been me with the mind of a child," she said bitterly.

"We have to keep him safe." The druid glanced around the room. If he was going to save the world, he was going to need the barbarian. But not in this condition. "I can't begin to tell you how vital this is. He'll need someone to watch over him."

"That would be me," Blundren said. "Until I can arrange something better."

"And I'll do what I can," the druid said.

"Why should you help?"

The druid hesitated. "Because I'm partly responsible."

"Partly? It's because of you that I'm here in the first place! That simple-minded barbarian over there came here to rescue me. That's the only reason he's here. Partly?"

"There's some truth to what you say. But before you get all high and mighty, think about setting someone on fire. In front of his daughter."

"You can't scare me. I know you stowed him somewhere. What are you really up to?"

The druid stared at her. "I'm not trying to frighten you. And frankly, I wish I could rethink bringing you here. But you need to understand the situation as it stands now. Dekatria's beside herself. She's gone to take her father's place at the head of the Qrudd warriors."

"I don't care what my…former friend…has done. I have to get back to my father."

"My plan was to get Snartglobber to send me to return you to him."

"Well, you failed. They were never going to return me."

"Snartglobber was easy enough to manipulate. Now things have changed." The druid turned away, looking skyward. One hand rested easily in the other behind his back. He inclined his head in her direction. "A terrible war is brewing, Princess. One that is beyond unnecessary. Innocent people are going to die."

"Why don't you do something to stop it?"

"We have to. There's more at stake here than I can say. But I need your help, or we have no chance."

"Funny," she said. "You kidnap me, hold me prisoner. Turn people to stone, set them on fire, then blame it on me. Now you ask for my help."

"It was not easy for me to reach this decision," the druid said. "You should be held responsible for what you've done."

"We both know I haven't done anything."

"So you keep saying. Regardless, we must consider the greater good here."

Blundren sighed. She propped her elbows on her knees and cradled her forehead in her hands. "I just want to go home."

"If there's a home left to go to. A question all of us may be asking soon."

Neither spoke for a while. She stared at the floor. "What would you need me to do?"

"First, we have to convince both sides to go no further."

"Things may have gone too far already," she said.

"Yes. But what if I were to return you to your father unharmed?"

"That might be enough for him. If he notices. Yes, he'd stop. What about the Qrudds?"

"They'll listen to me," Least High said.

"Even after Dekatria tells them about her father?"

"Yes, even then. I've lived among them for twenty years. I've known them for most of their lives."

"They'll scream for vengeance," Blundren said.

"They'll be angry. Tensions with Blisteria go back long before anything happened to Snartglobber. But it doesn't have to lead to war. I need to convince them of that."

"What about Dekatria? There's no way she'll listen to you."

"Not right away. Besides, she's not the true leader of the Qrudds—not by their tradition, anyway. She's a young lady who lost her father to an almost unimaginable horror. I'll deal with her gently. She'll be okay, given enough time."

Princess Blundren sighed. "And you believe you can convince all five clans to change course?"

"Well, the five clans don't always agree with each other. I'm sure I can reach some of them."

"It seems hopeless."

"But not impossible," he said.

"Look at how your plans have turned out so far, in the short time I've known you. I have more faith in the old ways than in what you propose."

"Failure is never the issue. It's all about how you adjust to what you couldn't have known in the first place."

Blundren blew out slowly, shaking her head. "Spin it any way you like."

"I'm the Least High Druid and mystical adviser to the five clans! Who better than me to deal with what's at stake?" *Granted, a comparison to what others might do is a low bar. But still. I never asked to be born with such talent and a destiny that beckoned.* "Have your father stand ready, in case I fail to stop them. He'll have nothing to lose by waiting a bit longer."

"True." The princess stood up. "How will I find him?"

"He'll probably move north with his forces, where the river is easily crossed. His scouts will be watching all along the river. They'll find you."

"When do we leave?" she asked.

"Now. We may already be too late."

"What do we do with the barbarian while we're gone?" she asked.

"We should take him with us. After a quick stop at Round Stones, he'll accompany you to your father's camp."

"Round Stones? You plan to set us free in the middle of Qrudd territory?"

"I can hardly blame you for not knowing who to trust. But you have to be there to convince them that your father will hold back."

"It won't work. They'll never let me go."

Blundren tapped Thundersquat on the shoulder. The barbarian followed her outside. When they stepped into the light, the barbarian dropped to his knees and shielded his face with his hands.

"What's the matter?" she asked.

Thundersquat squinted with one eye. He looked like he was trying to answer.

The Least High Druid helped the barbarian to his feet and gave him a little shove. "We have to go."

The druid took the lead north. Thundersquat followed, staring at the ground and blocking the sun with his hands.

"You spoke of unfinished business with my father," Blundren said.

"We've not spoken in over a dozen years."

"You knew each other?" she asked.

"Your father never told you?"

"Not one word."

"You're sure he never said anything?"

"I've heard of you. Who hasn't? But nothing having to do with my father."

"Then let's leave it there for now."

From the wood line a wolf howled. The druid glanced left. A white wolf slipped out of sight. Least High looked back at the princess.

"Bring it on," she said.

Chapter Thirty-Five

MISDIRECTION

DEKATRIA CHARGED the black stallion into the gathering of the clans at Round Stones, followed by two dozen warriors. All activity stopped and the crowd moved in from all directions. She identified three of the leaders. Thorn, the thick-headed but independent leader of the Egg Stealers, walked with the loud and charismatic Lumpface of the Rock Slingers. The whiny Bee Stings Behind led the yellow-spotted Jackals. Dekatria turned the steed in a slow circle as they clustered around. Her eyes drank them in, one by one. The crowd grew quiet.

"You ride the great one's stallion," Lumpface said.

She lifted the necklace of five bear claws. "My people! We've been betrayed."

"Where is the great one?" Lumpface asked.

Dekatria moved the black stallion forward toward the chieftain of the Rock Slingers. "My heart has been ripped from me. My father is no more."

"No!"

"This can't be!" Bee Stings Behind cried.

"How can such a thing happen?" Thorn asked.

She paused while a pall descended on the crowd. "He was murdered!"

"No!"

"Burned alive, right before my eyes. By the Least High Druid!"

"No!"

Thorn stepped forward. "Least High trained us, healed us. Gave us hope. Why would he do such a thing?"

Dekatria whirled the stallion. "The druid's not in his right mind. He was bewitched."

The crowd simmered.

"Who did this to him?" Bee Stings Behind asked.

"The sorcerer king's daughter." She locked eyes with Lumpface.

Lumpface's mouth hardened. "Let them come. They'll never get near you."

Thorn stared at the ground. Lumpface placed a hand on Thorn's arm. Thorn raised his head and looked at Dekatria. Her eyes connected and reeled him in.

"Yes. We'll protect you."

"Least High and I were like brothers," said Bee Stings Behind. "But he's not a Qrudd. We're through."

The black stallion reared as Dekatria tried to savor her triumph. It was hard to curb her disappointment. She had hoped for more resistance from these simple-minded aborigines. She jabbed her heels into the stallion's ribs, and he vaulted forward. Qrudds from all five clans dove out of her way as she galloped past, away to the hills to the north.

❧

Dekatria sat barefoot before the sorcerer king in the inner chamber of his tent. Her dress was tattered, her hair in disarray. She had already brought the old fool to the point of tears; he was breathing shallowly, trying to hold himself together. She would drive the Qrudd nation through his army like a stake through his heart, in a matter of days. He had no idea. Her mission was on the verge of being accomplished. It just had to play out. But why stop with that? She was like a cat that liked to toy with its prey before the inevitable meal. She loved that about herself.

Wolfmini's voice was higher in pitch. "Is there any chance that my daughter could've escaped, using the old ways? Faked her death, turned invisible?"

The sorcerer king was grasping at straws. Dekatria stared at the ground. "No. She was right there, in…" She broke off, as though she couldn't continue.

"Unforgiveable," Jermbog said.

She noted the lack of true distress in the magistrate's voice. To think that he thought he could put anything past her. *You want unforgiveable?*

Dekatria held her face in her hands and choked out her story. "I was there… They… When it was over…burned her… proper way…"

Her sobs made the rest unintelligible. She paused and breathed deeply. They were buying it.

"Forgive me, young lady." The sorcerer king faced an empty wall of fabric. His voice was thin, with a slight tremble that he barely managed to control. "I let my own grief get in the way. It must've been quite difficult for you to bear."

Dekatria stared at the ground without focus. "The Qrudds celebrated. I slipped away. Ran all night. I've been wandering for days, don't even… Lost count…"

The sorcerer king paced, slowly shaking his head. "Did she suffer?"

Why do they always ask that, as if it would matter? But suffer she will, she promised herself. And he'll get to see it. She let tears well again. "I have...it's been... I..."

Wolfmini placed a hand on her shoulder. "Perhaps we can speak more of this later, after you've had sufficient rest."

He looked at the magistrate. "Take her to a tent and make sure she's watched over tonight. She's not to be disturbed."

"As you wish, Your Eminence."

Jermbog was creepy, not just in how his eyes lingered on the curves of her body during the conversation. Jermbog's problem was that he was overly familiar, always moving in too close, as if he were a friend with shared secrets. Presumptuous. She fended off his hands when he reached for her arm to pull himself in close. She was near the point of asphyxiation from his cheap cologne, which failed to over-ride his odiferous sweat. Worst of all, he thought he was the one doing the manipulating.

When they were out of earshot, Jermbog asked, "How did you escape, my lady?"

"I can't talk about it now."

"I see." Jermbog seemed to weigh his next words carefully. "Suppose by some miracle Her Highness survived?"

"How can you even ask? After what I saw..." She pressed her hands to her cheeks and feigned distress, but she was on instant alert.

"It would present a problem, would it not? That is, for those who know her to be dead?"

Dekatria said nothing, not wanting to betray her suspicions.

"You study the old ways, my lady. Things happen that are

hard to explain, almost impossible to believe. But her father would no doubt be overjoyed if she lived."

"Yes, as would we all. But her father's enemies might feel differently."

"What do you suppose they would do if she were to reappear?"

"I suppose they'd try to capture her, like they did before," Dekatria said.

"Her enemies would probably even reward the scoundrel who caught her and turned her over to them."

Dekatria shrugged. "Perhaps. I guess it depends on what they had in mind for her."

"I'd hate for her to go through that again." His eyes narrowed. "But if the princess were to be found—extremely unlikely, I know—would you want to know?"

"Why are you asking all these questions? I told you..."

Jermbog stared at her feet. "You must be exhausted after running for several days. Well, as we said, we're only talking about remote possibilities."

She realized; he'd figured it out. She should've sliced her feet up. But it didn't really matter what he was up to. Blundren was still ensconced in her cell. He hadn't given away his suspicions—he was playing the angles. That would be his misfortune, when the time is right. But if he gives her away to the sorcerer king, it might disrupt her plan.

Jermbog reached for her arm. "Forgive me, I shouldn't even be discussing her, seeing His Eminence's grief. And yours as well."

Dekatria batted his hand away. "The thought of her death is never far from my mind."

Jermbog lifted the flap of a small tent and reached for her shoulder. "It isn't much, my lady, but for now it may provide what you need."

"I can't go in there. I need to be able to see if anyone comes."

Jermbog took her arm. "You're safe here, I assure you—"

Dekatria broke free and bolted into the woods. She paused just long enough at the edge to ensure that he chased after her.

When Jermbog started to fall behind, she slowed down. She stopped, as if she needed to catch her breath, and waited for him to close in. As he grabbed for her, she darted away and dashed into a clearing.

Qrudd warriors, archers with blue faces, and tall ones, tattooed, carrying spears, quickly surrounded them. One of them stepped forward, leading a black stallion.

The Chief Magistrate of All Things Pertaining and Otherwise puffed up his chest and held his hand up, needing to catch his breath. After a few deep breaths, he called out, "I know things. I would speak to your leader."

Dekatria sprang onto the stallion's back. "That would be me."

The lost expression on his face was priceless, as he no doubt replayed the past. After a moment, he flashed his gums at her. He was hers to play with now.

Dekatria rode north into the hills, alone, once again wearing warrior garb. She leaped off the black stallion and sashayed up to a small upright boulder. The dark-haired beauty opened a sack and scooped out a handful of dust and seeds. Her arm outstretched, she sprinkled the mix over a semi-circle of stones at the base of the boulder. She cupped both hands above the stones.

The brush ignited. Curls of purple, yellow, and blue

smoke rose from the shrine. They twisted into a dark brown cloud and expanded. When the cloud dissipated, it revealed an obese male wearing gold earrings and an open vest a few sizes too small. His thinning hair was combed over into a long ponytail on one side. He leaned over the boulder. He chewed a couple of times and swallowed.

Dekatria sent him her patented smile. "I summon you, Ax—"

"Thee."

"I summon thee, Axiom Punctilio, god of Stipulations a—"

"And Particulars. Yes. I know who I am. Who art thou?"

"I am Dekatria."

The god of Stipulations and Particulars made a rolling gesture with his hand.

"Dekatria, daughter of Pyrogenia."

"The goddess of Ethereal Thermodynamics?"

"Yes."

"What gives thee the right to summon me directly?"

"I'm the daughter of a goddess, am I not?"

"Not a very important one."

"She was once held in high regard," Dekatria said.

"There was the matter of an ill-advised marriage to a human."

"My father is—was—a powerful man."

"Powerful by what standard? One must be precise in these matters."

"It hardly matters now," she said. "She had a plan. It could've worked."

"As it is written, woulda, coulda, shoulda. Now she mucks out my stables."

"I called thee to draw attention to what I'm about to

achieve, so that there will be no doubt. I'm not my mother. I cannot fail."

"That remains to be seen, halfling."

"I've lived among humans. You can't count on them. I have to do everything myself."

Axiom Punctilio cradled his forehead between his thumb and forefinger, his elbow propped on the boulder. He rolled his hand again.

She seethed. Inwardly she swore to knock that bored look off his face once she attained the power she deserved. "I'll bring these unholy creatures back to the old ways. I'll restore the gods to their proper place of respect and devotion. They will—"

"Noted. My breakfast gets cold." Axiom Punctilio disappeared.

"She was a fool! I'm not my mother!"

He could choke on his breakfast, for now. Soon other gods higher than him would line up to secure my loyalty and influence. I'll deal with him then.

Chapter Thirty-Six

DISCOVERY AT ROUND STONES

THE QRUDD CAMP reeked. Blundren followed the druid into the camp. She held her head up and kept her eyes forward. The barbarian walked behind her. Warriors fell in on either side of them. As word spread, people rushed in from all directions, and the five clans closed in around them. Blundren searched the faces: she saw fear and hate. Angry shouting swirled throughout the mob. *This could get out of control in a hurry.*

They were escorted to a spot next to a large flat boulder, circular, about midcalf high above the ground. Five smaller stones surrounded it. On the eastern edge, a semicircle of upright boulders filtered the sun's rays as it peeked over the horizon.

A yellow-spotted Jackal, wearing a bear claw necklace, thrust his face in close to the druid's. "What did you do to the great one?"

"Old friends. I've done nothing."

"He lies!" the yellow-spotted chieftain shouted. "He's still bewitched!"

A plump chieftain pushed through the throng, a bear claw bouncing on the shelf of his stomach. Another chieftain with a rough-looking face brought an air of calm. The plump chieftain held the druid's gaze for a long minute. "The great one is no more?"

"He's gone," the druid said.

The mob ignited.

"My people." The rough-looking chieftain spoke in a loud, deep voice, accustomed to speaking in front of crowds. He held his arms wide and made eye contact with each and every member of the seething crowd. The simmer went quiet. The speaker opened his mouth slightly, as though he was about to say something, and paused. Many in the crowd leaned forward. "The great one is gone from us. We're angry."

Nods and whispers swept through the throng.

"And we're afraid of what the daughter of the sorcerer king might do."

"She's dangerous!" yelled the Jackal leader. "She could set us all on fire!"

"How?" Blundren asked. "I don't know how! And if I did, I wouldn't know how to control something like that. I mean I might have lit a few candles, and I think I helped create a burning tiger, but there's no way I set anybody on fire." Her voice faded out. "Not as far as I know."

The shouting resumed. They started to close in.

"Princess," the druid whispered, "best to say nothing else for now."

"What of Least High?" the plump chieftain asked. "We don't know for sure what he did. I'm not so willing to cast aside an old friend."

"Careful," the yellow-spotted chieftain said. "He may not be the same as he was."

"Your words are wise." The loud speaker nodded and spoke with authority. "But we need to find out. If we can fix him, then we must try."

"We need to find the truth," the plump one said. "Keep the sorcerer king's daughter under watch until we figure this out."

"Agreed. Let's meet with Least High," the loud one said.

The yellow-spotted chieftain threw out another jab. "And the great one. We'll make her bring him back?"

The plump one glared at him. "He's gone from us forever. But if she did something to Least High, we can rescue an old friend. He'll know what to do next."

The yellow-spotted chieftain threw his arms in the air. "If she could overpower Least High, what do you think she could do to one of us? What if she casts a spell on you?"

"I haven't done anything to you," Blundren whispered to the druid. "Tell them."

"Quiet," Least High said.

"Least High would never harm us, ever," the plump one said.

"Would you like to go into the tent with us, to make sure?" the loud one asked.

The yellow-spotted one hesitated. "Two of you should be enough. If anything happens to you, they'll need me out here."

A Qrudd war party burst into the camp. The blue faces indicated the Cloud Men, silent archers from the cliffs to the north. The taller ones were Raw Fish Eaters, from both sides of the river that divided Blisteria from Qruddlands. Their heavily tattooed skin was slick with oil, and they stank like rotting fish. A stir rippled through the crowd.

Among the warriors, chatting like they were old friends, walked the Magistrate of All Things Pertaining and Otherwise. When Jermbog spotted the princess, he revealed nothing in his face. He took in the situation. Then he tapped the bicep of the warrior next to him and nodded in Blundren's direction. She couldn't hear what he said, but several of the warriors looked at her.

Evidently, he'd made his choice. Blundren stifled a growl that percolated deep in her throat.

"Where is the great one's daughter?" the loud one asked the warriors. "She was was with you when you left."

Jermbog puffed up. "She went north to commune with the gods."

The plump chieftain inspected the magistrate. "Who's the little pink man?"

"He serves the sorcerer king," one of the warriors said.

"Then the sorcerer king is close," said the Jackal chieftain.

"Put him with the others," the loud one said.

Jermbog protested. "We had an arrangement. Ask any of these fine warriors."

A tattooed warrior took his arm. "She said not to trust him. Turn him over to the five chiefs."

"Watch the grease!" Jermbog snatched his arm away and brushed his coat.

The Raw Fish Eater seized his arm while a second warrior grabbed his other arm.

"She has big plans for me," Jermbog yelled. "Ask her!"

The chieftains turned their backs on the squirming magistrate and conferred around the central stone. The discussion was heated. The yellow-spotted leader of the Jackals waved his arms wildly. He shoved his reddened face nose-to-nose with the plump one and the loud one. At last, the argument subsided. The plump one spoke to the other chieftains, who all nodded. The yellow-spotted chieftain drew back in horrified astonishment.

The loud one raised his arms. The mob grew quiet. "Thorn and I will deal with the prisoners. We need a few of you to escort them to the tent. Bee Stings Behind will prepare the rest of you for war."

A ring of warriors formed a circle near entrance to the tent. The plump chieftain closed the flap behind him. The Least High Druid ambled toward the back.

Blundren guided Thundersquat to the corner. She addressed the druid. "So, I take it the Qrudds were not in a mood to listen. What about stopping the war?"

"When the time is right." The druid gestured to the two chieftains. "This is Thorn, chief of the Egg Stealers clan. And Lumpface, chief of the Rock Slingers."

The Least High Druid turned to the magistrate. "Jermbog, it appears we share a common misfortune. I trust you were able to deliver my message when we last met."

"Yes, Least High. To the sorcerer king, just as you asked."

"What message?" Blundren asked.

"Tell her," the druid said.

"That you had captured the princess and dared anyone to take her from you."

She got hot in a hurry. "That didn't last long. You turned me over to Snartglobber and his back-stabbing daughter. You were working with them."

"Yes, Princess. I worked with them. To keep you safe."

"Safe? As their prisoner? How about now? I had a chance to be free, but you brought me here, under the pretense of stopping you people from killing each other. And now I'm a prisoner again." She combed her fingers through her hair. "Rivers. Floods. Fake drama, lies, people turned to stone, burning. War. What's wrong with you people? I'm done with this. I'm done."

She sat and wrapped her arms around her knees. "I'm done."

"It's time she knew, Least High," Thorn said.

"Past time," Lumpface said.

"Perhaps so," Least High said.

"Wait," Thorn said. "What about him?"

The chieftains and Least High turned toward Jermbog.

"Not wise to let him know," Lumpface said.

"They know that I serve in the court of the sorcerer king," Jermbog said. "How far would I get?"

"You wouldn't get far from me," Lumpface said, stone-faced.

"Nor me." The druid moved in close, forcing the magistrate to look up. "I've been known to walk through a village unseen and deliver a fiery tiger from the gates of hell."

Jermbog's smile disappeared; he nodded and retreated to the back of the tent.

The Least High Druid searched the ground for a moment. "Princess, I've watched over you for more than a dozen years. I continue to do so now."

Arms still wrapped tightly around her knees, Blundren let the words sift. "What do you mean, you've watched over me?"

"The sorcerer king is my brother."

Her eyes shot up at the druid like lasers. "I don't think I heard you right."

"You heard correctly. I'm your uncle."

Blundren leaned back on her hands. "But you kidnapped me!"

"A plan to harm you was in place," he said. "I made myself part of it to protect you."

"Why didn't you just warn us?"

"They would've altered the plans. We'd be worse off."

"Why haven't I ever seen you?" Blundren asked.

"By staying hidden, I could watch over you while I searched for my brother. He was…not himself. It was a mad, uncertain time."

"You're referring to the frog story."

"Then you heard what happened."

"Recently. Like I said, I never saw you."

He gestured to the two Qrudd chieftains. "I don't suppose you saw them, either."

"Qrudd warriors?"

"Watched over you," Lumpface said. "Kept you safe. We were young warriors then, not old and fat like my good friend here."

"Surprised you never heard us," Thorn said. "Took all I had to keep him quiet."

Jermbog eased forward and leaned in. Lumpface gave him a hard stare. The magistrate developed a sudden interest in his thumbnail.

"Qrudds were not the concern back then," the Least High Druid said. "We were worried about the mystic witch. She was capable of just about anything."

"Why would she want to harm me?"

The Least High Druid hesitated.

"Did it have to do with my mother?"

"Yes. But—"

"It can't be worse than my father being replaced by a frog. Which is ridiculous. It just shows the power of stories. If you repeat them often enough, people believe them."

"You sound so much like my mother, your grandmother. She questioned everything, to the point where she refused to believe anything."

"I've heard that from others."

"From Herb, no doubt."

"You know of Herb?"

"Yes. He trained both of us."

"Herb said that my father might have had a brother."

"And that would be me," the druid said.

"But why did my father never mention you?" she asked.

"My best guess is that he wasn't actually there."

"If that's the case, why didn't you make yourself king and rule in his place, until he could be found?"

The druid laughed. "I wouldn't have been much better than the frog. The power I seek is of a different sort, inside us, in the world around us. No, the best plan was to find your father and restore him to the throne."

"The old ways couldn't help you to find him any faster?"

"There are limits when other sorcerers are involved."

"Naturally. I can see Herb's training coming through. By the way, we found the pond. It appears my father is back."

The druid's eyes brightened. "What?"

She frowned at Jermbog. "You saw my father as much as I did, before and after. What's your take on all this?"

"His Eminence was always there, Highness, yet he wasn't there so much of the time. I conferred with him, but he usually just sat there and blinked. He's different now. Better."

"Like you cared. Didn't I overhear you offer to sell out my father if the opportunity presented itself?"

"He made that offer to me," Least High said. "To betray my brother. I plan to take care of it before it becomes a problem."

Jermbog slid back a step. "I put myself in a position to save the princess. Like you."

Blundren stood. "You came into camp with Qrudd warriors. It looked to me like you'd joined them."

"I had to." Jermbog's gaze circled the group as he spoke in a confiding tone, as if he were sharing sage advice with his team. "I was deceived, like you. We need to be very careful who we trust from now on."

The Chief Magistrate of All Things Pertaining and Otherwise puffed up and sniffed as if he were about to add something. Abruptly, he spun around and fled through the tent flap. They heard warriors running and shouting outside.

Blundren glared at the Least High Druid. "We're on the brink of war. One you called unnecessary. Now that we're prisoners, and they want to kill us, what happens?"

The druid looked at the ground. "I meant what I said back at the castle, Princess. It's not worth it. We need to stop this war."

"What do we do, old friend?" Thorn asked.

The druid floated the question back to the group. "So, what do we do?"

Chapter Thirty-Seven

PRELUDE TO WAR

"ARE YOU READY" the druid asked.

She nodded. Thorn and Lumpface exited the tent, followed by the Least High Druid, Blundren, and Thunder-squat. A wolf howled. Blundren was about to release a howl in return before she caught herself and covered her garbled moan with a cough.

"It's just a wolf," Thorn said.

"I'm okay. I swallowed wrong." Her newfound uncle, who'd spun layers of lies without reservation, thinks he can persuade these people by telling them the truth. *It will never work.*

The two chieftains were confident in the plan. Maybe they hadn't felt the hate that radiated from the crowd when she entered the village. At any rate, they'd made up their minds. No way was she going to talk sense into them now. Her best bet was to keep her eyes open for the first opportunity to slip away unnoticed. In the eyes of this crowd, she could not be more conspicuous.

And what about the barbarian? If she saw a chance to

escape, she wouldn't have time to explain it to him. She regretted it, but he was going to have to be the druid's problem. It was the druid who caused the barbarian to lose his mind. Least High then convinced her to come to Round Stones. If his ideas were so good, let him come up with something to save the barbarian, too.

Qrudd warriors fell in around them. They returned to the Round Stones and waited for the crowd to fold in around them. Outside the ring of stones, next to the upright boulders, two warriors held Jermbog by his arms.

Lumpface stepped onto one of the stones and addressed the crowd. "First, the Least High Druid is under no one's power but his own."

Bee Stings Behind jumped up on one of the other stones. "You can't prove that. That's exactly what he'd make you say."

Least High joined Lumpface. "The sorcerer king's daughter never bewitched anyone. That was a lie, spread by the great one's daughter."

Murmurs swept through the crowd.

Blundren couldn't restrain herself. She hopped onto a stone. "We have to stop this war before anyone gets hurt." *So much for remaining unnoticed.*

"Don't trust her!" Bee Stings Behind shouted. "She defiles the stone she stands on."

The mostly white wolf raced across the open area into the center of the Round Stones. From the other side, Bolstrus broke through the woods and settled next to the barbarian. The crowd fell back. The wolf crouched next to Blundren, facing the Jackal clan, fangs showing. Blundren growled at the Jackal leader.

"Is that the same wolf that ate the troll?" one of the Jackals asked.

"She bewitches animals." Bee Stings Behind looked triumphant. "What more proof do we need?"

"Would you like to find out?" Blundren threw her hands out to the side and slightly back, fingers outstretched. She didn't have a clue what she would do next.

The Jackals hesitated. The Egg Stealers and Rock Slingers moved in to protect Thorn and Lumpface. They pulled the Least High Druid and the princess off the central stone and centered them inside their circle. Thundersquat drew her close and rested his hand lightly on her upper back. The Jackals and Raw Fish Eaters drew together and faced them. The Cloud Men moved to the north of the Round Stones and watched in silence.

Bee Stings Behind frowned at the Cloud Men. "And who will you stand with, my brothers?"

The Jackal chieftain was nearly trampled as the black stallion burst through the upright boulders and skidded to a halt on the central stone. The stallion reared. Dekatria held high the necklace with the five bear claws. "What goes on here?"

The crowd was silent. Thorn stepped up onto one of the side stones. "The five are no longer one."

The stallion spun around. The Qrudds looked down, holding perfectly still. Blundren felt the white-hot intensity of Dekatria's defiant glare.

Jermbog broke free and scurried toward Dekatria before warriors caught and restrained him. "Highness, hear me, please. I can be of use."

"What have you to say that I'd want to hear?"

"The real fight is not among the Qrudds. Well, partly. But not if we look deeper."

"Get to the point."

"The druid isn't bewitched. But he and the princess are working together."

"And why would the Least High Druid dare to work with the sorcerer king's daughter?"

He paused for effect. "Because Least High and the sorcerer king are brothers."

The stallion spun around again. The news radiated through the crowd. Only Thorn and Lumpface stood in silence.

"The druid has deceived us from the beginning!" Bee Stings Behind shouted.

"Enough!" Dekatria's single word immediately dropped their protests into dead silence. The stallion half-reared. "Magistrate. Approach."

Jermbog stepped forward.

"Perhaps you can be of use after all."

Jermbog puffed up and bowed. "At your service, Highness."

Dekatria stretched her arms out and pointed her fingers toward each other. As she twirled them, the air in front of the magistrate blurred and twisted in folds of changing color. A spiral ram's horn materialized, the length of an arm, suspended in air. Jermbog placed tentative hands near either end. He recovered his confident air and lifted it high in triumph for all to see.

"Now blow it," Dekatria said.

Jermbog inhaled and set it to his lips. The ram's horn sputtered. Several warriors stepped forward, but he waved them off. He took another breath and blew again. After an initial sputter, a pure, loud tone sounded through the valley.

"Good. Now I have one more thing for you to do."

The Magistrate of All Things Pertaining and Otherwise flashed his gums at the princess.

Blundren felt the heat rise in her head and chest.

Jermbog's eyes shot wide open as he burst into flames. He screamed. He threw himself on the ground and rolled. He sprang up and hopped in circles among the stones. Each scream sent shivers down Blundren's spine. The flames blasted outward in a brilliant white flash and extinguished.

Blundren and the druid ducked. Thundersquat and the wolf covered her. Her heart raced.

The Qrudd warriors scattered.

Tendrils of smoke brought the odor of burnt flesh and released a surge of nausea, which would have dropped her lower if she were not already crouched low. She grabbed the druid's arm. "Please, it wasn't me. I don't think. But maybe. Get me out of here before I hurt someone else."

"It was her," Least High said. "She killed her own father."

"Dekatria?"

"Stay alert. Stay close."

Dekatria reared the stallion once again. She held the bear claw necklace aloft. "You cannot trust any of your leaders. I return now, purified by the gods, to lead you to future glory!"

The demigoddess pointed her hand at the ram's horn, and it flew into her grasp. She blew another blast, long and pure.

A vast army poured over the rim of the hill to the north like molten lava, armed with golden shields outlined by the setting sun. The Egg Stealers and Rock Slingers gathered tighter around the druid and the princess.

Bee Stings Behind ventured out from behind the boulders. Others followed. The Jackal chieftain cast a quick look at the approaching army and back to Dekatria. He stepped up onto one of the five stones and raised a fist. "We'll be loyal to you as we were to your father."

"It's not your loyalty I seek but your servitude."

The yellow-spotted chieftain closed his mouth and stepped off the stone.

The Least High Druid, still on one knee, said, "The five have always lived free."

"They'll be my slaves, or they will die!" Dekatria shouted.

The druid approached the center stone. He spoke quietly, with an air of calm. "Forgive me, Highness. Your recent loss is beyond imagining, more than any one of us could bear. But what you suggest is extreme. Please, climb down. Let's talk."

"You want to see unbearable? Turn away from the true path. I'll sweep down over you and crush anybody in my way."

Blundren rushed to stand next to the Least High Druid. The wolf went with her. "You have no right to enslave these people."

"Who gave you the right to speak to me? I'm the daughter of a goddess. I'll do as I wish. And I'll take great pleasure in tormenting you. Until I get bored."

"The Qrudds are slaves to no one," Thorn said.

"Be sure and live, fat one." Dekatria pointed to Bee Stings Behind. "You. Call your warriors together."

The army of the north reached the valley. Dekatria surveyed the Jackals, Raw Fish Eaters, and Cloud Men. "The chosen few who survive will once again know the path to the gods. Fear me, but live true. Fight now and die, for gods and glory!"

The demigoddess waved to the Jackals and Raw Fish Eaters, who scrambled to line up where she pointed. She signaled to the Cloud Men. Silently they gathered behind the others, their back to the boulders. Each strung an arrow to their bows.

Thundersquat tossed Blundren on top of the silver stallion, who bolted for the woods to the west. The wolf streaked after them. Blundren bounced without mercy and clung to the horse's mane. The wind roared in her ears. She peeked under her arm.

"Archers!" Dekatria called.

The Cloud Men pulled the shafts back.

Dekatria waved, lighting the arrow points on fire. "Now!"

A volley of flaming arrows took flight toward the fleeing princess. The wolf and the stallion zigzagged to the left. Blundren nearly slipped off before she looped her forearms over Bolstrus's shoulder and neck. The arrows missed, but barely. She flopped against the stallion's right shoulder like a leather strap. As she slammed into his shoulder, she pushed off and used the momentum to swing a knee up to the stallion's back.

Bolstrus zigged to the right. Blundren whipped over to his other side. She managed to hook her foot over his shoulder and clung to a handful of mane. Her left knee dug into his ribs. She pushed her left hand against his shoulder in sync with his stride to reduce the jarring when his hooves hit the ground. With each leap, she inched her right leg farther and strengthened her grip. Blundren regained her balance just before they reached the safety of the woods, where she slid off the horse and scrambled behind a bush.

The Golden Horde from the north marched steadily closer. The Egg Stealers and Rock Slingers backed away from the other Qrudds. The Least High Druid and Thundersquat stood between them and the opposing clans. He'd saved her again. And she had been willing to leave him behind. He wasn't going to make it.

The Raw Fish Eaters let their spears fly as the Jackals fired their blow darts. The druid threw up his arms. The spears and darts bounced against an invisible wall of wind and dropped off to the side.

"Archers!" Dekatria ignited another round of arrows.

The archers set their arrows loose on the fleeing Qrudds. The warriors scattered. The druid waved his arm again, causing the arrows to change course. Several arrows found their marks anyway.

Many of the Qrudds had reached the wood line. Some lagged behind, dragging the stricken to safety. The archers loaded up again. The druid turned and fled. The barbarian grabbed a couple of the wounded and backed up slowly.

"Get out of there!" she shouted.

The archers released another barrage. Thundersquat shoved the two injured warriors behind him. The barbarian stood sideways with his hands raised in front of his face as a volley of arrows descended upon his position.

Blundren silently screamed at herself to do something, but her desperation failed to produce a single idea. She held her breath. Just before the arrows struck, the barbarian batted several arrows out of the way with backhand swipes, at the same time wriggling his body and legs just enough to dodge the rest. An arrow grazed the warrior to his right. Thundersquat threw an arm around each of the Qrudd warriors and sprinted toward the forest.

Chapter Thirty-Eight

UNTHINKABLE

THE SORCERER KING STUDIED the weathered fabric of the tent ceiling. A heavy weight pressed down on his chest. He thought of all those nights in the pond, meditating when he couldn't sleep. All those years, watching from afar, unable to protect her. Helpless, when the bats snatched her away. Then she rescued him from the pond. *She did that. She saved me.*

At last, reunited. Such relief, unimaginable.

New hopes. Dreams.

Only to see her taken again. Hope remained, back then; maybe the Qrudds operated from some core of reason. *What if they wanted something and would use her to force me to give it to them? I could've worked with that.* He wrapped his hands around the top of his head and squeezed.

It's over. Over.

Evil. Pure evil. Nothing I can do to stop it.

I can't think.

And I don't care.

He rolled onto his side and curled into a fetal position. He retreated into a roaring blackness, like crashing waves, scraping his soul against the broken-shelled shore. He embraced it. Beneath the battering, the thing he tried to ignore, but could not, was a soft, persistent, unwanted poke in the ribs. A quiet realization, one without force or a shred of commitment behind it. A tiny voice. "Tomorrow. They expect you to lead. No matter what."

His pain, his crushing grief, means nothing.

Wolfmini stood with his army on the hillside, facing the river. It was narrow and shallow there, one of the few reliable places he could always count on being able to cross. He stared straight ahead in a relaxed posture, hands cupped behind his back. People were going to die today. The sorcerer king felt his soldiers' eyes on him, searching for a signal to attack, for a way to face death. They would see that he was not afraid, and that would be enough. They didn't need to know he didn't feel anything at all. *What else could anybody do to me?*

Life was so much easier as a frog. Frogs didn't form attachments to tadpoles. If a passing snake nabbed one of three hundred siblings, one of thousands of offspring, of tens of thousands of nephews and nieces, frogs didn't even blink. Dusk came regardless, to signal another rousing chorus. From the start, life was neither empty nor fun. Frogs never demanded that it be anything more.

"It isn't what it isn't," a frog would say, and another would answer with a resounding belch; the statement made no sense, and that was probably the point.

Qrudd warriors emerged from the forest on the other

side of the river. Some were armed with curved throwing sticks, others with bolas and spears.

The Qrudds stopped. Wolfmini could see their faces now. They parted in the middle.

Behind them stood Blundren, a wolf at her side, the barbarian on the other. The sorcerer king's eyebrows knotted together. He blinked through the tears filling his eyes and looked again. *What sorcery is this?*

Blundren ran through. The emptiness inside him frittered away. Giddiness flooded in and propelled him forward.

The sorcerer king's army charged and swept around him. His daughter stopped. The Qrudd warriors drew their weapons and charged.

Wolfmini realized his mistake. "Stop!"

His army and the aborigines were in full battle cry. No one could hear him. His daughter would be caught right in the middle of battle. Wolfmini stretched his fingers out at chest level and pulled them into fists before sweeping them toward the sky. A wall of water shot upward from the stream in a thin sheet that divided the armies. The liquid wall undulated slightly and presented each side with smeared reflections and blurred distortions of their opponents. Both armies slowed to a jog and stopped. They lowered their weapons and looked questioningly at one another.

Wolfmini strode through his forces, fists held high. He flung his fingers outward in a violent twist, and the sheet of water dropped and splattered. He waded in ankle deep and held out his arms toward his daughter. She approached, and he hugged her tightly. "I thought I'd lost you."

Blundren wiped away her tears. "You'll have to show me how you did that. First, I have someone for you to meet."

Wolfmini glanced up at the barbarian standing behind her.

Thundersquat stepped aside. From the tree line across the river, a gaunt figure dressed in a loincloth and sandals, an amulet stashed in his belt, stepped out of the woods; his grayish-white beard billowed. The druid made his way to the river.

The sorcerer king squinted and frowned. Something in the way he moved was familiar. The druid stopped before Wolfmini and waited, clearly enjoying this moment. The sorcerer king mentally erased the crow's feet, filled in the hairline, and added color to the hair, beard, and eyebrows. "Can it be you, after all these years?"

The druid smiled. "Same question. We have a lot to talk about, brother." His voice was unmistakable, though huskier, partly, no doubt, from the emotion of the moment.

The brothers grasped each other's forearms and gazed at one another for a long moment. They broke the intense connection reluctantly and walked together, a hand resting on the other's shoulder, back toward camp. Wolfmini wrapped his other arm around his daughter.

"You have no idea what we're up against, Father," Blundren said.

Chapter Thirty-Nine

WAR

BLUNDREN STOOD BEHIND her uncle and her father, in the cover of the woods, overlooking the rolling hills that held the Qrudd encampment at Round Stones. She carried a thin bone dagger; the wolf was at her left. Dekatria's horde outlined the top of the ridge. Golden shields captured the sun and staged a fiery rim. A cold wave swept down Blundren's neck to the middle of her back.

Wolfmini turned his head. "I wish you'd reconsider."

"Like I told you last night," she said, "if they beat us, there's nowhere I could go that would be safe. You're stuck with me this time."

The sorcerer king, tight-lipped, gave his head a scarcely noticeable shake and faced forward. "There's so much more I should've taught you."

"And why didn't you?"

"I taught you some of the basics, beguilement and befuddlement. Fooling people, mostly. I thought if you believed there was nothing to it, you'd stay away from it. Not get sucked into it. You'd be safe."

Blundren surveyed the enemy forces. "How did that work out?"

Wolfmini lowered his head. "If I had more time, I could show you some things. How to work with elemental forces."

"So, telling me it was all a lie," Blundren said, "was in itself a lie."

"It wasn't the whole truth, no. But I had my reasons."

Blundren clenched her jaw. "Another time. If we're lucky."

To Blundren's right was the barbarian. He studied his fingers. The silver stallion next to him was antsy. Blundren placed a hand on Thundersquat's forearm. "Wait here."

She stepped up to her father. "What about the barbarian? Is it right to have him out here? He's still not sure where he is or what he's doing here."

"You told me he handled himself well against the archers. He'll either fight or run. Either way, for now he's one more man for the enemy to see."

"How much difference can it make?"

"Keep him close," Least High told her.

She spotted the Cloud Men, Jackals, and Raw Fish Eaters as they moved in from the right. Blundren backed up to the barbarian's side.

Wolfmini and Least High left the trees for the plain, followed by the Rock Slingers and Egg Stealers clans. Blundren followed with the barbarian, the wolf, and the silver stallion. The Blisterian army remained hidden.

Ahead of her surging army, Dekatria rode the black stallion, next to the leader of the Golden Horde. The commander signaled for the army to stop. The warrior priestess charged forward several strides, reined in the stallion, and turned him to the side. She raised an arm high, spun it in broad circles, and flung both arms forward. A tiny whirlwind of fire appeared, headed toward the sorcerer king and the Least High Druid. The whirlwind swelled into a blazing tornado about the height of three men. Dekatria's forces began to chant, beating swords against shields, spears against the ground, as they marched forward behind the tornado.

"Nothing to worry about." The Least High Druid pulled his amulet out from his waistband and stretched. The stone began to glow. He twirled the amulet and shot it forward, spinning out a whirlwind of his own, this one spitting water droplets in all directions.

"Not bad, brother." The sorcerer king swung his arms and tossed out another whirlwind just like it.

The two whirlwinds swelled into tornadoes, each about half the size of the one tossed by Dekatria. They flanked the larger tornado and crushed it from both sides. Steam hissed in a wild cloud. When the cloud dissipated, Dekatria's whirling fire advanced, twice its size. The Golden Horde flowed around Dekatria and followed the pillar of fire.

Wolfmini and Least High exchanged glances. They raised their arms again. Blundren and the wolf surged forward, splitting them. She mimicked the arm motions she'd observed, in sync with theirs. She could feel moisture being sucked out of the air. She threw out a spinning drizzle, as she went down on one knee. Hers was not much compared to the two tossed out by her elders, but it was something. The druid pressed his hands together. The three twisters danced around each other and merged. They exploded into a whirling, spitting spiral of water rivaling the size of Dekatria's firestorm.

The tornadoes collided with a thunderclap, and a cloud of steam shot out and enveloped both armies.

When the trio of sorcerers could see again, the fiery cyclone had doubled yet again, and billowing smoke darkened the skies. It bore down on the sorcerer king's forces. The heat was already intense enough to slow-cook a hog.

Blundren glanced at her father. The look he exchanged with her uncle was clear: they were out of answers. Bad enough that they were outnumbered, but they couldn't counter the fury of nature wielded by Dekatria. In short order, they would be burned to a crisp or hacked to pieces— maybe both.

Wolfmini drew his sword. The Least High Druid gripped his amulet.

Blundren surveyed the Golden Horde beyond the tornado and saw the commander remove his helmet. Thundersquat jogged past her, out into the open field.

"Wait! Come back!" Blundren watched helplessly. He kept going.

Dekatria spurred her stallion through her troops, past the whirling tower of fire, as if to run the barbarian down. Bolstrus bolted to his side, and Thundersquat swung up. The stallions lunged to attack.

"No!" Blundren snatched the amulet from the Least High Druid and dashed forward. She swung it high overhead and smashed it into the ground. With a blinding burst of white light and a thunderous crack, a knee-high ripple shot across the earth's surface in all directions. The ground began to undulate. Both stallions stumbled. The earthen wave tripped up half of the soldiers and warriors on either side. Blundren dropped to her knees. Her head was swimming.

A rupture tore into the earth with rumbling, splintering blasts and widened as it streaked across the battlefield. It passed beneath the fiery cyclone and swallowed it whole. The crack in the earth belched smoke, as it forked and shot a new branch in the direction of Round Stones. Boulders toppled into the breach. Warriors panicked and fled. They fell, rolled, and crawled through the smoke on the convulsing surface. The ground ripped apart beneath Dekatria's army, consuming those in its path.

Dekatria leaped back onto her stallion and whipped him into a mad retreat. The black stallion leaped into the cloud of black smoke as the earth split apart below her.

The fiery tornado was gone. The quake had finally run its course. Blundren glimpsed Dekatria in snatches through the billowing smoke, galloping back and forth among the fleeing troops, trying to restore control. She felt a mix of relief and disappointment at her friend's survival, followed by guilt that she shouldn't feel either.

The enemy forces were divided and reduced. The mixed forces under Wolfmini's command stayed put, most of them crouched low. Hysterical panic was on the table, but mentally they were much better off than their adversaries. Her father moved among the troops to salvage any calm that remained. Blundren flipped the amulet to her uncle as he walked by, headed toward Thorn and Lumpface. The three of them offered words of encouragement among the Egg Stealers and Rock Slingers.

Blundren spotted Thundersquat off to the left, staring across at the army to the north. She hurried through her father's forces and came up behind the barbarian, pausing a full stride away from the edge. Still feeling weak, she was careful not to look down into the abyss. "I'm here. Don't startle."

The princess pinched the back of his vest and guided him back. He looked like he wanted to tell her something.

"What is it?" she asked.

The barbarian stared across the divide with a pained expression. She took his arm and led him toward her father and uncle.

Dekatria's Qrudd warriors were trapped on the Blisterian side, the gaping fissure at their backs. Bee Stings Behind screamed at the Raw Fish Eaters. The Qrudds regained order. The Cloud Men strung their bows. The Jackals and Raw Fish Eaters advanced.

The Blisterian army approached the enemy clans from the left and middle, while the Egg Stealers and Rock Slingers closed in from the right. The sorcerer king's forces herded the remnants of the enemy clans into a tight mass.

The Cloud Men lowered their bows and returned the arrows to the quivers. Seeing that, the Raw Fish Eaters stepped back and planted their spears upright into the ground. They rested one hand loosely on the spear and placed the other hand behind their backs.

"What are you doing?" screamed Bee Stings Behind.

The Jackal warriors glanced at their comrades and flung their blowguns to the ground. Several scooted back to the edge of the crevasse.

"Pick those up!" the yellow-spotted chieftain yelled. He looked frantically across the divide.

From the other side of the rupture, Dekatria screamed at the surrendering clans. "Fight! You worthless nothings, fight!"

Dekatria turned and aimed her ranting diatribe at the commander of the Golden Horde. He stared impassively as she continued to scream. The commander replaced his helmet on his head, turned his horse and trotted away. His army pivoted like one organism and melted into the distance.

Dekatria set her wrath loose on the victors like a battering wind. "How dare you! Defy me? You'll live your worst nightmare! I'll make slaves of you all! Fight for the righteous path or die!"

The persistent tirade cost Dekatria the attention she demanded. Soldiers and Qrudds fell into myriad conversations. She upped the volume and continued to shout. An ear-piercing crack slapped the crowd into abrupt silence.

Blundren's heart turned a couple of somersaults. A brown cloud formed near Dekatria. The black stallion reared. The cloud dissipated to reveal Axiom Punctilio, the god of Stipulations and Particulars.

The Qrudds drew back. Dekatria glared at the god, who towered over her and the stallion.

"It appears that thou hast a grievance. I will assist thee, by bringing thee to a place to properly state thy case."

"I didn't ask for anything from you!" Dekatria screamed. Abruptly, she vanished, and the riderless black stallion galloped away.

Her father exchanged glances with her uncle. "Deus ex machina? I thought it was outlawed."

"It was," Least High said. "That's what we were always taught."

The god turned his head and regarded the druid. In a flash, he leaned over them. The Qrudd warriors and Blisterian soldiers scattered.

The Least High Druid bowed his head briefly. "Forgive my impertinence, but how would a deus-ex-machina ending pass muster with the very arbiter of rules and regulations?"

Axiom Punctilio nodded with half a smile. "Thou speaketh truth. The preferred convention would be for the protagonist to face impossible odds while everything blows up around him. He is permitted to emerge unharmed, but the second-in-command must die in a noble sacrifice."

"More creative, definitely. And just as plausible." Least High glanced at the sorcerer king. "I'm either first or third, not second."

"I'll take third," said Wolfmini. "I've had my day in the sun."

They both looked at the barbarian.

"What if I'm second?" Blundren asked.

"Let me put thee at ease," the god said. "I am not here to save thee, but to warn thee."

"Warn us?" the sorcerer king asked.

"I'm afraid so. The Braid of Time is frayed around the edges—unraveling faster than anticipated. Thy reality hath already been altered in ways that may be irreversible. Thy world will remain in precarious balance for half a moon."

"Then what happens?" the druid asked.

"The Braider of Time will no longer be able to keep this world distinct from those whose possibilities are in proximity."

"Are you saying the blending has gone too far?" Least High asked.

"In places."

"That barbarian over there is the one chosen to find the Half-Forgotten Stone," Wolfmini said. "Can he do it in half a moon?"

"He's only got half a mind," Least High said.

"At least we know where to start," Wolfmini said. "Take us a week to get there. That will only give him one week."

Axiom Punctilio hung his head and sighed. "Desperate optimism. Designed to reduce thy torment, but not mine. I'll have to generate a whole new set of standard operating procedures."

The god of Stipulations and Particulars disappeared in a brown cloud.

∾

Dekatria turned up her nose at the smell of the stable. She apprised the woman standing before her, wearing a sweat-soaked gray tunic. Errant strands of hair clung to her face and neck. "Hello, Mother."

Dekatria caught the pitchfork tossed in her direction.

"Start over there," Pyrogenia said. "I'm done on my side."

Chapter Forty

COTTAGE BOUND

"IT'S TIME WE HAD that conversation you've been wanting," Wolfmini said.

Thundersquat nodded. The barbarian was having a good day. He only lagged a sentence or two behind. The sorcerer king seemed to know more than he did about whatever they were talking about. The druid also looked like he knew.

"You've been tasked with finding the Half-Forgotten Stone."

With some hesitation, Thundersquat nodded. "Wouldn't deny it."

"When you first brought up the Stone, I didn't want to discuss it. Events associated with the Stone are still quite painful."

"Given what's at stake, you don't have any choice," Least High said.

"What does it do?" Blundren cut in.

"Shows you what's hidden," the druid said. "It anchors the Braid of Time. Keeps us apart from other possible worlds close to this one."

"You've seen it?" Blundren asked.

"I could have reached out and touched it." Least High looked sideways at the sorcerer king. "Then I lost track of it."

Wolfmini rubbed the back of his neck. "For a long time, the Half-Forgotten Stone was hidden in the magic fountain."

"Near the troll?" the druid asked. "I always wondered."

"Red-haired troll?" The barbarian smiled at the smell of blueberry cinnamon pancakes that penetrated his memory, unimpeded.

"Yes, he lived there, beneath an old tree. He fed us a fine meal."

"Melts in your mouth," the barbarian said.

"The troll knew about the Stone?" Least High asked.

"I don't believe so," Wolfmini said. "But even if he did, he might have forgotten."

"But it's not there now?" the druid asked.

"No. I blame myself," the sorcerer king said.

"I knew you weren't to be trusted with it," the druid said.

"What was I thinking?" Wolfmini swallowed. "The last time I saw it, the Half-Forgotten Stone was in the hands of the mystic witch."

Thundersquat's stomach growled.

"We have to get it from her," the druid said.

"We have to persuade her to tell us what she can recall," Wolfmini said.

"She won't exactly be overjoyed to see either one of us," Least High said.

"When do we leave?" Blundren asked.

"Perhaps it would be better if we dropped you off at the palace on the way," the sorcerer king said. "It's just a little matter, and we won't be gone long."

"Well, in that case, I might as well come with you."

"No. It's too dangerous." The sorcerer king jumped in a little too quickly.

"Just a little matter, but it's too dangerous?" she asked. "What's your idea of dangerous, besides the world coming to an end?"

"Your father's right, Princess," the druid said. "Danger far worse than anything you've seen so far."

"Well, let's see. That would include being carried off by bats and dropped in the woods in front of a wolf. Kidnapped. A raging river. Floods. Prison, a crazy chieftain, flaming arrows, war. A deranged demigoddess. Fiery tornadoes. Earthquake."

The sorcerer king and his brother silently conferred with each other.

"That'd be about right," the sorcerer king said.

"What are you walking into?" she asked.

"We just want you to stay safe," the sorcerer king said.

"Oh, I can be safe in the palace. But you're jumping into something so dangerous you can't even tell me what it is? You expect me to sleep peacefully, like nothing's going on?"

"Better if you didn't worry," the sorcerer king said. "But I couldn't take it if anything else happened to you."

"I just threw out a twister and caused an earthquake, in case you didn't notice. So, I'd say something already happened to me. And I'd like to know what. Am I safe? Is anybody safe around me?"

Wolfmini rubbed his face. "We can't say more."

"You've done enough damage by not telling me things before. You're just going to do more of the same?" The princess tried the barbarian. "Are you with them on this?"

"On what?" He thought for a moment. "Hard to tell."

"Why are all of you being so cryptic about everything?" she asked. "What's going on?"

"We've told you what we can, for now," the druid said, shooting a glance at his brother.

Halfway up the spiral incline on the twisted mountain, they encountered a fog, not unusual in the mornings when the clouds dipped low. The sorcerer king glanced at the druid and disappeared into the fog.

Blundren stepped into what she thought was a cloud. She passed through a wall of fog like a curtain, about two hands thick. It gave her an odd, tickly feeling. Her head was swimming. Her father was pale, hands on his knees. "What's wrong?"

"Nothing," he said softly. "I was just nauseous for a second. It's gone now."

"Same here," she said.

The path ahead was ornate, with carvings along the inner edge. At intervals, shrines filled cutouts notched out of the side of the mountain, adorned with ornamental gardens.

"What else has changed?" Wolfmini asked.

The druid and the barbarian stepped through the wall of fog.

"Whoa." Least High raised his hands and wavered, as he steadied himself. His eyes showed excitement, as he scanned the surroundings. "This is it. The blending. Has to be."

The courtyard gardens of the Onyx Palace were far more resplendent than before. The palace was still comprised of onyx, but with a more elaborate design. A series of keyhole-shaped niches had been etched into the surface. Gold outlined the rims of the towers and framed the windows.

A litter passed by, borne on the shoulders of Qrudd slaves. Two soldiers followed the litter and eyed the foursome with grim faces. One turned and signaled behind him. Soldiers poured out of the palace and surrounded them.

"What's the meaning of this?" Wolfmini asked.

The soldiers ignored him. The leader approached the Least High Druid and glanced up and down. "Your Eminence. What would you have us do with them?"

The druid exchanged glances with Wolfmini. "They're with me."

The soldiers stared impassively.

"Let us pass," the druid said. "I don't think I need to tell you what can happen if you don't."

The soldiers parted, and the four travelers entered the palace. At the far end of the great hall, a tall figure strolled toward them, dressed in flowing golden robes embroidered with symbols in black and red. As he drew near, Blundren gasped. His face was identical to that of her uncle, except for a neatly groomed beard and minus the leathery tan.

"I'm known as the Pinnacle Sage," he said, "the Utmost Exalted, the Wizard of Unsurpassed Charm."

"I like it," said Least High.

"It's self-evident," the Pinnacle Sage said, "but there's a tear in the fabric of space and time. The blending has begun. I'm to blame for having lost track of the Stone in this realm. You as well?"

Wolfmini coughed. "I believe I share more of the blame than anyone here."

"What did you do?" Blundren asked.

Least High said, "Time grows short. We need to focus on finding the Stone."

"Couldn't have said it better myself," said the Pinnacle Sage.

"This barbarian is the key to finding it," Least High said.

"From the Badlands? Intriguing proposition. In my realm,

it falls on a certain red-haired troll, a fearless outlaw. He seems to have gone underground. We can't locate him," the Pinnacle Sage said.

Least High's eyes danced around the palace. "You grabbed the Stone, didn't you? Went back for it later?"

"The very day Futhark the Meddler said I wasn't the one. I couldn't let him get away with that."

Least High nodded. "I let the moment slip by. I always wondered if he was holding me back, what I could've done. That one choice. It led to all this."

A woman's voice came in from the side. "Until in his utmost wisdom, he let the Stone get away."

The Pinnacle Sage held out his arm, and a woman of stunning beauty cozied up to him. The top of her head reached his chest. Her gown was comprised of exquisite fabrics Blundren had never laid eyes on. "My wife, the lady Caprice."

Wolfmini and the Least High Druid looked at each other, clearly taken aback.

"If you'd told me where it was, when I asked," Caprice said, "we wouldn't have ended up like this."

The Pinnacle Sage gave her a tender smile and stared at the floor. "You're right, of course. And yet I couldn't take that chance."

"You should have trusted me."

His face twitched. "The pull of that Stone is beyond esti-mation. I wanted to ensure that there was absolutely no chance you would ever touch it, even by accident."

She stood on her toes and kissed him lightly on the neck. "Perhaps Futhark the Meddler knew what he was talking about. You sold me short. Your desire to protect me has been our undoing."

"It hasn't ended that well in our world, either," Least High said. "Hence the blending."

The images of the Pinnacle Sage, his wife and the surrounding began to flicker.

"Find that Stone." The Pinnacle Sage locked eyes with the druid. "Don't even stop to sleep."

They were gone. The palace around them reverted to its original state.

"Let's get out of here, before everything switches back," Wolfmini said.

They raced out of the palace and courtyard and let gravity assist them in their jog down the spiral path. The fog curtain was gone. At the bottom of the mountain, they stopped to catch their breath.

"Her name was Caprice, like the mystic witch." Blundren caught the exchange of glances between her father and uncle. "What's going on?"

They ignored her.

"Now you have to take me with you," Blundren said. "I can't stay here—it's too unstable."

"No," Wolfmini said. "There has to be another way."

"What if we leave her with the red-haired troll?" the druid asked.

Wolfmini nodded. "She'd be safe there. Plus, last I talked to him, he felt pretty useless. This would give him a chance to do something important."

"I'm right here," Blundren said.

"Let's go," said Least High.

Thundersquat tapped Blundren on the arm. "Pancakes."

"Yes," she said. "There's that."

∾

At the old tree, in a slow boil, Blundren watched her father, uncle, the barbarian, and the stallion until they were out of sight. Not for one minute did she consider staying behind. Forces were at work here that defied explanation, and they had refused to help her understand. All her life she'd been led to believe that sorcery was just one big deception. What she thought was a lie was itself buried within a bigger lie. *But what's the truth?*

To top that, the world was apparently coming to an end. Yet they thought it was okay to wait while the barbarian had his fill of blueberry cinnamon pancakes. Thundersquat's thinking was still slow and labored, but they took him and not her. She eyed the troll. "We're going with them."

"We can't," Smidgel said. "You heard what they said. It's too dangerous."

"If they fail, we'll all die anyway. They don't have to know we're around. Just close enough, in case they need us."

The spotted lion moved next to the princess. The red-haired troll rubbed the back of his neck. Mudcat turned his head to the side and huffed.

"I can most definitely say no," the troll said. "I promised her father, and I meant it. We're staying right where we are."

The spotted lion raised an eyebrow.

"You promised to keep me safe," Blundren said, "not to hold me prisoner. How would you feel if something happened to them that we could've prevented?"

Blundren took off after the trio. The spotted lion trotted alongside. Blundren heard the red-haired troll scramble to catch up.

"They better not ever see us," he said.

"They better not ever need us, either," she said.

Chapter Forty-One

THE MYSTIC WITCH

WOLFMINI, THE LEAST HIGH DRUID, and Thundersquat conferred in the woods overlooking the cottage of the mystic witch. Bolstrus' head was high, ears pricked, head turned to afford a clear view of the valley below.

The mystic witch was outside, gardening. That meant she sat and pointed. She issued rapid-fire commands while the assistant scurried first one way, then the other, digging, trimming, pulling things out, putting other things in the ground.

Memories assailed the sorcerer king. Twenty years ago, he'd been slow to understand what was happening, until it was too late. His own blindness had played such an instrumental part in what took place. Yet even now his guilt was a light tap on the shoulder, when it should be grabbing him by his soul and shaking him like a rag doll. His knowledge of the dire consequences paid by so many was like a crawly thing he observed after he turned over a rock. Even the fear that awakened when he'd spotted the mystic witch was just another wiggly bug seeking shelter under the next little rock.

He wasn't insensitive or clueless. He'd learned how to compartmentalize—except where his daughter was concerned. Wolfmini regarded his brother. "After what we saw in the palace, can you do this?"

"Can you?"

"I never knew you were attracted to her."

"I'd forgotten how beautiful she was then." The druid thought for a second and met the sorcerer king's gaze. "She made her choice. Ultimately, she turned on you and put you in that pond. Changed all our lives. I have no problem separating from whatever happened back then."

"Or what might have been. You could've said something, you know."

"Right." The druid stroked his beard. "Funny, in the work we do, we distract people to keep them from seeing things as they are. Work their blind spots. No matter how good we get, it doesn't keep it from happening to us."

"Too easy. What we want, what we're afraid of. All the nonsense that competes for our attention. It's a wonder we ever see anything for what it is. For once, I'd like to stumble into a moment of true clarity."

"And recognize it when it happens, instead of after, when it's too late." The druid shrugged. "As if we know what we're doing now?"

Wolfmini smiled. "I missed this. Enough philosophy—we have a job to do. Ready, brother?"

"Don't choke."

The sorcerer king placed his hands on either side of Thundersquat's face and made sure the barbarian was paying attention. "Stay here. No matter what you see."

Thundersquat nodded. The two brothers stepped out of the woods. The mystic witch and the assistant looked up. She whipped an arm in their direction, and a bolt of energy shot from her hand. Least High threw his arms up; the bolt exploded, splashing splinters of light.

Wolfmini's heart raced. He'd scarcely had time to move his hands. He wasn't ready. Nowhere near ready.

"You'll pay!" The mystic witch flung her chair into the porch backhanded and stomped over to a nearby hedge.

Wolfmini sought to calm himself. Getting quicker meant getting rid of the time it took to decide what to do. Relaxed readiness. Let the first reaction be dictated by the opponent's first move. Then trust in your automatic training to follow two moves in rapid succession. He let his arms dangle and gave them a quick shake.

The mystic witch stretched her arms forward and aimed all her fingers at a point just above the hedge. Slowly she pulled her hands back over her head, spreading her fingers wide. The mystic witch glanced at them as she dashed into the cottage.

Above the hedge a dragonfly ballooned to the size of a mountain goat with oversized eyes. It twisted and contorted, emitting a high-pitched blast.

The brothers threw their hands over their ears.

A pointy snout punched out, trimmed along the jawline with scaly knots. Two curved horns jutted from the top of its skull, along with a third horn on the snout. The exoskeleton grew scales that flashed blue. Filamentary legs morphed into masses of muscle on powerful hindquarters. Its tail stretched and curled around. Two sets of translucent wings thickened along the topmost edge and stretched. The beast was now half again larger than an aurochs. The reptilian insect displayed its wings and opened its jaws wide, revealing rows of saber-like teeth. The dragon drew its head back and shot forward, spewing flames.

The Least High Druid cast an invisible shield. Flames

curved around the shield as a blast of heat swept over them. An acrid smell lingered. The creature soared above in a slow vertical loop before dropping toward them. The druid blew on his fingers.

"What do you have that'll bring down a dragon?" Least High asked.

Wolfmini's insides sloshed wildly up and down. "Nothing."

"That shield took a lot out of me. I might be able to do it once or twice more."

"I never learned how to throw up a shield against flames."

"Fear can paralyze you. Don't think about the object you're trying to block out. It can't exist for you. Just focus on the shield."

"I can do that, but not fast enough."

The dragon cast another volley of fire and smoke. The shield held, but the heat was intense. The creature's tail bounced against the new shield and narrowly missed the druid's head. It was hard to draw a breath; there wasn't enough air. The brothers' eyes met. The Least High Druid wasn't defeated, but he looked like he didn't have much left.

The dragon flew at them again. The flames curled over the shield. The heat singed Wolfmini's beard and seared the top of his skull. He knocked his helmet off, now smoking on the grass.

The druid was on his knees. "That's it. The next one won't hold."

A lot was said in that last look between them: a rush of what might have been, dissolved into a whisper, and replaced by the simple feeling of what they meant to each other.

Wolfmini squinted at the creature as it soared through its final turn. "I didn't come all this way to lose now."

About to be fried by an overgrown dragonfly. Was this karma?

He'd feasted on his share in the pond, one dragonfly at a time, to survive until the next meal. In order to eat, he had to learn how the creature thought, what it could see. Then it came to him. *Just an overgrown dragonfly.* Wolfmini relaxed. He gave the druid a pat on the shoulder as he stepped past. "I've got this, older brother."

The dragon shot forward.

Wolfmini blew into his palms and flung them out with a flourish. Across the sky, celestial light reflected off specks of dust too small to see and coalesced into a sparkling image of a giant toad. Wolfmini opened his mouth and tapped his fingers on his throat. The toad projection's throat undulated rapidly. From the image the sorcerer king emitted a deep resounding belch that vibrated in his bones.

The dragon veered sharply to the left and hovered, staring at the projected image. The dragon darted away and disappeared in the distance. Wolfmini dropped to his knees; the toad vanished.

The brothers caught their breath.

The sorcerer king jerked as something electric stabbed and seared into his ribs. As he fell, the druid leaped over him. Least High fired a ray at the same time as the mystic witch. The rays exploded. The mystic witch backed into the cottage and slammed the door.

Least High dragged Wolfmini into the cover of the woods.

The pain was intense, and Wolfmini was lightheaded, struggling to regain his focus. "I don't suppose she's amenable to conversation."

The druid laughed. "I'd rate it on the other side of impossible."

"The assistant, then. He might recall something."

"Our best shot." The druid's hands hovered above the sorcerer king's injury.

Wolfmini felt the burning subside, replaced by a cool sensation. "Who knows what she did with the Stone? She could've buried it, concealed it with magic. Given it away."

"Somebody else could've stumbled across it and taken off with it," the druid said. "But even if they did, they would've lost it yet again, given the mess we're in now."

"Not looking good."

The door opened. The assistant stuck his head out and peered at them. Wolfmini planted a thought for him to approach them—a prodding, like he really ought to consider it. It would still have to be the assistant's choice.

The assistant closed the door quietly and hurried across the clearing toward the brothers. "You okay, cousins?"

Wolfmini nodded. "You know why we're here?"

"She doesn't want to talk to you."

"It's okay, cousin," the druid said. "But maybe you can tell us what we need to know."

The assistant's eye twitched. "I can try."

"I know it's been years," Least High said. "What do you recall of the Half-Forgotten Stone?"

The assistant's forehead knotted up. "Blue, wasn't it?"

"Remember where you saw it last?"

"No."

"A lot depends on it," Wolfmini said. "I can't emphasize enough how serious this is."

"I'm not sure."

Least High grabbed him by the shoulders and shook him. "We all know she had it. Try."

"Easy, brother."

Least High released him. The assistant cocked his head

and stared at the ground. He tucked his elbow into one palm and rested his chin in the other.

"Can you ask her?" Wolfmini asked.

The assistant blanched. "Maybe."

The druid moved his face in close and stared until the assistant's nostrils flared. "You have to do this. Come out before tonight and let us know what you learned."

The brothers followed the assistant down the ridge toward the cottage and settled behind a bush around the corner from the front door.

The evening light faded. Thundersquat saw the assistant slip out the back. The sorcerer king and the druid couldn't see his exit from where they hid. They told him to stay here. His eyes felt dull, like the vacant stare of a bison, pressed down by the heavy weight of decision, such as whether to move forward to the next sprig of grass. If he were a bison, he'd go forward. But he could stay where he was, too. For a while. Stay here, they told him.

Now that he thought about it, a bison steak would taste pretty good about now. Bolstrus nudged him from behind. Thundersquat snapped his attention back to the present. *Never said how long I had to stay.*

Thundersquat and the stallion followed the assistant into the woods. They almost walked up on him and ducked behind the trees. When he went forward again, they moved only when the assistant moved. The assistant stopped now and then to study the surroundings. They wound through the hilly terrain, across and along creek beds holding thin streams of running water.

The assistant dropped next to two flat boulders in a tiny

clearing. He spread his hands out and explored the ground. He lifted his head and slowly rotated it.

Thundersquat strolled over.

"What are you doing here?" the assistant asked.

Thundersquat gave it a minute to sink in. "Nothing. What about you?"

The assistant shrugged. "Trying to remember something. I don't know if I've been here before or not."

Thundersquat nodded slowly. "That's what my days are like."

"Things were starting to feel vaguely familiar," the assistant said. "Now I just feel lost."

Talk about familiar. He'd been lost and without a clue before. Many times. It never bothered him like it did now. A puzzle. He could solve it, if he could figure out what it was. "If I was planning to remember... something I was sure to forget... where would I put whatever it was?"

He stood on the boulders and looked out along the line that divided them. The line pointed to an old tree with roots jutting out of the ground. On the right side of the tree, at the base of the trunk, was a hollow opening. The barbarian peered in and felt around. *Nothing.*

He leaned against the tree with his back to the opening. Straight ahead two trees had grown together, split near the base of the trunk. Another tree beyond intersected the angle. Thundersquat spun around the joined trees and approached the tree beyond. He ran his hand along the side of the trunk and scanned the surrounding ground. He scraped the groundcover aside with his feet and uncovered a flat stone, about elbow to fingertip in diameter. The barbarian stooped and flipped it over. He pulled out his stone blade and stabbed it into the hard ground, digging, scraping.

He froze when he felt the chill on the back of his neck.

Someone else was out there. He flipped the blade around in his hand. Familiar smells put him at ease. He struggled to find the words. "Come out. Get a better look."

Four of them stepped out from the nearby trees: Blundren, the wolf, Smidgel, and the spotted lion. Bolstrus trotted out and joined them. Thundersquat resumed digging. The group peered over the barbarian's shoulder.

Thundersquat gingerly peeled away layers of crumbling dirt. He uncovered a patch of leather, which turned out to be an old pouch, the size of his hand. He brushed it off. It was heavy. Inside was a single dense rock. He flipped the pouch upside down. A stone dropped out, oblong in shape, slightly translucent, with dozens of facets chipped off the surface.

Blundren snatched it up. It began to glow, casting a blue light on her face. She looked up at Thundersquat, her eyes wide. The princess stared at Smidgel, then the lion. She tilted her head at the assistant. Her eyebrows knotted together; her mouth was slightly open. Blundren stared at the Stone once again before she fled, taking it with her.

Thundersquat took off after her. He wasn't sure what was wrong, but something wasn't right. The princess raced through the trees into the clearing. She stopped and stared again into the Stone.

As Thundersquat and the others reached the edge of the clearing, Blundren bolted past the sorcerer king and the Least High Druid to the front of the cottage and dashed inside.

"Didn't you tell her not to touch it?" Least High shouted.

"She's not supposed to be here!" Wolfmini yelled.

Chapter Forty-Two

OLD SECRETS

"YOU!" THE MYSTIC WITCH fired a bolt at the princess.

All Blundren's muscles seized, and the princess dropped to the floor. The Half-Forgotten Stone rolled into the middle of the room. A viselike grip grabbed the back of her neck and the base of her spine and yanked hard. She screamed. Unseen forces pulled her spine taut and strained, as similar pressures spread to her upper and lower jaw. Lights flashed as she felt a crushing pressure across the top of her skull, and her eyeballs swelled. Something clamped down on her fingers and stretched, but not at the joints—between them. The pain ceased and she lay panting, disoriented. *Since when could I taste air?*

As her mind started to clear, she beheld the Stone a few feet in front of her. When she reached for the Stone, her arms stopped short, barely reaching past her eye. Blundren looked at her hands. Her palms were shrunken, her fingers stretched and misshapen. Skinny talons jutted out from where her nails used to be. Brown oblong faces stared back at her from multiple facets of the blue Stone. *Why am I turning my head to see in front of me? And how can I see behind me at the same time?*

With her other eye, she took in the sepia and maroon stripes along her back. Her dress draped loosely over her elongated body, leading to a tail of iridescent blue.

She registered her transformation into a salamander and the peculiar aftertaste that came with it. Yet it was but a tiny blip among screaming sirens sounding off in her mind. In that flash of an encounter with the mystic witch, the Half-Forgotten Stone had uncovered a secret. If what she learned were an earthquake, it would have leveled a major city. It would have carved gaping fissures, hissing with sinister fumes from the netherworld. The far-flung devastation would have leached the survivors of everything but hopeless resignation.

According to the Stone, the mystic witch was her mother.

The wolf burst through the door and leaped to the fallen salamander princess. He stood over her, snarling, as Wolfmini and Least High rushed in.

The mystic witch drew her hand back. Blundren rolled into the wolf's legs and darted to the wall. She bounced off a split second before a blast tore a hole in the wall and zigged toward the open door.

Wolfmini and the Least High Druid leaped over her and blocked the mystic witch. Thundersquat scooped up Blundren and slung her over his shoulder before he leaped off the cottage porch, followed by the wolf. When the barbarian hit the ground, it knocked the wind out of her.

They raced through the clearing. Blundren bounced hard as the barbarian charged down the steps to the creek. Light exploded behind them. He eased her off his shoulder and set her down on the grassy streambed.

Blundren scrambled into the water, her only thought to

get as far away as possible. Her tail swiveled back and forth, propelling her through the shallow creek. The wolf splashed alongside. Thundersquat raced along the bank and dove in, his hands clamping down on what used to pass as shoulders. She tried to push forward, but the barbarian's weight pressed her down. She rolled and broke his grip, but he wrapped his arms around her and held firm. She wriggled furiously as he carried her out of the water and pinned her to the ground.

Blundren stopped struggling, but her heart continued to race. Her gaze flitted back and forth from the wolf to the newly arriving troll and the spotted lion. The barbarian holding her was warm. He wasn't hurting her, but her predominant urge was to escape. To anywhere. Her head was spinning. Splashes of color with tails like comets ricocheted inside her skull. Images collided: the mystic witch, her expression enraged; fragments she'd picked up through the Stone, of the barbarian crushed beneath the abysmal.

Behind them the flashes and bangs in the cottage ended in a few fizzles. Shortly thereafter Wolfmini and the Least High Druid hurried down the steps and caught up to them by the stream.

"What happened?" Smidgel asked.

Least High's eyes lit up with exhilaration. "We were kicking her butt. She quit."

"She got a migraine," Wolfmini said. "It used to happen a lot whenever things didn't go her way."

Wolfmini stood staring at his daughter, head slightly tilted, eyes narrowed.

The druid looked over Wolfmini's shoulder. "Not a problem, brother," he reassured the sorcerer king.

Least High ambled over to the creek, filled his hands, and returned. To Thundersquat, he said, "Hold her tight. She's terrified."

The barbarian cradled her firmly in his arms, and the salamander princess couldn't budge. Her heart pounded. The druid
held his cupped hands over her, flung his fingers open, and let
the water drop. Eyes to the sky, he chanted mysterious nonsense
syllables. He placed one hand behind her head and let the other
hand hover over her belly. Tingling vibrations radiated through
her entire body as she transformed back into human form.

The barbarian set Blundren on her feet and steadied her
with warm hands on her waist and shoulder. His face was
close, his voice gentle. "Brown stripes are fading."

She touched her face. The princess slipped through the
barbarian's hands and slumped to the ground. She felt where
her tail used to be. "Weird. That was so real."

Blundren's glance darted toward a passing dragonfly. She
smacked her lips. The wolf sat next to her, and a couple of
times they jerked their heads to the side at the same time.
Her father studied her closely. She drew back. "What?"

"Nothing," her father said. "Do you feel anything out of
the ordinary?"

"Why do you ask?" She stretched her left arm and examined it.

He shook his head. "Just worried. I'm glad my brother
knew what to do."

"To know what he does and how to control it, that's..."
Blundren looked around. "Speaking of which..."

The druid was gone.

"He was right here," Smidgel said. "Why would he leave
without saying anything?"

"Where's the Stone?" Blundren asked.

"He grabbed it off the floor just before we left," Wolfmini
said.

No one spoke. The troll scrambled up the steps, and

Thundersquat trotted to the creek. The spotted lion picked up the druid's scent trailing off into the woods.

"Back at the palace, he saw what he could've had," Blundren said. "Power...riches...a beautiful wife..."

"Let's not jump to conclusions," Wolfmini said.

"What harm would it do to just let him keep the Stone?" the troll asked.

"No one person should have that kind of power," Blundren said. "Incredible and devastating, all at once."

"Worse than that," Wolfmini said, "those who hold the Stone often regret it. It can do irreparable damage."

"What kind of damage, Father?" Her tone was partly accusing, with a touch of fear.

Wolfmini frowned. "You know, don't you?"

Warmth filled her eyes, and soon a tear rolled down her cheek. "Yes."

"It was my biggest mistake. I never dreamed anything would go wrong."

"What were you thinking, Father?"

"Nothing. I simply gave it to her as a gift. I didn't know it would do that to her."

"Gave what to who?" Smidgel asked.

Blundren looked at her father. Her lower lip trembled. "The Half-Forgotten Stone. He gave it to my...to her. The mystic witch."

Wolfmini placed a hand on his daughter's shoulder. "The mystic witch—Caprice—is my beloved wife. And her mother."

They could've heard a spider tiptoe on sand.

"Futhark the Meddler warned me, but I didn't listen." The sorcerer king placed his hands behind his back and paced back and forth. "The Stone changed her. In time she no longer knew who she was. She became paranoid. Eventually she tried to kill me and her own daughter."

Blundren's tears flowed freely now. To hear it out loud…

"That Stone is dangerous," Smidgel said.

"It needs to be put in a safe place where no one can find it," Wolfmini said.

"We should be able to track him," Smidgel said, looking up at the barbarian.

Blundren said, "My uncle's not invisible. He caught us not paying attention."

Smidgel approached the sorcerer king. "Your Eminence… I mean no disrespect in saying this…the Least High Druid is very powerful. Are you able to—?"

"Therein lies the problem," Wolfmini said. "Twelve, fifteen years ago, different story. Now…he's at least as powerful as I am, likely more so. He's definitely faster. And now he has the Stone."

"He could be safeguarding it," Smidgel said. "Like you're talking about doing."

"If that's true, there'll be no danger in following him. But it would be wise to be cautious. Be ready for anything."

"We can't possibly plan for everything," the troll said.

"Agreed."

Blundren's heart quickened. "Don't go. Never mind what I said earlier. Let him have it, if he wants it that bad."

"What will it do to him?" the troll asked.

"His choice," Blundren said.

"Cruel justice," Wolfmini said. "But he's not the only one who'd get hurt. We need to end this."

"We?" Blundren felt again for a tail. "I can't control any of this."

The sorcerer king's voice was gentle. "We have no other viable choice."

"I'm lost. I know I made certain things happen. I felt it. But I don't know enough. I can't tell when it's real or when I'm just fooling myself."

"Why should that stop you?" Thundersquat asked.

She looked at him in surprise. She'd gotten used to discounting him in conversations. "Are you keeping up with us?"

He paused a little longer than necessary. "Catching a lot of it."

"What do you think I should do?"

He tilted his head and frowned, like he was straining to decipher ancient symbols. With the delay, she wasn't sure he was going to reply.

"You agree with my father?"

Thundersquat shrugged. He shook his head. He looked lost.

"Do you think we should try to get the Stone back?"

The barbarian nodded slowly. "Need to put it somewhere safe."

"Since you found the Stone once," Wolfmini said, "you're under no obligation to retrieve it now. We can take care of it without you."

Thundersquat tossed his head toward the princess. "Doesn't know what she's doing."

"I can handle not knowing what I'm doing a lot better than you ever could. Just go."

The barbarian gave a scarcely noticeable nod and walked away, toward Mudcat where the druid's trail led into the woods.

"That's not what I meant."

Bolstrus trotted in and joined the barbarian.

Wolfmini followed Thundersquat. "Let's go, daughter. We need you."

She watched her father go. The red-haired troll scampered past him. They disappeared into the woods. Blundren recalled the blending at the palace. Anything they could do at this point would probably be futile. Her uncle will never give up the Stone. She had felt its pull. Her choice was clear: sit here and wait to see if it all ended, or spend what little time was left at the center of it. Where hope and trust fell short, she had plenty of curiosity. She strode after them until she caught up with her father.

Thundersquat and the stallion walked in front of them, just ahead of Smidgel and the spotted lion. The wolf was not in sight, presumably in the lead. She wasn't sure how she knew, but she knew.

"Think we'll find him?" asked the troll.

After a pause, the barbarian said, "Maybe."

"What exactly would you want me to do?" Smidgel asked.

Another pause. "Think of something when we get there."

"You do that on purpose, don't you?" the troll said.

The barbarian shrugged.

The spotted lion huffed.

"I should've learned what by now?" Smidgel asked Mudcat.

The lion grumbled.

"You don't know what they know or don't know," the troll said. "Show a little faith."

Blundren called ahead, "Whatever you do, don't anyone touch that Stone."

Chapter Forty-Three

THE CHASE

BLUNDREN SLOWED. Suddenly the druid's scent was fresh and strong. The princess cocked her head and maneuvered her ears in all directions. She zeroed in on the Least High Druid, standing off to the left in the darkness. Blue light from the Stone lit half his face.

"What is it?" Smidgel asked.

"He's over there," she said.

"Where?" her father asked.

"Over there, to the left, by that tree."

Wolfmini raised his hands in a defense-ready position and scanned the area. "I can't detect him."

"He's…not here, but I can see him."

"What's he doing?" the troll asked.

"He's sad. It's going to be okay." She watched her uncle's brows contract; his mouth hardened. "Why is he… I don't… He hates me."

Her upper lip curled. She felt a growl emerge from deep in her throat.

Wolfmini peered into her eyes. She shrieked. Not far

ahead, a wild animal yelped at the same time. Her body stiffened.

"What did he do to you?"

Blundren strained to move, but could not. She took note of her father's concern. Thundersquat and Smidgel crowded in over Wolfmini's shoulder. She tried to speak, but only produced a muffled gurgle.

When the blue light went out, the Least High Druid slipped into the forest. The mostly white wolf, encased in rock, strained to follow. His face and shoulders emerged momentarily and snapped back. After a few seconds' rest, he threw his weight onto his right shoulder and yanked his left forepaw free. He pivoted and tugged until he freed the right. The wolf crouched low and drew back. He stretched the elastic essence that anchored him to the stone. Gathering his strength, he hurled himself forward and tore loose along his left rib cage. With another lunge he tumbled free. He rolled and bounced softly against a tree. His shoulder slipped through the outer layers of the tree before he fell away.

The wolf stood, yet he felt like he was hovering. He sniffed the hard rock sculpture of himself. He curled around and spun as he examined his body. The ground cover intruded through his feet. He was translucent. Despite the unsettling discovery, he bounded after the druid. His paws sank below the surface before propelling him up. The wolf floated down, like the mist that hangs over ponds in the morning. After a few awkward strides he adjusted better to the weightlessness and picked up speed, skimming across the surface.

Blundren rocked back and forth, then tumbled forward and rolled. She rubbed her shoulder and stared at her feet. "Strange. I felt so heavy before. Now it's like I'm floating."

She leaped up and eased into a trot, trying to conceal how

unsteady and lightheaded she felt. The red-haired troll hovered alongside, like he was ready to catch her. "I'm fine."

They spread out and searched the woods ahead. The group came upon the statue of the wolf. Smidgel knelt in front and studied the face. He placed a hand on the top of the head. The face crumbled, and the troll flinched. When he pushed against the stone wolf's back, the entire statue caved in, sending up a cloud of dust. Smidgel coughed and backed away.

"What do you think happened, Father?"

"I believe it's a warning."

"It could be an illusion, to scare us," she said.

The red-haired troll coughed again. "It's working."

The spotted lion stopped.

"The druid's nearby," the red-haired troll whispered.

Thundersquat plucked a praying mantis from a branch and placed it gently on the top of his hand.

Smidgel tugged at the barbarian's vest. "Did you hear what I said?"

"I don't think his mind is fully back," Wolfmini said.

"I agree," Blundren said. "What do we do?"

"I'm sure my brother's watching us now, through the Stone. We can't hide from him." Her father looked grim. "Time for us, daughter. Be ready for anything."

Wolfmini leaned toward the troll and the lion. "When we find him, surround him. Keep moving—don't cluster. Make it harder for him to keep track of all of us."

The sorcerer king moved quietly into the bushes on the right. At intervals, the lion, the troll, Bolstrus, and Blundren followed the path of her father. She glanced back. Thundersquat slowly rocked his hand and studied the praying mantis.

They discovered the Least High Druid in a clearing. The Stone rested on a log, casting a blue light onto his face. He touched the top of it with one forefinger.

They inched closer.

"Give it up!" Wolfmini shouted. "We have to stow it in hallowed ground."

"No! There's got to be another way!" the druid cried.

"You know there's not!"

"You never could see the possibilities. I can do this."

"You live in a fantasy world," Wolfmini said. "You're blind! If you weren't so arrogant, you'd see it. And the rest of us will have to pay for your mistakes."

"Who else should be in charge of the Stone? You? How did that work the last time?"

"He's beyond reach. We have no choice now." Wolfmini tapped the troll on the head. "Run. Change speeds. Random patterns. Never together."

The five of them—minus the barbarian, who wandered aimlessly—ran in circles around the clearing, adding abrupt starts and stops when they were concealed by trees and undergrowth. The druid's head wavered back and forth. The next time Blundren caught a glimpse of the clearing, the druid was gone. She froze, listened, took another step, and listened again.

When the red-haired troll caught up with her, they found her father staring at a statue of the spotted lion.

"Probably another illusion to scare us, don't you think?" The troll held his hand over the statue's back. "It's so lifelike. You have to admire the druid's craft."

Smidgel hesitated, then lay his hand on the head of the lion. It failed to crumble. "This one's different."

Blundren touched the lion's back. Cold rock.

"Mudcat!" The troll swiveled his head and scanned the darkness. "Mudcat!"

The troll's legs gave way. As he dropped to his knees, his breath came in staccato gasps.

Wolfmini slapped his upper back. The troll collapsed. He lifted his face out of the dirt and pulled up into a crouch, still struggling to breathe. His face was pale.

"For now, put it behind you," Wolfmini said to the troll. "We need you. More than ever."

The troll thumped a fist lightly against his thigh. His trembling hands scraped through his beard. He swallowed. He looked down for a long moment.

Wolfmini offered a hand. Smidgel took it. The sorcerer king helped him up, and his breaths evened out.

Thundersquat ambled up to them, still fixated on the praying mantis.

Chapter Forty-Four

WIZARD'S DUEL

A LIGHT GLOWED up ahead. Blundren exchanged glances with her father. Bolstrus trotted past her father, around the perimeter. Wolfmini nodded to Smidgel. The red-haired troll took a deep breath and jogged after the stallion. The sorcerer king paused for a few seconds and followed the troll.

The Least High Druid backed up slowly in the middle of a clearing, forefinger held to the Stone like before. His head wavered slightly as he stared into it. He stumbled slightly on a broken limb, but never broke his concentration.

Blundren went left. She felt an odd sensation, as if someone had brushed the back of her eyeballs with a feather. She glanced behind and saw her father step from a curtain of fog. His hair was longer, a bit straggly, sticking out below a leather head covering that sprouted antlers instead of twisted horns. He was dressed in a combination of animal skins and cheap wool, like the rural peasants she saw in the market. "How did you get over there? Why'd you change clothes?"

"What about you?" he asked.

A twig snapped deeper in the woods, and a second figure emerged from the fog. Blundren stood face-to-face with her mirror image, likewise dressed in rural clothing.

"The blending," the two said, taking each other in.

"We spotted the Pinnacle Sage in the clearing up ahead," the rural princess said.

"He's not the Pinnacle Sage. He's the Least High Druid."

"No matter. He's got the Stone. We need to get it from him."

"He's powerful," Blundren said. "How well do you know the old ways?"

"I can do anything he can do. The Pinnacle Sage raised me, taught me everything. Unless he held something back— you can't trust him."

"The Least High Druid is full of surprises. I don't know what to think any more."

"Secrets come out." The alternate Blundren nodded toward the rural Wolfmini. "I found my real father, in spite of the Pinnacle Sage's lies."

"Who knows what else they're hiding?" Blundren asked.

"If we had the Stone, we'd find out," her duplicate self said.

"We need to get it away from him, for sure. But I don't want to get close to that Stone again. Once you've touched it, it pulls you to it, like a desperate hunger that can never be filled."

"We'll help you with the druid. Then, if our worlds are still blended, you join us in the fight against the Pinnacle Sage."

"Agreed. My father, Wolfmini, is the sorcerer king. He's on the other side of the clearing."

The red-haired troll came upon them and stopped. His wide-open gaze passed from one face to another.

"The outlaw," the rebel princess said. "You've come out of hiding to join us?"

"I'm not… Yes." Smidgel's expression remained startled.

"I know it's confusing," Blundren said to the troll. "They're with us now. Tell my father."

Smidgel nodded and resumed his jog around the perimeter.

The reinforcements infused Blundren with confidence. She stepped to the edge of the clearing, and when her father approached from the other side, she felt the now-familiar brush against the back of her eyeballs. She glanced to her left. The rebel doppelgangers flickered and disappeared. In their place stood the Pinnacle Sage.

Blundren wheeled to face him. Her heart raced.

He held his hands up. "I'm not your enemy, miss. I raised you, or one like you, as my daughter."

"But she wasn't your daughter, was she?"

The Pinnacle Sage's face tightened. "Nevertheless, we need to focus on the druid there. The other two couldn't give you the help you need. But I understand him. I know how he thinks. Least High got a taste of what he could've had. Unless he willingly gives up the Stone and stows it properly, the Braid of Time will continue to unravel."

"He won't give it up."

"No. We have to take it from him."

From the corner of her eye, she watched her father step into the clearing. "We have to go," she said with a little desperation.

Everything went dark.

Blundren was flung into the night, twirling, tumbling in midair. Something tugged at her spine, her limbs, her fingers, stretching them. She screeched. She heard yelps and epithets from the men around her. She was deposited on her feet. The pain subsided. She felt behind her. No tail. Much less pain than when she'd been transformed into a salamander. More in her arms and legs, less in her face. She crouched, ready for anything.

The light gradually returned. Two sorcerer kings stared at her from the other side of the clearing, wearing helmets with twisted horns. A third Wolfmini entered to her left. On the ground in front of each of them was a Half-Forgotten Stone. One lay before her as well. She snatched the Stone, and it started to glow. The other three did the same.

Something was off. This Stone had no power, not like it felt the last time. The glow was an illusion. Also disturbing was the fact that her hands appeared rough and weather-beaten. She realized she was dressed in the same robe as her father. The princess raised her hand to her cheek and ran her fingers through the beard there, feeling the tingle in her cheek. She gave the beard a tug. Her fingers wandered up to the helmet that pressed down on her skull.

The sorcerer king in the center raised the Stone high. "This Stone is fake. Which one of you is my real father?"

"What are you talking about?" Blundren asked. She heard her father's voice tumble from her throat.

"Father, he's Least High!" the center sorcerer king yelled. He shot his hand forward and zapped a ball of light at her.

Blundren dove to the right and rolled. She smelled something burning. Blundren huddled among the gnarled roots of a tree. A second ray whizzed past, then a third. She jerked with each explosion.

Blundren sat, paralyzed. The events of the past couple of months came rushing back. Tears welled up. The one who fired at her had to be Least High trying to kill her. Unless it's a duplicate of herself from a blended world, thinking that she was the druid. Another burst singed her sleeve. Something snapped inside.

"Enough!" The princess spun to the right and whipped her left hand forward. A blaze of light fired at the fake sorcerer king but fell short. She ducked behind the tree. The palm of her hand tickled and burned. She glanced at it and then peeked at the other sorcerer kings, their stones tucked under their arms and their hands poised in front. They looked back and forth between her and the one who had fired at her.

"Father!" She dodged a ray and dove to the right. "Do something!"

"Don't listen to him, Father," the other sorcerer king shouted. "He's trying to confuse you."

She fired one back, high and right.

A bright flash blinded her. Blundren was snatched into the air again, twisting and spinning and dropped hard. She caught her balance. No pain this time. Instead, she'd felt a warm tingling ripple through her entire body.

As the light faded, blurred silhouettes coalesced into three princesses standing next to each other on the other side of the clearing. They were dressed like she was, at least like she had been earlier. She glanced at her hands, relieved to see they were back to normal. She felt her cheek. It was smooth again.

Thundersquat wandered through the clearing, rolling his hand, staring at the clinging mantis. It gave Blundren time to think.

"Who are you?" one of the princesses asked the other.

"Only one of us can be her," one said.

"Neither of you is me," said another.

Blundren tossed her Stone to the ground. One of the

others backed away and did likewise. He had to be her father or the Pinnacle Sage. They looked at the two remaining princesses. One of them nodded and let the Stone drop.

The one who still held the Stone had to be the Least High Druid. Blundren shot a ray of light at him, as did the other alternative princesses. The fake-princess druid jumped to the side and fired back at all three of them.

Another bright flash left her sightless. She was jerked into the air in a backwards somersault. Forces wrenched her insides as she twisted. Her whole body was wracked with pain, almost as severe as the salamander experience. She felt her limbs stretch once again. She rolled out of a tumble and felt her foot graze the ground. She slammed the other foot down and her knee gave way. She staggered forward but stayed on her feet.

As her vision recovered, dancing lights dimmed to reveal three druids standing across from her in the clearing. They looked at her and at each other. Blundren glanced down at her loincloth and wrapped her arms around her chest to cover herself. Warmth rushed to her cheeks, offset by the cool breeze across the top of her bald pate.

Each druid stared into a glowing blue Stone.

"This Stone is fake," one of the druids said. "I've felt its power before."

"Mine has no power either," Blundren said.

"Nor has mine," said the druid on her right.

"How did I get over here?" the druid on the left asked. "I was over there."

"Which one of you is my father?" Blundren asked.

"I am," two druids claimed.

The one who didn't answer had to be the Pinnacle Sage. One of the other two is her father. The other must be lying: the druid. But which one?

The ghost of the mostly white wolf bounded into the clearing, trailing mist. Blundren was abruptly bombarded with scents. And she knew. She picked out her uncle and her father. A whiff from the other smelled like her uncle, but with a hint of cologne: the Pinnacle Sage. The wolf crouched and pointed at the true Least High Druid.

Thundersquat ambled by. The druid swung behind him and shot a bolt at the wolf. It passed right through. The druid was startled. He stared into the Stone before he fired a shot at Blundren.

As the fireball whizzed past her head, Blundren pivoted. The Pinnacle Sage and her father shot bolts at her uncle. Least High deflected the bursts with his free hand. Lights sparked and fizzled a meter in front of him. The three of them fired at him again. His shield held.

Least High used the barbarian for cover. Thundersquat raised his hand and rolled it over. The mantis repositioned itself. The druid's eyes darted back and forth between the Stone and his three adversaries.

Bolstrus charged out of the woods up to the druid and reared. Least High drew back. Adroitly, the barbarian snatched the Stone, flipped a cloth over it, and dropped it into a pouch.

The druid dropped to his knees and grabbed his head. Thundersquat stuffed the pouch inside his vest.

Blundren and her father reverted to their original forms as they dashed over to the druid. Smidgel jogged into the clearing and stooped over, hands on his knees, chest heaving. The wolf glided past him into the forest. The Pinnacle Sage joined them and placed an arm around Blundren. She stiffened, and he removed his arm. Thundersquat returned the mantis to a tree and sauntered back to the group surrounding the druid.

The Least High Druid looked up at the barbarian, disoriented. "I knew you were there; I could feel you. But the Stone never warned me what you were up to."

"Saw you stumble back there. Can't see what you're not looking for."

"Something snapped in my head when you grabbed it from me."

"That's the point when my head cleared."

The Least High Druid looked at the crowd that surrounded him. "Forgive me."

"Why did you run off with the Stone?" Wolfmini asked.

"To keep it safe. But it grabbed me."

"What do you mean, it grabbed you?" the Pinnacle Sage asked.

"It was like it sent tendrils inside my skull and pulled me away." The Least High Druid squinted. "Very strange. I watched what I was doing, but from a distance. Like my arms were tied."

"I understand," Blundren said.

The Least High Druid pressed his hands into his head. "I only touched it for a moment. But I wanted it, more than anything I wanted in my entire life."

Blundren nodded. If the mystic witch hadn't blasted it out of her hand, she might not have given it up, either.

"What do we do now?" Smidgel asked.

The Pinnacle Sage patted the barbarian on the shoulder. "You did well. We need to keep the Stone safe. Give it to me, I'll take care of it."

"No, don't," Blundren said. "Something doesn't feel right."

Least High jumped up. "He'll take it to the other world. He'll use it for his own purposes. Our world will still be in danger."

The Pinnacle Sage inserted himself between the druid

and the barbarian. "Don't let him twist your thinking. Least High wants access to the Stone. I can make sure that never happens."

Wolfmini said, "Neither of you should have it. My brother's right about our world being in danger if you take it."

"Your history with the Stone is tainted as well," said the Pinnacle Sage.

The Pinnacle Sage rested a hand on Thundersquat's shoulder and held his other hand out.

"Not giving it to anybody," the barbarian said.

"That's most unfortunate." The Pinnacle Sage strolled over to Blundren. "Help him to change his mind."

"Why would I want to do that?"

"Consider this."

A flash of smoke engulfed the two of them. As it cleared, Blundren felt a hand wrapped around her throat, points digging into her neck. Sharp talons hovered in front of her face.

"I don't think my husband should have the Stone, either," purred the mystic witch, Caprice, from the other world. "Besides, he's somewhat incapacitated at the moment."

Caprice jerked the princess close, using her as a shield.

"Not giving you the Stone," Thundersquat said.

Blundren's heart pounded. "Don't. If she takes the Stone into the other world, I'll die anyway, with all the rest of you. You can't ever give it to her. No matter what."

Caprice tightened her grip. "Noble, my dear. Don't you know I could obliterate the lot of you now with a snap of my fingers? Besides, you don't really know for sure that this world will end. It might just be different. You'd have to adapt."

"To think you could've been my mother, in the other world," Blundren growled.

"Oh, please," the mystic witch said. "None of you ever cared one iota for me—not you or the sissified buffoon I married. He was just a tool for me to get the Stone, which the fool lost. But now I can take yours instead. I deserve to have it."

Blundren felt queasy; she detected a vortex of energy spiraling out from the mystic witch's core. As the force swirled around each of the others, Blundren could sense it—almost see it—though it was invisible. Tiny disturbances sparked around the Least High Druid and, to a lesser extent, her father. She recoiled as she realized that whatever had to be done must invoke the old ways. She was the nearest to the witch. In direct contact. The others would not risk hurting her. *It has to be me. It has to be now.*

Blundren had never been blessed with the notion that she knew more than she did. She'd admitted to herself that she'd brought on that earthquake. Everybody saw it. But she'd done it on impulse, without forethought or plan. When she smashed the druid's amulet into the ground, it could just as easily have formed a tiny puddle of honey or sprouted butterflies. She could not afford any illusions about what she had to do now.

Even if she'd possessed the knowledge and skill—a dubious presumption—Blundren didn't know if she could bring herself to do what must be done. She recalled her horror at Dekatria's callousness when the priestess incinerated her own father and, later, the magistrate. Blundren reexperienced the fear and revulsion she'd felt when she thought she'd started the fires herself, by accident. Two choices became clear: either live with what she might do, or die, along with everyone she loved, knowing that she hadn't tried.

This is it, then. Incinerate her. Or failing that, splash her with honey. And/or butterflies. Forget that I wasn't very good at lighting candles. That I failed to ignite the door in Snartglobber's castle. Why not run through all the reasons I might fail, here at the biggest moment of my life?

She pictured herself on the edge of a precipice. Her fear seethed like a bubbling cauldron. The warmth rose in her chest and radiated down her arms. She braced herself for the agonizing screams to follow. *Now or never.*

A talon pierced the skin on her neck, and a cold blast cascaded through her body. Her head felt like she'd eaten too much snow too fast, only ten times worse. Paralyzing pain wracked her from head to toe.

"Amateur," Caprice whispered. "Do you think I can't feel what you're trying to do?"

Thundersquat reached inside his vest. He leaned toward Wolfmini and Least High. "Is there a way to cross over into the other world?"

"I know a way," Least High said.

"We're out of time," Wolfmini said. "We'd never find her soon enough."

"You might find me sooner than you'd like," Caprice scoffed.

Thundersquat pulled out the pouch. "She could kill us all and take the Stone anyway. At least this way we'd have a chance."

"No!" Blundren cried. The cold began to subside.

The barbarian held the pouch out toward the mystic witch. "Don't stop to rest. We'll be right behind you."

She removed her claws from Blundren's throat and seized the pouch. The mystic witch flashed a triumphant smile. "See you on the other side. If you dare."

She shoved the princess aside, leaped toward an opening in the underbrush, and vanished. Wolfmini and Least High fired bolts that hissed through empty space. Tiny wisps lingered and faded away.

"How do we get across?" Blundren asked, jumping to her feet.

"Grab hands," the druid said, "while the link's still fresh. Once she stashes that Stone, we'll never get through."

"Do you trust him, Father?"

"No." Wolfmini seized his brother's hand. "But he knows more than I do. We have no other choice."

Blundren clutched her father's free hand and held an outstretched hand toward the barbarian.

"No one's going anywhere," Thundersquat said.

"We're going to die otherwise!" Blundren yelled. "How can you back out now?"

The barbarian thrust a hand inside his vest and pulled out a leather packet folded around an object the size of the Stone. He held it up. "Gonna be surprised when she opens that pouch."

Chapter Forty-Five

SAFELY BURIED

BLUNDREN THREW her arms around the barbarian and squeezed tight. His shoulders and arms stiffened.

She withdrew and stowed her hands behind her back. "Your brain's not half bad, when it's working."

"Ought to talk to UncleCousin Sumac."

"His isn't the only opinion that counts." She searched his face.

He held her gaze.

His eyes gave the impression that he had a lot to say, but his mouth was grim. It felt like the end of something, not the beginning. "You're leaving. You're going off to hide the Stone, aren't you?"

"Need to finish this job. After that, well…"

"You won't be coming back."

"No need to protect the village anymore. Got to find my father. Waited my whole life."

"I need to tell you something." Blundren took his hand in both of hers. "When I held the Stone, I saw what you saw during the battle."

"The Commander of the Golden Horde." His eyes were unfocused. "Thought maybe I saw him before."

"From what I received from the Stone, he looked like your father."

The barbarian tilted his head. "Long time ago. Hard to tell."

"I saw you as a boy when you found out he was gone. What an awful day, I'm sorry."

His face tightened, and he took refuge behind a distant veil that allowed him to appear fully present, yet completely disconnected.

Are men born being able to do that, she asked herself? She thought of how she felt all those years when her father was there, yet not there. Thundersquat's father had been taken away. The two of them never had a chance. "What if we were to take the Stone to the Badlands? Show me where he disappeared."

"You want to use this Stone to find my father?" Thundersquat asked.

"It would work. The power I felt—"

"No!" Wolfmini grabbed the barbarian by the shoulders and pulled him halfway around. "You know what the Stone can do! You can't ask her to do that. It would destroy her."

"Father, you don't know what he's been through."

Thundersquat gripped the sorcerer king's wrists and lifted his hands away.

"Please, I can't lose her again," Wolfmini said.

Thundersquat exchanged a long look with Smidgel. "Don't have to ask what you'd tell me."

He looked back at the princess. "Might find my father someday, might not. But not this way. Need to bury this Stone somewhere safe."

Maybe he should try the same place he hid his emotions.

Nobody would ever find it. Her face also shifted to neutral, and the irony didn't escape her notice. "Go now, then, before the mystic witch discovers the switch."

"She's right," Least High said. "Where to?"

"No," Wolfmini said. "You're not going to know where it is."

"What if the mystic witch shows up? Don't you think he'll need me then?"

"We already saw what the Stone does to you," Blundren said.

"That was before. I'd never hurt anyone."

"What about Mudcat?" Smidgel asked.

"The lion? Came out of nowhere." Least High shrugged. "I reacted."

"Can you reverse what you did?" the troll asked.

The druid lowered his head. "That spell's irreversible. It's unfortunate."

Smidgel quivered. He spun around and hurried to a tree at the edge of the clearing. He leaned against it with a stiff arm.

"You don't know this," the druid said, "but he had a powerful craving for meat. I saw it in the Stone. He almost ate you. Many times."

The druid walked behind the troll and placed a hand on his shoulder. "It was more than he could bear. He's probably better off. At least you have the statue, to remember him."

"Enough," Thundersquat said. "Leave him alone."

Wolfmini's eyes were open wide, his nostrils slightly flared. "Brother, could you ever have imagined you'd do what you did?"

"It wasn't me, younger brother," Least High said. "The Stone..."

Wolfmini's voice was cold, devoid of emotion. He looked at the druid like he was a stranger. "Time for you to go away. Anywhere—it doesn't matter. I never want to see you again."

"But all those years… I tried to find you. I watched over your daughter."

"And tonight, with the Stone, you attacked her. You tried to kill us." Wolfmini shook his head. "You're not the same. I feel it. I can't trust you. Ever."

"All those years I searched for you. I never lost hope. You're going to throw that away?"

The sorcerer king replied, "You threw it away the instant you grabbed the Stone and ran off with it. *You* set all this in motion."

"This was my chance!" the druid yelled. "For once, I had the power!"

The others grew quiet.

"I was going to be the one."

Blundren slid next to her father. "My father's right. You're not the same. What could have been is not possible now."

The Least High Druid sneered at her. "You touched the Stone, too."

"I never tried to hurt anyone."

Thundersquat clamped down on the druid's biceps. "Come with me."

Least High glanced up at the barbarian and smiled. "At least someone's listening to reason."

They walked together back to the center of the clearing. Thundersquat turned him loose with a shove. "Now go."

Least High's smile vanished. His eyes narrowed. "I swore I'd never let anyone stand in my way again."

"Do what's right and nobody'll have to."

"Our paths will cross again. This isn't over."

Blundren watched the druid slip into the forest. She turned at the sound of the barbarian walking over to the troll, who leaned against the tree and stared at the ground.

Thundersquat stood behind him, struggling to find words. "Mudcat was...Friend like that doesn't come around too often."

The red-haired troll nodded.

"Couldn't have done this without you," Thundersquat said.

Smidgel swallowed and turned toward the barbarian. His voice was thin. "If you ever need me, just ask. But please, not anytime soon."

"No more adventures for a while." Thundersquat pulled Smidgel away from the tree and lifted him in a tight bear hug. When he put the troll down, he patted him on the shoulders. "Gotta go."

"Well," the troll said. "Well. I'll say good-bye, then."

That was almost emotional, Blundren thought.

The silver stallion trotted into the clearing, and Thundersquat swung up onto his back. After a few strides forward, they stopped. The stallion turned to the side, and Thundersquat looked at Blundren. Her heart picked up a beat. The barbarian nodded, and then Bolstrus galloped away.

He nodded. I got a nod. Her throat constricted. She mentally ticked off all the times he'd showed up when she needed him. She'd tried to reciprocate. But in the end, he didn't owe her anything. And he should not matter to her, at least not in any personal way. That would make no sense whatsoever. *So why do I feel so empty?*

She sought her father and discovered he was watching her. She gave him a half smile. "Let's go home, Father."

Maybe they can light a stupid candle later.

When Thundersquat reached the edge of the Badlands, the past caught up with him. The haze that flickered on the horizon became pieces of bodies, a writhing heap in puddles of blood. The farther he rode into the Badlands, the stronger the stench. He knew it wasn't real. At night he awoke soaked in sweat, half buried among the bodies, unable to move or dig himself out. Ten times a day cold shivers persuaded him to turn around and run, to forget this foolish mission. Nobody would ever know what he did with the Stone. He could go anywhere. But he'd made up his mind.

He pushed on toward the granite towers. A raptor circled above. Thundersquat had noticed the bird tailing him three days ago. The barbarian stopped at a waist-high crack at the base of the granite structure. He glanced again at the bird, dismounted, and squeezed through the entrance.

Back at the Onyx Palace, the sorcerer king gazed into the concave depression in the pedestal. He saw the crack in the granite tower widen into a small cave. Wolfmini spotted the raptor, as it swooped past the entrance to the cave. Whoever was using the bird as a scout would not be able to follow the barbarian inside.

The cave narrowed into a tunnel that opened on the left. The image through the pedestal was dark, hard to distinguish. Thundersquat waded into a shallow pool. He reached into his vest, removed the pouch, and dumped the heavy object into the pool. He retrieved a handful of loose rocks and let them spill over the object until it was covered. Thundersquat exited the cave.

An idea popped into Wolfmini's head, and he smiled. *Not exactly ethical. But what harm would a little invitation do, in the long run? He'd still have to choose.*

Chapter Forty-Six

CONCLUSION

SMIDGEL RAKED around the old tree. He missed a few leaves; he left them there and moved on. He gazed at the worn patch in the shade where the spotted lion used to nap. The troll sighed and leaned on the rake. He let it drop and left it with the teeth facing up.

The red-haired troll trudged over to the magic fountain. He studied the mirrored surface, where the nearly bare branches pierced the gray afternoon sky. Two stubborn leaves fluttered in the last gasp of a dying breeze and lost their grip. They drifted down to merge with their reflections. The dried leaves lay still and lifeless. The heavy mugginess weighed on what was left of his spirit. "Mudcat, you'd have something to say about Thundersquat's judgment. And maybe mine."

The troll wrapped a rag around his hand. He reached into his pocket and pulled out a package. With care, he peeled back the edges of the leather wrap. Blue light lit up his face as the Half-Forgotten Stone came to life. Smidgel glanced at the empty spot in the shade. "When Thundersquat hugged me, he slipped it into my pocket."

The troll tossed the Half-Forgotten Stone into the magic fountain. "I had no idea he had that much trust in me."

The blue light glowed for several minutes and then faded. The ripples disappeared, and the surface was smooth again. He ambled over to the shady spot and stretched out on the ground. He sighed. "They say the Stone was hidden here once before. I should remember something like that."

Thundersquat exited the cavern and draped an arm over the stallion's neck. At last, the faux mission was over. He could kiss the Badlands good-bye forever and leave no stone unturned in the search for his father. He glanced to the west, where the battle with the abysmal had occurred. Images flickered. Smells ambushed his brain. He turned his head away. Every fiber of his being urged him to get out of there as fast as he could. But he could never escape by running. The abysmal didn't die back there; it was born. The abysmal went with him wherever he went, ready to torment him at every turn, whenever he lowered his guard. Pain had been a blessed escape, and for a while he found respite in a simple mind. But that was no life. When he grabbed the Stone, his life returned. It was good to be aware again, to have all his faculties back. But it came with a price.

Maybe there was another way. All his life, whenever the Council of Elders told him not to do something, the barbarian took it as a challenge. They came up with one rule after another to control him. He found ways to twist around them, not out of disrespect, nor to defy their authority. He did it to show them how they were holding themselves back.

Can't let new ideas get in your way, as long as you don't do any harm. He just liked to play. A little twist on what they expected. Something new.

Now he'd imposed his own rules. Don't go back there. Stay away from anything that brought to mind the monster he carried within. Never revisit what happened on the other side of that ridge. It was forbidden, prohibited by fear, by horror, by the suspicion that he he'd never get through it. If he tried, he'd go bonkers for sure. Thundersquat flinched at the idea of going back, but the thought of running was worse. "Too many rules. And I'm the one who put them there."

He couldn't go back there. He shouldn't go back there. Nothing good can come out of it. But there was no real escape anywhere else.

It was time to find out how bad it could get.

It was worse.

For a week, maybe two, Thundersquat plodded onward, Bolstrus by his side. He headed straight toward the field beyond the ridge where it all took place. Memories swarmed with each passing hour. Each time he stopped and took the hits and lumbered on when he could.

When exhaustion at last prevailed upon him to lie down to snatch a few hours of sleep, he lay on the ground and watched the moon move through the stars. It seemed slower than usual. He must have drifted to sleep, because he bolted up, cold, soaked in sweat. He climbed to his feet and continued his journey.

Man and horse paused at the top of the ridge. On the other side were the same empty, scrubby grasslands as behind him. It was where the abysmal had pummeled Grandfather's last breath out of him. The barbarian had reached his weakest point: exhausted, emotionally drained.

Sweat beaded on his forehead. He felt cold. His fingers trembled. If he waited until he was ready, he'd never go. Thundersquat and Bolstrus passed over the ridge.

Bones were still scattered far and wide, picked clean by scavengers and swathed with gray from blowing dust. He strolled over to where he'd begun, to retrace the threads he had pieced together before. He reached down and grabbed a handful of the fine dust and let it slip through his fingers. The first time, he had zoomed in and tarried just long enough to draw out the clues; he'd blocked out the big picture. To do more at the time would have expunged his soul and left him lying there, a useless pulp. Back then he couldn't afford to imagine more, to dwell on what they went through as it happened. This time he was all in, determined to scrape out the remnants of his soul and stretch the definition of useless. He watched each scene unfold over and over while he stood there, emotionally raw. He pictured the villagers' faces, pored over their final moments. It stirred flashes of encounters he'd had with them across his whole life. Unacceptable losses. Painful feelings pounded him until they wore themselves out. He moved on to the next clue and did it yet again.

Two or three days later—he'd lost count—he worked his way over to the skeleton of the abysmal. He blinked when an image of Grandfather's last stand punched through. Even though he hadn't seen the battle, the state of Grandfather's remains and the words of UncleCousin Sumac were clear enough.

Thundersquat reached down and ripped the spear from the abysmal's ribs. Crumbled fragments of dried blood near the point flaked off as he ran his hands over the shaft. Grandfather had held this spear in his hands and had given his life to drive it home. The spear had probably weakened the monster, perhaps what allowed them to defeat it. In a way, he and his grandfather had vanquished the monster together—with the help of a few friends and a raptor that picked that exact moment to lose its mind.

He broke the spear over his knee and tossed the pieces to either side. Beneath the bones of the abysmal lay the raptor's crushed skeleton. Two creatures, like any others. Hunting their next meal. Fighting to stay alive while they could. The barbarian kicked some of the loose, dry dirt over the abysmal's bones.

He stretched and let the sun's strength run through him. Once again, he felt a tiny part of the vast oneness proffered by the unbounded blue above and the land that stretched as far as he could see. Thundersquat curled up near the trees and slept the rest of the day, through the night, and halfway through the next.

Half a rainbow pinned a wisp of a cloud into the distant hills. Fenestral Smogen stepped out of the cavern's mouth and stretched both arms wide. A warm smile cracked the fossilized leather of her face in ways long forgotten. In her exuberance, she tossed her cane aside and listened to it careen down the mountain slope. Then she realized what she'd done. "Dramblunkit."

She became aware of a presence hovering on her right. "The barbarian came through, didn't he, Herb?"

"It looks like it," Herb said. "But I'm not sure it's over."

"Don't tell me you don't feel this."

"I do. But I've seen some things this time around that I've never seen before. I don't know how it might shape what's yet to unfold. The future's so tricky to remember.

You have to use Calculus Ten. Can't do it in my head anymore."

Fenestral Smogen rubbed her hip. "That Braider of Time was getting on my last nerve. Reduced to tears, and she's supposed to be a goddess. Never saw anything like it."

"It happens more than you think. I remember when I thought they all knew what they were doing."

"As far as I'm concerned," Fenestral Smogen said, "it's over."

"Probably," Herb said. "Or maybe it's just beginning. I mean, once you consider the inverse root of the infinity confabulation matrix, and—"

"Not today, bub." Fenestral Smogen hobbled back to the cavern. "When you get a chance, fetch me my dog-blasted cane."

Thundersquat and Bolstrus halted at the eastern edge of the Badlands. To the north, the mountains blocked out half the sky. The range extended into the lands of the Qrudds. If he went due east, he could parallel the range until he reached the battleground. Turn north and track down the commander of the Golden Horde. Maybe find his father.

As he skirted the edge of the ridgelands, his eyes revisited the twisted mountain to the southeast. The Onyx Palace. Somewhere in the wilderness lurked the Least High Druid. *Should be able to handle him, father and daughter together. If they see him coming in time.*

Thundersquat's eyes followed the line of the northern range to the point on the horizon where they disappeared. The answers were right there in front of him. All he had to do was follow the trail to quash all those years of not knowing. If he didn't go, he was sure to regret it. So why wasn't he excited, at long last?

He glanced again at the twisted mountain. He could feel the squeeze of her hands when she offered to use the Stone to help him. She was willing to destroy her own mind in order to ease his. Clearly somebody dropped her on her head at some point.

The silver stallion wouldn't budge. Thundersquat let him have his head. He'd move when he was good and ready. Most of the time he couldn't stop the horse from moving; this was a welcome change, even if it wasn't destined to last. The barbarian took a final look at the twisted mountain. *Practicing her skills right now, most likely. The druid shouldn't be any trouble. If she sees him coming.*

If.

Bolstrus half-reared and spun to the right, plunging into the forest, straight toward the Onyx Palace. Thundersquat leaned forward and hugged the stallion's neck to dodge the trees. *Never did anything that made any sense. Why start now?*

At the base of the twisted mountain, the old stallion was winded and lathered up, his stride off kilter. Thundersquat slipped off and charged up the spiral path alone. He slowed to a jog and finally paused to catch his breath. Until this point, he'd known exactly what he was doing. He suddenly realized he hadn't come just to defend her.

His body went cold, and his mouth went dry.

Thundersquat looked behind him. He could go back and resume the hunt for his father. But the druid was still out there somewhere. *Need to be here.*

No.

I want to be here.

The princess knew him as a barbarian. A fool. Damaged

goods. On a mission central to his heart, never to return. He came here to protect her, that's all. *One thing I'm good at.*

But not really. He wasn't there when his village needed him. The blue tiger got the best of him. The only way he beat the abysmal was with the help of a deranged raptor. When he barged in to rescue her, Blundren ended up taking care of him. He was absolutely useless when the druid took out the lion.

Mudcat. Fought with him against the abysmal. Stood with him against the blue tiger. The way the troll carried on when he realized the lion was gone.

Grandfather. If only I'd been there when it mattered.

Here to protect her. Do what I can, anyway. That's all. Improve her chances if the mystic witch or the druid come for her. That's all it could ever be.

Thundersquat crept into the courtyard like a halfhearted suggestion. He paused when he saw her. Blundren leaned out over the outer wall, staring at the western horizon. The breeze blew through her hair. *What's she gonna think now? Out of the blue. Uninvited.*

Blundren turned her head. They gazed at each other. Her face registered no reaction. *Such a mistake. Stupid.*

Thundersquat moved a step forward. The barbarian looked at the palace door, like he had something to do. He glanced her way and shrugged. He strode toward her.

She watched for a moment and took a few tentative steps in his direction. They picked up the pace. He was unable to contain a half smile.

A few steps away, Blundren broke out a smile that lit up the garden. She ran and leaped into his arms. She squeezed his neck as he swung her around. He let her slide down, his hands wrapped around the small of her back, their gazes still locked, eyelids half-closed. *If this moment stretched out another month or two, I'd just have to live with it.*

Their faces pressed together, and he felt the warmth of her cheeks against his. Her fingers lightly caressed the back of his neck. Their mouths slid together at last into a long, soft kiss.

He jerked his head back. "Been eating bugs?"

"Not that many."

The barbarian watched her expression waver—from open and eager to concerned, afraid, then impatient. He realized he'd taken too long to reply. To be fair, it wasn't entirely clear what he was supposed to say. Small talk with any other woman would no doubt take a while before it worked around to her time as a salamander. Not that he would've fared any better if she'd always been human. He shrugged. "Could be worse."

She placed a finger on his lips. "You probably shouldn't talk."

"Story of my life."

They turned toward the palace. Her hand slipped naturally into his. It was time for another conversation with the sorcerer king. His tongue puffed up against the roof of his mouth; there was not enough moisture left to swallow.

What could possibly go wrong? 'Dropped by for a visit. Thought I'd take your daughter away with me. Yeah, thirteen years in a swamp does sound like a long time. No, don't know how many times you almost lost her since then. Two, maybe three? Math's never been —what's that, where would we live? Haven't had a chance to talk about it. Out there somewhere with monsters, evil witches, druids with a grudge. No worries. Glad we have your blessing.'

As they neared the palace entry, rivulets of sweat trickled down his back. He hesitated.

"What's the matter?" she asked.

The last thing he needed was to feel like this. To hope. To take a chance on losing someone else. He noticed the knots in his forehead and took a minute to let them dissipate. Thundersquat inclined his head in her direction and squeezed her hand. "What can go wrong?"

Her eyes sparkled. "Should we make a list?"

"Life's scary enough." Thundersquat turned his attention to the palace door. He took a deep breath. Shoulders back, he escorted the princess up the steps. The last time he needed to talk to the sorcerer king, it was one obstacle after another. *With any luck, he'll send me away to wrestle a great bear first.*

AFTERWORD

This book had its genesis in stories made up by father and son before Zack invaded the school system. Flash forward a couple of decades, when a benevolent entity recommended for no apparent reason that someone straighten out the storage area. None of that stuff was hurting anybody. While engaged in the task—enthusiastically, according to some—I rediscovered the dot matrix printouts and dusted them off. We remembered the stories as having been better than they were. Zack challenged me to try to write for real. We reworked the stories more in line with our collective age, which was somewhere upwards of twelve. We resurrected several characters and they brought uninvited friends.

I had always considered myself to be a fast learner, but learning to write was like sprinting waist-deep through molasses. In my previous career I had learned to distrust the sense that I knew what I was doing. Instead, that idea always spurred me to investigate further, to find out more information that would shed light on what I didn't know but thought I did. That attitude translated well to the ups and downs central to learning to write. It helped me to scale down the excitement of seeing how far I'd come, as well as the discouragement that followed the next time I realized something that should have been obvious all along. Let's just say that there were many opportunities to learn.

If all goes according to plan, this book is the first of many. I hope you enjoyed it. Meanwhile, be wary of attics and other havens where project monsters lurk. Benevolent entities are still out there looking for things for a body to do.

AFTER THE AFTERWORD

Why revise, when that time and effort could have been spent writing another book? Simple. It was fun, and the book is better. The first version wasn't terrible. But learning did occur in the process of writing it, and I couldn't let it go. If you keep growing, it's natural to be dissatisfied with what came before. Granted, I'm hyperfocused on the next thing to learn and overly critical of what I've done in the past. But it's how I learn. It's what keeps me fresh.

Of course, it's possible to devote 10,000 hours to master a skill and end up worse than where you started, as Swedish psychologist Anders Ericsson points out. But not if you focus on a level of skill that's just out of reach and strive to discover what you need to know and do in order to get there. Once you get there, do it again. It's inevitable for some learning to slip through whatever barriers you started with.

Was the revision worth the time and effort? I think so. What's different in the revised edition? By the time I started plotting the sequel, I had a deeper understanding of the characters and their development through the story. I get why

Stephen King described the process of writing as an excavation. Minor scrapings resulted in better flow, crisper dialogue, and more clarity regarding what a character was thinking and feeling in each situation. Where possible, I modified the plot to heighten tension, by stretching the degree of commitment or entrapment perceived by characters at critical points. In addition, I wanted to play with the cover illustration and the blurb on the back.

Enjoy, while I move on to the sequel.

ACKNOWLEDGMENTS

Many thanks to my son and co-creator Zack, for issuing the initial challenge to write for real, and for the creative discussions along the way. I thank my wife Nettie, son Ben, and Aunt Peggy for their patience and fortitude as they pored through early versions of what evolved into this manuscript (triple points to Nettie for reviewing every major draft). I value their honest feedback, which is not easy for many to give, but which enabled me to move forward and not prolong anyone else's agony. Thanks to our friend Debby for her careful review of a late draft.

I am grateful to my editors. In an early manuscript review, Lynnette Labelle highlighted a handful of areas that I needed to study with regard to the craft of writing. She pointed out useful directions to take toward that end, and I benefited from her advice. As the manuscript matured, Sue Ducharme gifted me with astute questions and commentary. This book would have been far less without her insight and attention to detail. Any errors or deficiencies that remain are mine.

Special thanks to Nettie for pushing me into a painting class. Thanks to Emily Shipe for helping me get to the point where I could produce the cover for this book. Whereas the goal to produce the cover myself prolonged the process, and though I still have much to learn, this experience has greatly enhanced the pleasure of this adventure. Once again, I appreciate my wife for her encouragement, for accommodating my schedule, and for listening to me when I had her trapped in the car.

ABOUT THE AUTHORS

 Q. E. Daniels is a retired psychologist who lives with his wife in the southeastern United States. They share space with a mini golden doodle who cheats at games she invented. Zack Daniels is a successful IT consultant who has traveled extensively and lives with his wife and children in the southeastern United States. This is their debut novel, revised.

QE Daniels illustrated the cover.

www.ingramcontent.com/pod-product-compliance
Lightning Source LLC
Chambersburg PA
CBHW050919250626
47155CB00001B/303